D0011602

Berkley titles by Barbara Dunlop

MATCH MADE IN PARADISE
FINDING PARADISE
STRANGERS IN PARADISE

Strangers in Paradise

BARBARA DUNLOP

JOVE
New York

A JOVE BOOK
Published by Berkley
An imprint of Penguin Random House LLC
penguinrandomhouse.com

ISBN: 9780593333006

First Edition: May 2022

Printed in the United States of America
1   3   5   7   9   10   8   6   4   2

Book design by George Towne

Strangers in Paradise

Chapter One

IT WAS A GLASS-HALF-FULL KIND OF DAY FOR HAILEY Barrosse. Sure, it had been a slow summer season in the tiny town of Paradise, Alaska. In fact, it had been an excruciatingly slow year, particularly for the bush pilots who flew for West Slope Aviation. They were paid by the mile. So, no miles, no money.

Not that Hailey had a lot of day-to-day expenses. She lived in WSA staff housing: a small rustic room, just a bedroom, a bathroom and a tiny sitting area. But it stayed warm in the winter and had a great view of the mountains during the long summer days. The company provided three tasty meals plus snacks in the staff cafeteria, so if her bank balance suffered a little in the short term, she could live with that.

Today, however, was a bright spot for the entire town. It was the first day of principal photography for the superhero action movie *Aurora Unleashed*. The production had brought new jobs to town. Local residents had been hired in catering, carpentry, hair and makeup, as well as in logistics.

That wasn't even counting the business spin-offs for everyone from Galina Expediting and West Slope Aviation to the Bear and Bar Café and Rapid Release Whitewater Rafting.

Today, practically everyone had assembled at Mia Westberg and Silas Burke's house on the banks of the Paradise River to check out the action. It was a picturesque location: a wildflower meadow with soaring mountains and snow-capped peaks in the distance with the newly built two-story villa at the center of it all. The spectators clustered behind the surveyor's tape boundary that ran to the river's edge. But as the official pilot to the location scouting team, Hailey was allowed on set with the rest of the crew.

"Grab a snack," Willow Hale told her, stepping up to the heavily laden craft services table.

"Is eating all anybody does here?" But Hailey joined Willow to check out the assortment of fruit and nuts, cookies and treats. In addition, enticing smells wafted from the catering tent, even though they were halfway between breakfast and lunch.

"We have to keep up our energy level," Willow said, selecting a peanut butter granola bar and peeling away the wrapper.

Hailey was tempted by a bag of white chocolate–covered cashews. The delicacy was new to her, but how could you go wrong with cashews, white chocolate and crunchy toffee?

You couldn't, that was the answer. She picked up a package.

"Besides," Willow continued between bites, "they're tossing me off the sundeck into the river this morning."

Hailey stopped tearing open the crimped foil. "They're *what*?"

"That's the first scene. I mean, not the first scene in the movie, but the first one they're filming. Probably want to get it done before the weather cools. I have to say, I'm all for that." Willow took another bite.

"Do you know what you're doing?" It was a twenty-foot drop from the sundeck into the water. And the water was freezing. Well, nearly freezing, just barely liquid. The river was fed year-round by glaciers high up in the mountain peaks.

Sure, Willow was athletic. But she wasn't a professional stuntwoman. She was a Californian who loved adventure sports and had been drafted by the production based mostly on her enthusiasm for Paradise and the project.

"Not exactly," she said.

"Well, did you rehearse it?"

"Are you kidding?" Willow's voice rose. "Do it *twice*?"

"Good point." Hailey had to agree. "Plus, the first time might kill you."

"Well, hopefully not dead, dead," Willow said matter-of-factly. "There'll be a safety diver in the water."

"It's three minutes to hypothermia in that river." Hailey didn't see how a safety diver would help in such a tight race against time.

Willow pulled the high collar of her shirt down to show a patch of white fabric. "Dry suit. I'm brave, not suicidal."

Hailey felt a little better about that precaution. She tore open the bag of cashews. "What about the current? If the diver misses, you'll be swept all the way to Weaver Lake."

"Riley and Nicholas are downstream in rafts. If it all goes bad, they'll catch me."

"Oh." Hailey popped a nut in her mouth.

"See that?" Willow grinned and squeezed Hailey's arm. "You're not getting rid of me today."

"These are delicious," Hailey noted, taking an appreciative look at the shiny blue bag. "Where have you been all my life?"

"So, that's it?" Willow asked on a pout, gesturing to herself up and down. "No more worrying about me?"

"You said it yourself, Riley will save you." Riley had had a soft spot for Willow since her first trip to Paradise nearly two years ago. Hailey held out the bag. "Have you tried these things?"

Willow took a couple of nuts, biting one in half and checking the inside. "Yum."

"Right?" Hailey ate another.

Willow focused on a spot past Hailey's left shoulder, her gaze holding there. "Oh, hello. Who is *that*?"

Hailey turned to look then convulsively swallowed. Who *was* that? Had they replaced Cash Monahan, the actor playing Archvillain Dax Vanquich?

"Is he the new Dax?" She was embarrassed by her fangirl reaction. She wasn't a fangirl of anyone. But this guy was . . . it was hard to find the right words: *rugged*, *sexy*, *buff*? The camera had to love those deep mysterious eyes.

"They didn't replace Dax," Willow said. "They'd have replaced his stunt double too. And look"—she pointed to where the crew was getting the shot set up on the sundeck—"Buzz is still here."

Hailey didn't want to look at the stuntman. She wanted to keep watching the man striding their way with such power and composure, like he owned the place.

"He looks like money," Willow said.

Hailey agreed with that. "An executive producer?"

"Mia's the executive producer."

"Maybe she needed another backer. Does he look like he's from LA?"

The film's financial backer, Mia Westberg, was a former fashion model who had moved up from LA nearly two years ago to marry local pilot Silas Burke. Not that this guy's demeanor said fashion industry, not by a long shot. Although, he was wearing a dark, custom-fitted suit with a crisp white shirt and a blue silk tie, so he was definitely dressed the part.

"I wouldn't say LA," Willow answered. "No tan, and that body doesn't look like it was sculpted in a gym."

"It looks good," Hailey said, trying to keep her voice even but wanting to sigh like a teenage girl.

The stranger caught her gaze. He stopped walking and his eyes narrowed, as if he was trying to place her but couldn't.

It was then that Hailey noticed the woman beside him. She was dressed as suavely as he was in a black-and-white-checkerboard blouse, a short, tailored steel-gray jacket and a matching slim skirt. Her dangling earrings looked terrific below her short dark hair. But she'd made a bad choice in shoes. The heels were too narrow for walking over the meadow.

"She looks more like New York," Willow said.

"What are they even doing here?" Hailey wondered.

"On set?"

"In Paradise."

The woman said something to the man. He tilted his head to listen but kept his quizzical gaze on Hailey.

"He's staring at you," Willow whispered.

"Do I have something on my face?" Hailey wondered if she'd smeared chocolate in her enthusiasm over the cashews. But even if she had, the chocolate was white. He wouldn't see it from that distance. She glanced down at her mottled blue T-shirt and gray cargo pants. Nothing seemed off with her outfit.

Her leather hikers might be scuffed and worn, but they were eminently practical. And she'd popped a WSA ball cap over her ponytail to keep off the sun. There was nothing remotely noteworthy about her appearance.

Willow studied her for a minute. "You're good."

Then a bad feeling came over Hailey. "Oh no."

"Oh no what?" Willow asked, sounding worried.

"He might be from Atlanta."

"Atlanta?"

"My family might have sent him." Hailey's stomach turned queasy at the notion.

"Why would they do that?"

"Because they want me to come home." Hailey's sister had sent three texts yesterday alone, and Hailey had flat-out ignored the recent phone calls from her mother.

"They'd send a guy?" Willow sounded skeptical.

Hailey knew it was unlikely they'd send someone to fetch her. Sure, her family wanted her home for the annual shareholders' meeting, just like they always did. But she never attended. She just gave her sister, Amber, her proxy for the votes.

Then again, unlikely wasn't impossible.

"He's coming this way," Willow said with a thread of excitement in her voice.

The man's attention had definitely zeroed in on Hailey.

She considered making a run for it, but he looked like he'd have some speed. And even if she made it to her pickup truck, what then? Head for the airstrip and commandeer a plane?

She wasn't letting this guy run her out of Paradise.

He was only yards away now, and she braced herself, planting her feet, squaring her shoulders and lifting her chin.

"Hello," he said in a deep honey-smooth voice that sent a ripple up her spine.

She waited, gaze narrowing, prepared to tell him she wasn't leaving Paradise and he could march right back to where he came from.

"I'm looking for Raven Westberg."

Surprise tumbled through Hailey, and it was immediately followed by embarrassment. He was clearly not here for her.

She almost laughed at her own absurdity.

"I'm not sure she's on set right now," Willow said, glancing around.

"Is Raven expecting you?" Hailey asked.

He might not be here for her, but this guy didn't fit in Paradise, not by a long shot.

"We don't have a specific appointment." His assessing gaze told Hailey it was none of her business. Unfortunately, the smoldering look also made her heart beat more deeply in her chest.

Residual adrenaline, she told herself. Not that he could have bodily removed her from Paradise. But she hadn't wanted to argue with some brash stranger about returning to Atlanta.

The professional-looking woman handed Hailey a business card. "If you do see Raven, could you ask her to call?"

The card read *Dalia Volksberg, PQH Holdings*, embossed in gold letters.

"What can I tell her?" Hailey asked, growing curious and slightly uneasy. Were these people lawyers? Headhunters? What did they want with Raven?

The man answered, an edge to his deep voice. "That we'd like to speak to her."

"About?" Hailey wasn't going to be intimidated by him.

His lips thinned as he stood in pointed silence.

Hailey's back stiffened in response. People obviously hopped to it for him in his world. But she wasn't part of his world.

She handed the card back to the woman. "I don't expect to see Raven anytime soon."

She felt Willow's surprise. The man clearly noticed it too, because his suspicious gaze slid to Willow then back to Hailey.

"Alaskan hospitality?" he challenged Hailey on a drawl.

"Urban entitlement?" she returned with the same level of defiance.

For some reason, he smiled at that. "I guess we'll track her down ourselves."

He turned to walk away then, tossing a steel-eyed look over his shoulder.

"Wow," Willow said.

"High on himself or what?" Hailey asked rhetorically.

"I wonder what he wants with Raven."

"I hope he doesn't find her."

"How could he not find her?"

Willow was right. A person couldn't hide in Paradise if they were trying.

PARKER HALL HAD GROWN UP IN ALASKA, BUT PARA-dise seemed quirky even to him. To be fair, he'd spent the last ten years in Anchorage refining his image to better fit in with his expanding business circle.

He'd expected the town's mood to be gloomy, given the tough times they'd faced over the past year. But what he'd found was optimism, almost a festival air.

"You do know it's going to come out," his business manager, Dalia Volksberg, said as they threaded their way through the trailers, equipment and people crowding the set. Pickups and semitrucks were parked in a neat line beside the long gravel driveway and multiple generators rumbled in the background.

"I know it will," Parker agreed. "But not because I gave it away to a curious woman."

"You cut her off pretty quick," Dalia observed.

"There was something about her," he defended himself.

He couldn't quite put his finger on it. He'd sensed an underlying hostility, then a stubbornness, and he hadn't wanted to give an inch.

"Well, those shoes for one," Dalia responded airily. "I mean, seven pockets in your slacks are bad enough, but there's no excuse for mismatched laces and mud-caked hikers."

"You're a pocket snob?" Parker hadn't noticed what the woman was wearing. He'd been too busy taking in those clear blue eyes. He could admire the intelligence he saw behind them, even the curiosity. But her obstinance sure put him off.

Not that they weren't beautiful eyes. And not that she wasn't a beautiful woman. Even without makeup, her eyelashes were thick and dark in contrast to her light whisps of auburn hair beneath the olive-green ball cap. Her cheeks were flushed against her pale skin, and he'd caught the slightest hint of freckles on her cheekbones.

He couldn't help but be fascinated by her deep pink lips that looked highly—he stopped his thoughts in their tracks, giving himself a mental shake.

"The women here . . ." Dalia's tone was searching as she gazed around at the people they passed.

He resolutely redirected his attention but didn't see anything strange. "What about the women?"

"They don't even seem to . . ." She paused, clearly searching for the right word. "*Try.*"

Parker gave a wry smile. "It's a working town, Dalia."

At least it had been a working town. It was more of a depressed town now. Well, except for this film. He hadn't known about the film until they'd arrived. It had to be a one-off, a temporary respite from the economic downturn. There was nothing about Paradise that would qualify it as Hollywood far, far north.

Everyone's attention suddenly swung in a single direction, so Parker looked too. There were three cameras in place on the big sundeck, their operators at the ready and the lighting bright on the actors. A man and woman were circling each other like they were about to engage in a fight.

The woman was the quieter of the two he'd just encountered. He glanced over his shoulder, scanning the crowd until he caught a glimpse of the obstinate one.

She was just as pretty in profile, her pale auburn ponytail sticking jauntily from the back of her green ball cap. Like everyone else, she was intently watching the action on the sundeck. Her teeth scraped her bottom lip, and his chest went tight with desire.

He hadn't felt arousal that fast and that intense in a very long time. Okay, maybe never. Interesting.

A gasp came up from the crowd, and he looked back to see the woman in the fight go over the railing and drop twenty feet into the swift, icy river.

"I sure hope that was on purpose," Dalia said.

Parker knew it had to be a stunt, but he watched along with everyone else until the woman waded out of the river with support from a scuba diver who'd obviously been waiting under the water with a rescue line.

"That was impressive." Dalia gazed around the film set, taking in the trailers and equipment and crew. "This seems higher budget than I would have thought."

Parker agreed and checked for a film title or a production company name, wondering why anyone would spend the money to come all the way up here for a wilderness setting. Surely there was something equally suitable in northern California or even Colorado.

"Is that Raven over there?" Dalia asked, angling her chin into the crowd.

Parker looked. "I see her."

They made their way past people who were gesturing and chatting excitedly, sharing their thoughts and going over the nuances of the stunt.

Raven was talking to a tall blond woman who looked vaguely familiar to Parker. He wondered if she was a famous actress.

"—so hard to believe it was her first time," the tall blonde was saying.

"You guys are off to a really great start," Raven responded.

"Natasha Burton was a find as director. She's so patient with everyone." The blond woman's gaze met Parker's. "Hello?" There was a grace about her, a cultured air, even though she was dressed in jeans and a sweater.

She was one of the few women he'd seen in Paradise

wearing makeup, lending credence to his theory she might be acting in the film.

"Good morning," he said. Then he looked to Raven. "Raven Westberg?"

"That's me." She waited expectantly.

"I'm Parker Hall, and this is Dalia Volksberg." They all shook hands before he continued. "Is there someplace the three of us could talk?"

Raven looked from Parker to Dalia and back again. "Am I being audited?"

"No." Parker glanced at the blond woman again, hoping she'd be polite and step away. "But it is a private matter."

Raven's brow furrowed as she took in both Parker and Dalia. "Are you from the bank?"

The blond woman canted her head, peering suspiciously at Parker.

He ignored the look, but he wasn't surprised to learn Raven was wary of bankers. "We're not from the bank."

"Why so cagey?" Raven asked.

"Is everything okay?" The obstinate woman was suddenly at his elbow, looking ready to defend her friends—which was ridiculous, since she was the smallest of them all.

"This man wants to talk to Raven," the blond woman answered. Then she turned back to Parker. "I'm Mia Westberg. Raven is my cousin."

"Do you work at Galina Expediting?" Parker asked her. Hugh hadn't mentioned a cousin in company management, but it was possible this Mia was a pivotal player.

"No. But you're on my property."

A tall, fit-looking man in cargo pants and a T-shirt positioned himself next to Mia, brushing her arm and facing Parker. "Something I can help you with?"

Parker met his level gaze. "I'm only looking to speak to Raven."

"About?" the man asked.

"It's a private matter, but Hugh Oberg is aware of it."

"You know something about this?" the man asked Raven.

She shook her head.

"I'm here to explain," Parker said.

"*We're* here to explain," Dalia put in, shifting forward, obviously hoping to defuse any conflict between the two men.

Parker wasn't worried about conflict. The guy wasn't aggressive. He was only curious. Parker couldn't blame him for that. He'd explain if he could, but he owed it to Hugh and Raven to talk to her first.

"You can talk inside," the man offered to Raven, and Parker realized this must be Mia's husband. It made even more sense that he'd step into the conversation.

"I'd appreciate the opportunity," Parker said, keeping his tone cordial. They were off to a rocky enough start here as it was.

Raven hesitated for a moment, but then stretched her hand out, palm up, gesturing toward the front porch.

"Thank you," Parker said to the man.

"Silas Burke," the man introduced himself, and held out his hand to shake. "I'm Mia's husband."

"Parker Hall."

"Let me know if you need anything," Silas said to Raven.

As they walked, Parker sized up the large, newly built two-story villa set beside the river. It was impressive, particularly compared to the aging buildings he'd briefly seen in town. They passed a canopy array surrounding the director's chair. The space was filled with a jumble of tables, cables and computer screens, the electronic equipment blinking hundreds of colored LED lights.

A cluster of people huddled beneath it, listening intently to a woman who was clearly mapping out their next shot. He couldn't help but wonder what they'd film next and if he'd recognize any of the actors. He wasn't immune to the magic and mystery of moviemaking.

Raven had her phone to her ear while she opened the front door and gestured them both inside. The living room was bright and airy with big windows and high ceilings. The floors were smooth wood, polished a warm honey tone, and a huge stone fireplace took up nearly an entire wall.

A natural wood staircase led to an open loft above a dining room overlooking the river. He could see the film crew outside on the sundeck taking down equipment, some of them picking up the scattered pieces of what Parker assumed was a prop barbecue that had been destroyed in the fight.

"How do you want me to do that?" Raven said into the phone as she closed the door behind them. She glanced to where Parker and Dalia had stopped to wait.

"This is impressive," Dalia whispered to him, taking in the leather furniture, glass-topped tables and a shelving unit featuring photos and attractive abstract sculptures.

A glassed-in wine rack was built into the wall of the dining room, and Parker eased a little closer to it, curious about the labels.

"Well, he already talked to Mia and Silas," Raven said, sounding doubtful. She paused. "You know they will."

Parker was regretting tracking Raven down in what turned out to be a busy event full of curious people. He'd originally intended to draw her unobtrusively aside for a quiet talk. But it sure hadn't worked out that way.

Then again, walking straight into Galina Expediting Monday morning would have caused even more speculation.

"I can," Raven said. "Bye." She pocketed her phone and blew out a breath. "So." She gestured to the sofa and armchair grouping, indicating they should sit down.

Dalia took one end of a love seat while Parker sat down in an armchair. Raven sat opposite Parker in a matching chair. A low glass-topped table with a carved wooden bowl was centered between them.

"I assume that was Hugh," Parker opened.

Raven nodded without offering anything further.

"I assume he confirmed we spoke yesterday?"

"He did."

"I'm the owner and CEO of PQH Holdings." Parker stretched forward and set his business card on the coffee table.

Quick on the draw, Dalia did the same, setting hers down beside Parker's.

Raven glanced but didn't pick them up.

"We're predominately a mining company," Parker said, while Dalia shifted and shot him a look. She'd made no bones about wanting him to move away from mining as his corporate image.

"We've diversified over the years," he added to appease her.

"And you're interested in Galina," Raven said.

"We're interested in Galina," he acknowledged. "It's not a secret that you've had a tough year financially."

"It's a private company," she stated. "Our financials aren't public knowledge."

"You've laid off staff."

"Nearly everyone's laid off staff."

"True," he nodded.

PQH Holdings hadn't had to lay off staff, but her point was still valid.

Parker had been in the fortunate position of hiring over the past year, skimming the cream from companies who'd been forced to let people go. Economic downturns were hell on the majority, but the minority of companies that were cash rich and in industries that hadn't suffered as much could come out of them as winners.

Parker intended to come out of this as a winner.

Raven's back was ramrod straight, her shoulders square, chin up. "Hugh asked me to show you two around the warehouse."

"We'd appreciate that," Parker said. "Your assets and operations, financials, clients, the area. Whatever you think is pertinent."

"You're looking to buy the company?" she asked.

"Invest in it." He paused. "Maybe." He was nowhere near to making a decision, but buying Galina Expediting outright didn't seem like a plausible path forward. Parker didn't get the sense Hugh was ready to let it go altogether.

"Invest how?" Raven asked, tilting her head, her gaze narrowing on him.

"I don't know yet. I don't know much of anything. As you said, Galina is a private company." He'd like to reassure her that her position was safe no matter what he did, but that would be premature. Depending on the investment, depending on the deal, if something did go ahead, there were no ironclad job guarantees.

Every new deal was a risk—for everyone involved.

CURLED UP ON THE SMALL SOFA IN WILLOW'S RENTED cabin, Hailey searched for information on Parker Hall and PQH Holdings while Willow showered off in the compact bathroom. They'd left the film set an hour ago, picking up a leftover pizza from the catering trailer on their way out. Now the aroma of fresh-baked crust, pepperoni, mushrooms and cheese blended with the cozy smell of wood.

Willow had scored one of Riley Stern's whitewater rafting–company cabins—newly built and considered premium accommodations—because the two had grown close during her visits to Paradise over the past couple of years. The other four cabins were assigned to the two stars, the

director and cinematographer Vanessa Tracy. The rest of
the visiting cast and crew were in temporary trailers on set.

Since there was a good eighteen hours until her next
flight, Hailey had opened a beer and was sipping from the
chilled bottle as she surfed the web. She couldn't be sure
she'd found all Parker's holdings, but what she'd cobbled
together from websites, permitting applications and news
releases showed he owned at least six operating gold mines,
a fuel supply company, a mechanical repair company with
locations in Anchorage and Fairbanks, a machine shop, and
a small but growing transportation company. She also put
together what she could for a timeline to see how he'd
grown his business interests over the years.

The sound of water hitting the shower stall abruptly
ended as a text popped up on Hailey's screen. She saw it
was her sister, Amber, and quickly squeezed her eyes shut
to block the view. She set her tablet away from herself and
took a long pull of the beer.

She didn't want to read Amber's text. She knew what it
would say, and she didn't want to feel guilty all over again.
She had enough on her mind.

Parker Hall was circling Galina Expediting. Hailey
didn't know for sure, but she'd be a fool not to guess Galina
had suffered financially over the past year. They'd laid off
a few staff members in the spring, and WSA's slow season
was a direct result of the Galina slowdown.

Parker was obviously looking for a bargain. Problem
with that—well, problems with that, plural—were that Galina and WSA were inextricably linked. The two companies were the driving force of Paradise itself. Anything that
changed Galina altered the equilibrium and messed with
the town.

Raven had run Galina forever, where Brodie Seaton had
bought the fledgling West Slope Aviation more than a de-
cade ago. The two of them worked hand in hand, making
both companies great places for their employees to work

and giving Paradise its unique character. Hailey didn't want it to change; nobody did.

Her tablet pinged again—a reminder of her sister's text.

"I'm starving." Willow emerged from the bathroom in a cloud of steam. She wore a loose T-shirt and a pair of gray sweatpants, her feet pushed into woven slip-ons and her short dark hair still damp around her shiny, clean face.

She detoured to the fridge to get herself a beer, twisting off the cap and tossing it into the trash. She flopped down on the opposite end of the sofa. "Nothing like physical exercise to get your appetite going."

Willow's second stunt of the day had been a dirt bike chase along narrow trails, up and down steep hills. The spectators couldn't watch much of it, but there was one spectacular jump visible from the road in front of Mia's property. Quite a few people stuck around to watch, gasping at the one bad moment where Willow fell off the speeding motorcycle.

"Are you sore?" Hailey asked. "Any bruises?"

"A decent one on my thigh." Willow pointed to it with a grimace. "But the dirt was soft, so it didn't hurt all that much."

"I don't know about your job, girl."

"If it wasn't risky, it wouldn't be nearly as much fun."

"I suppose that's one way of looking at it."

"Says the bush pilot who flies in marginal weather and lands on crappy little airstrips all over Alaska."

"It's mitigated risks." Hailey peeled a sheet of paper towel from the roll they'd set out on the coffee table and helped herself to a thick slice of the pepperoni and mushroom pizza. "We take every safety precaution."

"You don't think I do the same?" Willow set down her beer and dug into the pizza. "Man, this looks good."

"I'm glad to hear you do." Hailey took a first bite. It was lukewarm but tender and flavorful—exactly what she was in the mood for.

"I had body armor, a helmet, leathers and proper boots. I'd have to come down pretty hard to get injured."

"You got a bruise."

"That's hurt, not injured." Willow took a big bite of the pizza, then smiled and nodded her head. "Oh yeah." She swallowed. "Another benefit of an active job. You can ramp up the calories and do no harm."

Hailey heartily agreed with that. Yesterday she'd hauled a full load of building supplies out to a mining exploration camp, then brought some heavy mineral-core samples back to Paradise. She and fellow WSA pilot Xavier O'Keefe had help with the loading and unloading at the Paradise end. But they'd been on their own in the camp since all the drillers were out in the bush.

It was a better workout than any gym.

Her tablet pinged with another text, drawing Willow's attention. "Something going on?"

Hailey glanced reflexively down. "My sister, Amber."

Willow took another bite of pizza followed by a swallow of her beer. "You're not going to check it?"

Hailey shook her head.

"You mad at her or something?"

"Not Amber specifically. She just drew the short straw."

Willow turned on the sofa, folding one leg in front of her so she was facing Hailey, looking amused. "Texting you is the short straw?"

"They want me to come home."

"And?"

"They know I'll say no. So, it's not much fun to ask."

Willow cocked her head. "Explain?"

"It's the annual shareholders' meeting. For the family corporation." Hailey's tone stayed level, though her shoulders tensed with a momentary quiver. "They want me to show up and vote."

Willow squinted. "You have a family corporation?"

Hailey drew a breath and took a bracing swallow of her beer. Then she nodded. "Magnolia Twenty."

"Weird name."

"My great-grandfather's goal was to build the corporation up to twenty companies. And, you know, Atlanta . . . magnolias."

"That seems like a lot of companies. Did he make it?"

Hailey coughed out a laugh. "And then some. And after that we added more." She paused, contemplating the tasty-looking strip of pizza crust left in her hand. "I mean *they*. I'm not part of it anymore."

"Oh?" Willow reached for another slice.

"It's a cutthroat thing, always angling, plotting, positioning yourself and your interests above everyone else's. I'm not into that." Hailey took a satisfying bite of the chewy crust.

"Plus, you'd have to work behind a desk."

"That's true."

"We're way smarter than that."

"We *are*," Hailey agreed.

The text gave its follow-up ping, and Willow looked to the tablet sitting on the table. "You should probably still answer her, even just to say no."

"I will. I just don't feel like duking it out with her right now." Hailey leaned forward for her second slice of pizza. "If I wait an hour, with the time zone change, she'll be in bed."

"Solid plan," Willow said with a nod. "So, did you hear what Parker wanted with Raven?"

"No. But I did a little digging."

Willow's brow rose with interest. "And?"

"PQH Holdings. I found six mines and four service companies."

Willow waved a dismissive hand. "A mere ten companies to his name? Slacker."

Hailey grinned. "Well, he only got started ten years ago."

"Still, I hear twenty is the benchmark."

Hailey sobered, worried by what she'd found. "He's a go-getter all right. And for some reason, Galina's on his radar."

Chapter Two

PARKER CLICKED TO OPEN THE PHOTO THAT HAD JUST popped up from Lucky Breach mine manager Colin Woodside. "Well, *that's* not going to hurt the bottom line," he said to Dalia, reaching across the dining table to show her the image on the screen.

They were finishing dinner in the Bear and Bar Café, the only restaurant in Paradise, and also the establishment below the small B and B where they had slept last night.

She squinted at the nugget. "Is that real?"

He understood why she'd ask. "They think they might have hit a rich vein."

"What are we looking at? I can't tell the scale."

"He says it's eleven ounces."

"That sounds big."

"It's *huge*." The miner in Parker was itching to explore the find.

The Lucky Breach mine was fly-in only. They'd barged in some heavy equipment when the river was high last year, but everything else went in by air from Anchorage. His expenses had been high, the venture his most risky to date. But if there were more nuggets like this to be found, or even nuggets a fraction of the size, the property was going to show a massive profit.

"I've *got* to get a look at this." He made up his mind as he spoke. Lucky Breach was less than forty minutes by bush plane from Paradise.

Dalia looked up from her laptop. "You mean now?"

"Why not now?" All the picture had done was whet his appetite. He wanted to see the nugget in real life.

More importantly, he wanted to see the ground they'd pulled it from. What was the geology? How far might the deposit go? And he wanted to look at it now before they started digging and sluicing their way through the ground.

He pulled up his contact list for WSA and tapped to dial.

"It's eight o'clock," Dalia said.

"It's light until nearly midnight in June," he pointed out.

She rolled her eyes. "What about the Galina financials?"

"You can look them over while I'm gone."

The call clicked through. "West Slope Aviation. Brodie Seaton here."

"Hi, it's Parker Hall calling. I'm looking for a flight out of Paradise tonight. To the Lucky Breach mine."

There was a pause. "I'm not familiar with that one."

"We're a new start-up, just south of the Broken Branch airstrip."

"Oh, Broken Branch. Sure. We can do that. What do you have for passengers and cargo?"

"Just me, one passenger. No cargo. I'll only be on the ground for a couple of hours."

"So, you'd want us to hold there," Brodie confirmed.

"Yes, I would."

Dalia sipped coffee from a white stoneware mug, looking amused while she watched Parker talk.

"I can send you over in the 185," Brodie said.

"Sounds fine." Parker didn't much care which plane they used.

"We'll need to fuel up . . . eight forty-five work for you?"

"Eight forty-five is perfect. I'll be there."

"Great. See you then." Brodie ended the call.

Dalia set down her mug. "Well, that was impulsively expensive."

"It's a strategic assessment of the mine's geology." Chartering a small plane would be well worth it.

"I know you'd rather tromp around the mine than look at the financial reports. But they do matter."

"We won't be tromping." He paused. "Okay, there'll be some tromping."

She looked him up and down, taking in his suit jacket, slacks and dress boots. "Did you bring any grubby clothes?"

He didn't appreciate the term *grubby* for his work clothes. But he hadn't brought any along since he hadn't planned on leaving town. He'd lose the jacket and tie and change his dress boots for the casual pair he'd tossed in at the last minute. "I'll be fine."

Dalia shook her head while Parker polished off his coffee. He paid the bill and made a quick trip upstairs to his room to change. A short time later, he was driving down the main road out of town, north to the airstrip, pulling into the parking lot five minutes early.

He could see the Cessna 185 at the edge of the parking lot. A pilot in an olive-green flight suit was at the back of the plane checking out the landing gear and control surfaces while a ground crew member in coveralls filled the fuel tanks in the wings.

Parker rolled up his shirtsleeves as he headed into the office to hand over his credit card. It was dim inside the building, with a fluorescent light high above his head and a small stream of sunlight shining through a window next to the metal door. He assumed the man behind the scarred wood counter was Brodie Seaton.

The office was old, clean but battered from years of wear and tear. It smelled faintly of aviation fuel and coffee. The linoleum floor was faded to beige. It might have once had a discernable pattern. If so, it was long gone.

Beyond the counter was what looked like a crew area, three tables and assorted chairs that had obviously been randomly collected through the years. A circa 1980s fridge stood in one corner next to a small strip of orange counter, faded to golden in a few spots, with a coffee maker standing next to the sink.

"Parker Hall?" the man asked him.

Parker nodded. "You're Brodie?"

"That's me." He looked to be in his early thirties, tall, fit-looking with a skin tone that indicated he spent a lot of time in the outdoors.

He pushed a clipboard across the counter. His broad, calloused hands said he was a hard worker. "At the bottom," he said, handing Parker a pen.

"Is there a deadline to get back tonight?"

Brodie shook his head. "Legal daylight lasts twenty-four hours in June."

"Perfect." Parker signed his name.

"Fueled and ready," a woman's voice came from behind him.

Parker recognized that voice, and its softness seemed to cloak him in honey.

He turned to see her crystal-blue eyes go wide.

They stared at each other in silence.

"You're a pilot," he said.

"Is that a problem?" she asked, lifting her chin.

"Not for me."

He'd been curious about her since yesterday. Sure, she might be contrary, but he wasn't necessarily put off by contrary women. They could be both challenging and fascinating. Who wanted mannerly chitchat when they could have something that made their brain work harder?

"You two have met?" Brodie asked.

The woman focused on her boss. "Briefly. At the film shoot yesterday. He was looking for Raven."

"You're interested in Raven?" There was a thread of steel in Brodie's voice.

Parker wondered what it was about Raven that brought everyone in this town to her defense. She'd struck him as a perfectly capable woman. There was no need to protect her—least of all from him.

He half turned to look at Brodie again. "We only met yesterday."

Brodie's eyes narrowed as if he was suddenly suspicious of Parker.

"It was business," Parker added, in case Brodie thought it might be personal.

There'd been nothing remotely personal about his reaction to Raven. In fact, the only person he'd reacted to in a personal way was Hailey. And his physical attraction to her—he slanted a brief look her way right now—was muddled by a peculiar fascination.

Sure, she was pretty. But plenty of women were pretty, many much more glamorous than Hailey. Her eyes might be one in a million, and her sassy mouth might get him thinking about kissing her to silence. But that was just fantasy. He'd never do anything about it.

After a long pause, Brodie spoke to Hailey again. "Hold at Broken Branch for—" He looked to Parker.

"Two or three hours." Parker confirmed his earlier estimate.

"No problem," Hailey responded. Then she backed up to open the door, holding it open for him.

His chest hitched unexpectedly as he brushed past her.

Anticipation, he told himself. Anticipation of an interesting flight and an impressive gold nugget.

* * *

AFTER GIVING PARKER THE STANDARD SAFETY BRIEF-ing, Hailey handed him a headset and pointed to where he should plug it in. She settled a ball cap on her head, threading her ponytail through the back. Then she pushed on her sunglasses before settling her own headset. They were flying southwest into a lowering sun, and it was going to be bright.

She checked the controls and tested the engine revs, glancing to make sure Parker had done his seat belt up properly. "WSA radio, this is Three-Seven-Zulu taxiing for Paradise airstrip. Flying forty minutes to Broken Branch strip return, three hours fuel on board."

"Three-Seven-Zulu, wind three knots east-northeast, ceiling unlimited all the way, clear for taxi and takeoff," Shannon Menzies answered through Hailey's headset. "Have a nice flight."

"Thanks, Shannon. Three-Seven-Zulu, out." Hailey switched to intercom and brought the little Cessna up onto the strip. She only needed about a quarter of the runway for the takeoff, so she took an immediate turn and accelerated, lifting off to the west.

"You're going to the Beecham property?" she asked Parker as they climbed out along the river valley. The Beecham family had run a small placer mining operation off the Broken Branch strip for many years.

"To the Lucky Breach mine." His voice was clipped and slightly static through the intercom.

"It's new?" She'd flown over the strip a couple of times this year and had seen they'd widened a trail to the south. She knew someone new was working in the area.

"An exploration camp right now."

"Yours?"

"Mine."

She digested the information. "It must look promising." If the property was moving into development and production, it could explain Parker's interest in Galina. They'd likely flown their camp supplies in from Anchorage up to now. But it was an expensive route for a property this far north.

"Getting more promising by the hour," he said.

She looked his way to see if that was a joke.

He looked serious.

"Literally?" she asked, wondering what he'd meant.

"They unearthed an eleven-ounce nugget."

Hailey didn't like the sound of that.

An eleven-ounce nugget was a once-in-a-lifetime find. It was great for Parker and everyone connected to his mine. But it made his property more valuable, and it was way too close to Paradise for her liking.

"And you have a plan to develop," she concluded. It was a no-brainer, really.

"I don't have anything so far."

She sent him a skeptical frown. Galina was obviously already part of his plan.

"They just found it today," he said.

"Today?"

His expression said she was slow on the uptake.

"So, what were they doing before that?"

"Mining gold." His lips curved into a smirk. "How do you think they found the nugget."

She was confused now. "What about Galina?"

"What about it?"

"You're here looking at it."

He was silent for a moment before answering. "I am."

"*Before* they found the nugget."

"The property hasn't moved."

His interest was obviously about more than a single find, and her anxiety settled into a hum. Silence came up between them as the miles slipped past: Crisp Falls, the Green Narrows, High Sheep Pass. The landmarks fell away one by one until Hailey could see the Broken Branch airstrip in the distance.

She adjusted her altitude, engine speed and flaps, doing a pass over the strip to gauge its condition. Then she circled around and lined up, bringing the Cessna down on the bumpy ground, slowing quickly and spotting an ATV at the edge of the trees.

"Your guys, I assume," she said.

"That'll be Colin."

She taxied close to the ATV, pulling onto a strip of long grass off to the side, out of the way on the off chance another plane wanted to land while she waited.

She started through the shutdown list, peeling off her seat belt and removing her headset, then pushing her seat back to give herself some leg room. She gave a wave to Parker's friend Colin, thinking she'd sit tight for a while, maybe read the mystery novel she had going on her phone before getting out to stretch her legs.

Parker cracked his door and turned to climb out. Then he paused and looked back. "Are you coming?"

Hailey was surprised by the invitation. "I wasn't planning on it."

"You don't want to get a look at an eleven-ounce nugget fresh from the ground?"

She was curious. "I thought you'd bring it back to the plane."

"Why would I do that?"

"We're not here to pick it up?" She'd assumed that was the point of the trip.

"We're here to check out the geology of where they found it. It can sit in the safe with the rest of the gold until we do a transfer to Anchorage at the end of the month."

He cocked his head toward the outside. "Come and see."

Since seeing the nugget seemed more interesting than waiting here alone for two hours, Hailey took him up on the offer, climbing out and chocking the plane's wheels to secure the aircraft.

"Hailey, this is Colin Woodside," Parker said of the man

leaning against the four-seater ATV. He was wearing dusty cargo pants tucked into worn work boots with a T-shirt and a plaid flannel shirt atop. His hair was messy, and his hands needed a wash.

In short, he looked like most of the other men she'd seen working in mining camps.

Colin grinned. "Hop in, Hailey." To Parker, he said, "You have got to see *this*!"

Hailey climbed into one of the back seats, while Colin took the wheel and Parker sat down beside him. The ATV revved beneath them, and they took off with a lurch onto the narrow bumpy road through the woods.

Hailey hung on, bouncing in the seat and leaning around corners. Colin was obviously familiar with the route and got them quickly to a row of canvas wall tents erected over wooden floors and half walls. There was a cookshack across the clearing from the tents with a washing lean-to beside it and an outhouse down a trail out back.

It was typical Alaskan bush living.

Colin parked the ATV and shut it down. "Gold room is this way," he said as he climbed out. He was clearly excited to get to the nugget viewing.

"How far to where you're working the claim?" Parker asked as he straightened and started to walk.

"About a half mile along the river. Don't tell me you want to go there first."

Curious, Hailey waited to hear Parker's answer, wondering if he'd be seduced by the shiny gold or be more interested in the future potential.

"Show me the nugget," Parker said easily.

Hailey got the feeling he was humoring Colin.

"You won't regret it," Colin said with a grin, taking off at a brisk pace along the row of four wall tents.

Hailey had to do a little hop-skip to keep him from getting away.

"He won't leave us behind," Parker assured her.

"He seems very excited."

"He'll have major bragging rights when he gets back to Anchorage."

"Is he heading back soon?"

"Not for a while. He can usually last out the season."

Hailey knew what Parker meant. "Some people are better in the bush than others."

In her years of flying people in and out, she'd identified two types of people: those who chose their careers for their love of the wilderness, and those who practically sprinted for the airplane as soon as she landed to take them out on days off or at the end of the season.

She liked the wilderness a whole lot better than a big city, but she could sure understand the yearning for a hot shower and proper bed. She struggled to get a good night's sleep on a camp cot, and a lot of the guys on the mining claims were twice her size. She admired them for being able to bear it.

"Colin has always been great in the bush," Parker said.

"You've known him for a long time?"

"Ten years."

"What about you? You ever had to spend time in the camps?"

Parker laughed at that.

"What?" she asked.

"I grew up in a mining camp."

She drew back, pointedly taking in his unsuitable dress shirt and suit slacks. "Didn't learn much, did you?"

His grin stayed in place. "I didn't bring work clothes to Paradise."

"Why not? Paradise is exactly the kind of place where you should bring work clothes."

"I'm here as an investor, not a miner."

She scanned the camp around them. "Could've fooled me."

"I didn't plan on them finding a monster nugget."

She lowered her voice to a mock singsong level. *"Nobody* plans on a monster nugget."

"Geologists sure try," he responded in kind. "They would if they could."

"Where'd be the fun in that?" she countered.

Over the years, Hailey had learned that all miners were gamblers at heart. If finding gold was too easy, they'd have given it up to try something more challenging. They were like Willow that way. It seemed the risk was half the fun.

"Come on," Colin called out, standing in a small shack with the door open.

Hailey realized her steps had slowed and he was now quite a way out in front. She stepped up her pace.

When they got to the shack, Parker stood back to let her go in first.

When Colin switched on the lights in the windowless building, Hailey noticed she could hear the low throb of a generator in the distance.

He bent to turn the dial on a bulky old safe, yawing the door open and removing a white plastic tray with a cloth covering. He set it down on the raw wood table in the center of the room and pulled off the cloth with a flourish.

Hailey's eyes went wide, and her chest fluttered as the lumpy, oblong nugget shone under the lights. The surface was irregular but smooth, giving it a polished sheen. She'd never had gold fever, but she could see how something like this would set a person's heart beating faster. She knew it was just a rock. But she also knew that for people in civilizations throughout the ages, it was a life-changing rock.

"Isn't it a beauty?" Colin asked breathlessly.

"I thought it would be rough," Hailey said, reaching out to run her fingertips over the cool surface.

"Polished by nature," Colin said.

"We can easily sell it as is," Parker said, walking around. He looked a lot less starstruck than Hailey felt. He also looked more mercenary, like the only magic for him was in the dollars and cents—probably why he'd been so successful in business.

"The large-nugget market is hot right now," Colin said. "I can reach out to a couple of brokers if you'd like."

Parker gazed at it from the back, and Hailey moved around to see what had caught his attention. It seemed equally compelling from every angle. She guessed that was probably good for pricing.

"Hold off on selling for now," Parker said.

"You want to keep it?" Colin asked, looking as if he liked the idea.

If it had been Hailey's, she'd have liked to keep it. Although she supposed it was a huge investment to have locked up as a souvenir. If a person sold it off instead, they could do something practical, like build a small house, even at Paradise's high building prices.

Then she smiled to herself. It seemed unlikely that someone as wealthy as Parker—who was acting like he could afford this nugget as art—would ever build a house in Paradise, Alaska.

"What?" Parker asked, and she realized he was looking at her smile.

"It's amazing." She said the first thing that came into her mind, since her musings were embarrassing.

"Are you getting a little gold fever?" he asked.

"Possibly," she admitted. "I've never seen this much up close."

"Try picking it up," Colin said.

Parker lifted the nugget, hefting it a little as he held it out to her. "Check it out."

Hailey wiped her palms on her pants and reached out so he could set it down in her hands.

He let go of it slowly.

"Wow. It's heavier than it looks." She drew her hands closer to her body to balance the weight.

Colin grinned. "She's such a beauty."

Parker took the weight back. His fingers skimmed her hand as he did, sensitizing her palm, sending pulses through her skin and up her arm. They both stilled for a second.

She met the mirror of his eyes just as a sharp breath hissed through his parted lips.

ONLY HALF PARKER'S ATTENTION WAS ON THE DIRT AS he dug into the old, dry creek bank. The other half was on Hailey. As brief as their touch had been, it had shot right through to his core. It was the strangest sensation, half heat and half buzzing electricity.

"How far in do we have to dig?" she asked, surprising him by picking up a shovel and sizing up the bank.

"I've got it," Parker said, although she looked pretty comfortable with that shovel in her hand.

"Try a little farther down this way," Colin said, then caught Parker's disapproving look. "I mean, only if you really want to," Colin finished.

"I'm game." Hailey picked her way along the bank.

Parker clamped his jaw. He wanted to tell her to stand back. She was the pilot, not a laborer. Plus, it still annoyed him to see women toiling in the dirt.

He knew where his attitude came from—his history with his mother and sister. They'd both been forced to work to exhaustion by his demanding father.

He knew some women liked physical work, and they were perfectly entitled to their own career choices. Still, watching Hailey struggle to wedge her shovel into the packed soil hit him on a visceral level.

"If you go a couple of feet in, it'll give us a good test sample," Colin said. "That nugget was abnormally close to the surface. Could be an anomaly, or it could be a huge find." He took his own shovel several yards farther down from Hailey.

Parker dug in again, setting aside shovelfuls of topsoil and overburden until he came to some cleaner gravel that looked promising. It was coarse with stones, and he turned to drop a sample into the gold-mining pan behind him.

He moved to where Hailey was shoveling. "How's it looking?"

"Not quite there," she answered, pushing the shovel in with her foot.

"Want a hand?"

"I'm good."

He moved a little closer, itching to get in. "I can just—"

She turned to glare at him. "What? My shoveling's not up to your standards?"

"No, no. I didn't mean that."

"I got this, Parker."

"I can help, is all I'm saying."

"You don't think I'm strong enough to shovel?"

"I don't want your hands to get sore."

She looked like she might laugh. "Seriously? How wimpy do you think I am?" She turned back to her work.

"Fine," he said, spreading his arms, shovel and all, in surrender.

Down the way, Colin clattered some dirt into another of the gold pans.

The wind picked up, rustling the leaves in the poplar trees that lined the upward slope behind them, cooling Parker's bare forearms and cutting through the cotton of his shirt.

Hailey hit a promising-looking patch.

"That looks good," he told her.

She turned his way again, eyes narrow. "Are you always such a micromanager?"

"No." He wasn't.

"Then step away from my test site."

He eased backward, staying clear as she dumped the dirt into a pan. Then they all set their shovels down, lifted their pans and headed for the rushing water of a nearby creek that had been rerouted decades, maybe even hundreds of years ago.

"Have you ever panned for gold?" he asked her as they crouched beside the water.

"Why do I get the feeling I'm going to get a lesson."

"It's a legitimate question. If I grab the yoke on the Cessna, are you going to ask questions?"

Her expression went hard. "Don't you touch my yoke."

"It's a hypothetical, Hailey."

She glanced at what Colin was doing, then dipped her pan into the water. "I'm not going to crash your pay dirt into the ground."

Parker couldn't tell if she knew what she was doing or was just copying Colin's technique. "You might send my gold floating down the creek."

"Gold doesn't float."

Parker dipped his own pan into the clear, rushing water. "You are the most contrary person."

"That's because you're a meddler."

"A meddler?" He was insulted by that. He'd only been trying to help.

"Trust me." She shook the pan, rhythmically rotating it, sluicing water in and out and letting the loose dirt flow out over the lip. It looked like she knew what she was doing.

He focused on his own pan. "All you had to do was answer my first question." He switched his voice to a higher pitch. "Yes, Parker. I've panned for gold before."

She kept her focus on her pan, but he could see her stifled smile.

"Would that have been so hard?" he asked.

"Would you have asked if I was a man?"

He didn't know the answer to that. Maybe. It depended on what kind of man. If she'd been obviously urbane, he would have asked. If a guy had looked Alaskan outdoorsy, probably not.

He shifted his gaze her way again. Okay, if she'd been a man dressed as she was, who seemed as capable as she did, he wouldn't have asked.

"Got you," she said under her breath.

"I admit nothing," he countered.

"I've got flakes," Colin called out.

Parker looked over, envying the man's speed. Colin was far more practiced than Parker right now. It had been a few years since Parker had spent time out in the field at all, never mind done any panning.

"No nuggets," Colin said, sounding disappointed as he scooped some more water to finish.

Parker stared into the fine gravel as he continued swirling water through his pan. Gold flecks appeared. There were plenty of them, but not a single nugget.

"I've got something!" Hailey called out, coming to her feet.

Parker and Colin moved in from either side for a look at her pan. A small nugget poked up from the gravel.

"Nice," Colin said with appreciation. He reached to pluck it out.

"How big?" Hailey asked, her eyes aglow with excitement.

Parker had thought they were clear blue, but in the bright sunshine, they took on a green tone. Or maybe they turned green when she was excited. His body warmed to that particular thought, and he quickly tamped down the unwelcome sensation.

"Maybe a quarter ounce," he said.

Her expression fell. "Is that all?"

"No, that's good," Colin quickly put in. "It's really good."

"It means there are more nuggets in this ground," Parker added. He gazed back at the old creek bed. One nugget was an anomaly. But more were geologically significant. "This could be a serious find."

"Here you go." Colin dropped the nugget into Hailey's palm.

She shifted it around in a stream of sunlight. "It's so pretty. Can we pan for some more?"

"You want to keep it?" Parker offered, liking the idea of her enjoying the results of her work.

She looked up at him in shock. Her eyes were back to blue again, lending credence to his theory that her emotions changed their tone.

"I can't keep your gold," she said. "It's yours."

"You found it," he reasoned.

"You're the one who owns the claim."

"Fifty-fifty," he offered. "We'll keep what's left in the pan, and you can keep the nugget."

"I don't think that's fifty-fifty."

Parker caught Colin's curious look. Then watched Colin's expression turn to a knowing grin.

But Colin had it wrong. Parker didn't have designs on Hailey. He was simply entertained by her budding gold fever.

"It's close enough," Colin said to her, backing up Parker's statement. It was clear he thought he was being a good wingman.

"We should get going," Parker said to Hailey.

"But we're on a roll." She looked eagerly back at the dry creek bank.

"It's also coming up on midnight."

"Are you about to turn into a pumpkin or something?"

He couldn't help but chuckle. He gestured to the pay dirt behind them. "Fine. Pan away. But I'm keeping half of what you find."

"Hang on," Colin drawled. "Is that the deal? Can I keep half of what I find, too?"

Parker rolled his eyes. "Sure. Tonight, everybody keeps half."

Hailey's green-blue eyes narrowed as she tipped her chin his way. "So, you get half of what I find. And you get half of what Colin finds. And you get everything you find?"

"That's right."

"Hmph," she said. "I believe you'll be buying the drinks."

"Anytime," he said. His tone came out unintendedly intimate, and Colin gave him another knowing look that he chose to ignore.

Chapter Three

HAILEY ROLLED THE LITTLE NUGGET AROUND IN HER fingertips, trying not to think of it as a bribe as she sat on the deck of the Bear and Bar Café, sipping an iced tea, scrolling through information on Parker's company, PQH. Maybe he'd meant it as a gift, no strings attached. It had certainly felt that way in the moment. It felt like they were having some fun, off on a lark panning for gold.

But later . . . later, Hailey started wondering what it had meant. She'd started wondering about his entire demeanor, his smile, his jokes, the light in his eyes as they'd found a few more nuggets. They were even smaller than the one she'd first found, but both Parker and Colin insisted it was a great sign for the potential of the ground.

If she was a mistrustful person, she might suspect Parker had been working his way into her good graces. Because after a while, she'd started wishing him well with the mine. She'd hoped he'd find big nugget after big nugget. But then she remembered what it would mean for Raven and Paradise. The more successful Parker's business ventures became, the more determined he'd be to invest in Galina. And once he invested in Galina, he'd want to make the company work for him.

She'd seen her family do it dozens of times. They'd get their hooks into a smaller company, woo the owners with promises of expansion and greater profitability. It was a best-case scenario for the Barrosse family when the target company was already in financial trouble—like Galina. There were few things more compelling to a struggling company than the promise of ready cash.

It was like her gold fever last night. Sure, she'd admit that's what happened. When she saw that shiny nugget in her gold pan, showing up so quickly with so little effort, she couldn't help but think about the riches in the ground around her, all of them just waiting to be discovered.

Even now, she remembered the excitement and anticipation. Her hand wrapped around the warming nugget as she remembered her other emotions as well. Parker's touch had been the first jolt to her system. His hands were warm, strong, broad and slightly calloused. There was an energy to his skin, an energy that her skin seemed to like. Her flesh liked it too, and her bones, maybe even her soul.

She shook herself, realizing she was wandering off on some silly fanciful poetry. It had been merely a touch. It was light and fleeting—even if the look in his smoky eyes had made her feel like she was the only woman in his world.

He probably practiced that smoldering look in front of a mirror, using it as part of his schmoozing repertoire. A person didn't get that rich that fast without a talent for winning friends and influencing people. If a guy like that wanted something from you, you were instantly his target.

It wasn't clear what he wanted from Hailey. He might not even know himself. It could be no more than a reflex. She was in front of him, so he turned on the charm.

She shut off her screen and took a sip of her drink, admitting to herself she wasn't going to find anything more from public sources. Plus, she'd already worked out the pattern of his acquisitions and how he seemed to run them all as a single entity. It was enough to make her suspicious.

She knew that pattern. She recognized that pattern. If it were only about her, she'd be ready to convict him on that alone. But it wasn't only about her. She needed a lot more evidence before she went to Raven.

And to get more evidence, she'd need insider information. Too bad there were only two insiders in town—Dalia Volksberg and Parker himself.

"*There* you are." Willow breezed through the open doorway that led from the Bear and Bar lounge to the sundeck. "Breena said you were out here drinking."

"It's iced tea," Hailey pointed out, holding her glass up as proof.

"Why? It's nearly four." Willow pulled up a chair.

Theirs was one of three occupied tables on the café deck. The other two were taken up by couples, both sets clearly into each other, laughing, whispering and gazing sappily into each other's eyes. Romantic attraction was clearly in the air out here, and it had her wondering if their pheromones had infected her too, making Parker seem sexier in her memory.

"What's that?" Willow pointed to the nugget.

Hailey had forgotten she was still twisting it in her fingers. She looked down. "Gold."

"Nice. What for? Are you getting something made?"

"I flew a passenger to a mine yesterday."

"And they gave you gold? Man, I need to switch jobs."

Hailey *wished* gold nuggets were a regular perk of her job. "Are you done stunt-womaning for the day?"

Willow nodded, reaching for Hailey's iced tea with a question in her eyes.

"Go for it," Hailey told her.

Willow took a swig. "Easy day. I had to scramble up a

rock face, but it wasn't all that steep. We didn't need to rope in or anything. Plus, they had me do a couple of trail runs and some weight training for the transition sequence. That Hope Martindale sure isn't much of an athlete."

"They didn't hire her for her fitness." They'd hired her in part because she looked like Willow.

Probably it was strange to hire the stuntwoman and then find a star to match. But Willow had been in on the ground floor of the film.

It had happened when Mia Westberg had partnered with her cousin Raven to organize Finding Paradise—a match-making project that brought LA women north to meet the working men in town. Nearly two years ago, fellow match-making tour participant Scarlett Kensington had fallen for pilot Xavier O'Keefe and convinced Mia to finance a film in Paradise. Scarlett was determined to have her new friend Willow do the stunts.

Enter Hope Martindale, a little known but rising actress, and the plan came together. It seemed to be working out well for everyone.

"How about you?" Willow asked. "Any more flying today?"

Hailey shook her head. "It's a quiet day. Xavier and T are on a grocery run to Wildflower Lake. Silas and T-Two took a Twin Otter on a fuel haul to Viking Mine. They're welcome to that trip." Loading and unloading fuel drums took a whole lot of muscle. Hailey wasn't sorry to miss the heavy work.

Willow nodded to Hailey's tablet. "Did you answer your sister?"

"Not yet." In fact, Hailey had pushed her family problems out of her mind both last night and today. "I've been creeping on Parker Hall some more."

"Ooh, what else did you find?"

"Not much that's new. With private companies, there's only so much they disclose on the Internet."

"What were you looking for?" Willow polished off the iced tea.

"Information on his companies and investments. When he got involved in them. How they work together. But I think I'm going to have to go analog to get anything more."

"I'm in. Do we grill Parker? Schmooze him?" Willow waggled her brows. "Cozy up to him and get sexy?"

Hailey ignored the last part, especially since it sounded like fun. "Either him or his sidekick, Dalia Volksberg."

"You mean the woman sitting in the dining room? You want more of this?" Willow waggled the empty glass.

Hailey's attention perked up. "Dalia's in the dining room?"

Willow nodded.

"Is she alone?"

"She was when I came through."

Hailey came to her feet and collected her tablet. "Let's go get a drink."

Willow stood. "Now you're talkin'."

Inside the restaurant, Hailey spotted Dalia right away. At a table by the window, she was dressed in a midnight-blue blazer over a silky white blouse with chunky silver necklaces, straight-legged black slacks and a pair of tan heeled ankle boots. Her hair was up in a messy knot, showing off dangling multistrand earrings.

Hailey guessed that was Dalia going casual. She wasn't self-conscious about her own cargo pants, scuffed, dusty work boots and boxy, hunter-green T-shirt. But the contrast was a little stark.

"Hi, Dalia," she greeted her from a few feet away, not wanting to intrude, and not sure that Dalia would even remember her from their meeting on the film set.

Dalia glanced up and closed her laptop screen like it was confidential, which it probably was. "Hello, Hailey."

"Do you remember Willow Hale? She's working on the *Aurora Unleashed* film."

"I remember you both," Dalia said.

"Do you mind if we join you?" Willow asked, making a move for a chair on the opposite side of the table, not giving Dalia a chance to refuse.

"I . . . uh . . ."

Willow slid to the window and patted the other chair for Hailey.

"Do you mind?" Hailey felt compelled to ask Dalia for real, giving her a chance to refuse.

Dalia fluttered her hand in a gesture of surrender. "Sure."

"What are you drinking?" Willow asked her.

"Coffee."

"Any interest in martinis? You seem like a classic woman. Am I right? Or maybe you want a metropolitan or a crantini?"

Dalia gave a little shudder at the word *crantini*.

"Vodka?" Willow asked.

"Extra olives," Dalia answered.

"Three vodka martinis, extra olives, coming up." Willow pushed back her chair, squeezed out and headed for Badger at the bar.

Hailey and Dalia blinked at each other from across the table.

"She's—" Dalia started and then stopped.

"Energetic?" Hailey finished for her.

"High-octane," Dalia responded.

"She is from LA."

"Recently?"

Hailey grinned. "Yes. She's only in town to film *Aurora Unleashed*. Well, she was up here two years ago too. She was part of the Finding Paradise matchmaking project."

"Matchmaking project?" Dalia looked curious.

Hailey was happy for the innocuous conversational topic. "It was quite the event. Raven and her cousin Mia decided there weren't enough eligible women in Paradise, so they brought some up for a long weekend. Willow was one of them. Another participant, Scarlett, happened to be a film producer. Mia happened to be willing to invest in a film. And voila. Here we are." She took a breath, deciding it was safe to nudge the conversation in the right direction. "And how do you like Paradise?"

"I've only been here two days."

"From?" Hailey was quite curious about that.

"Boston by way of Anchorage."

That explained Dalia's great fashion sense. Downtown Boston was both formal and professional.

Hailey kept the topic going. "What brought you to Anchorage?"

"Parker."

Something shifted inside Hailey. It felt irritatingly like jealousy. Were Parker and Dalia, Parker *and* Dalia?

She'd thought theirs was a business relationship. And it was obviously that. But nothing said it couldn't be more. In fact, it made sense that it was more. The two of them made a compellingly great couple, almost a matched set, both cultivated and refined, both poised and successful. Why wouldn't they be a couple?

It wasn't any of Hailey's concern if they were. It didn't change her objective one iota. She was still determined to figure out Parker's interest in Galina, and if he was looking to hurt Raven or Paradise.

"He offered me a job," Dalia continued, smiling to herself at what must have been a happy memory. "Completely out of the blue. Alaska was *nowhere* on my radar at the time."

"Parker was a draw?" Hailey probed.

"His ambition and corporate balance sheet were compelling."

Hailey felt a rather worrisome sense of relief. The two could still be a couple, but Dalia wasn't making it sound like they were.

"How did he find you?" Hailey asked, searching for more.

"I wrote an article in *Weekly Enterprise*."

Last night, Parker had said he was born and raised in Alaska. What would lead him to read an East Coast business magazine?

"Was it about him?" Hailey asked, trying to understand.

Dalia looked puzzled by the question. "No. I'd never even heard of him."

"Heard of who?" Willow asked, arriving at the end of the table with two of the martinis in hand.

"Parker," Dalia said.

"I thought you worked for him." Willow set one of the martinis in front of Dalia, then put the other in front of Hailey.

"I meant before I worked for him," Dalia said. "I hadn't heard of him before he offered me the job."

"Oh. That makes more sense." Willow turned and headed back to the bar.

Dalia gave Hailey an amused smile and stirred the skewer of three olives through her chilled martini. "Maybe I should wait until she gets back."

"Good idea." Hailey lifted her own olive skewer and slid an olive off the end with her teeth, crunching down on the tart morsel.

A moment later, Willow returned with her own martini and sat back down. "So, what did I miss?"

"Dalia is from Boston," Hailey said.

"No kidding." Willow seemed impressed. "I have an aunt in Boston. Haven't seen her since I was a kid. I think she's an accountant or something."

"Accountants are cool," Dalia said.

"Never heard that phrase before," Hailey couldn't help but add.

Dalia frowned. "It's not all about numbers."

Hailey felt guilty for coming across as insulting.

"It's not exactly your hot career though," Willow put in, smoothing the moment over, making Hailey grateful. "Not like Mia the high fashion model."

"Mia's a model?" Dalia asked, looking intrigued by that revelation as she took a sip of her martini.

"Former," Hailey said, taking a drink herself. The martini felt both cool and warm going down. She realized she was in the mood for something just like this and silently thanked Willow for the idea.

"Should we get snacks?" Willow asked. "I could go for some gooey loaded nachos."

Dalia drew back, taking Willow in with what looked like surprise. "You're so trim."

"Calories in, calories out," Willow said with an airy wave. Then she eyeballed them for their reactions. "So, yes to nachos?"

"Sounds good to me," Hailey said, then turned her attention back to Dalia, hoping to keep the conversation on the right track. "What was your article about?"

"Conglomerate Diversification in Supply Chain Management."

"Sounds riveting," Willow said.

Dalia didn't seem bothered by the sarcasm. "It was a case study of Australian Prime Metals."

Hailey had already made a mental note of the publication name. Now she made a mental note of the article and the company Dalia had studied. They were both information threads, and either could be a valuable clue to Parker's plans for Galina.

"What was your conclusion?" Hailey asked.

"I'll go order the nachos," Willow said, pushing her chair back again.

"That diversification into supply chain companies provided financial predictability and security in the mining sector."

"And Parker liked that."

"He seemed to. He called. Then he flew to Boston and, well, made me an offer I couldn't refuse."

IT SEEMED AN UNLIKELY GROUP TO PARKER—DALIA WITH Hailey and the stuntwoman from *Aurora Unleashed*. Her name was Willow if he was remembering right. The three women were engaged in a lively conversation as they sipped martinis at a window table in the Bear and Bar. They also seemed to be about halfway through a large platter of nachos with all the fixings.

He was guessing it wasn't the first round of martinis, especially since Dalia selected a cheese-covered chip and dunked it into a small bowl of sour cream before popping it into her mouth. Then she daintily blotted her lips with a paper napkin in her perfectly manicured hand, swallowed and laughed out loud at something Hailey had said.

Baffled by the unexpected scene, Parker made his way to the edge of their table. "Hi, Dalia." He couldn't stop himself from glancing Hailey's way and remembering their moment at the mine.

She was dressed in what he'd come to recognize as her uniform of multipocket cargo pants and a plain T-shirt. She didn't seem to wear makeup or do anything beyond a practical ponytail with her hair. Still, she looked beautiful, more so with the sun highlighting the pale amber of her hair and reflecting off the blue-green of her eyes.

"Parker," Dalia greeted him in a lilting voice. Her eyes looked suspiciously bright with what he guessed was martini consumption. "Did you know Mia was a famous model?"

He'd clearly walked into the middle of a conversation. "Mia?"

"*Raven's* cousin." Dalia sounded like she was scolding him now. "She's rich. She's from LA. She's financing *Aurora Unleashed*."

"My first stuntwoman gig," Willow added.

Parker glanced at Hailey again.

"Hello, Parker." Her patiently amused smile made him think she might be slightly behind on the martini count.

"Girls' night out?" he asked.

Dalia slid over to the chair by the window, moving her martini with her. "Sit *down*, Parker."

Willow reached over to shift Dalia's nacho plate, leaving space for him.

"Hungry?" Willow asked him. "I was thinking about ordering some wings."

"Don't you ever stop eating?" Dalia asked Willow.

Parker caught Hailey's gaze and gave her his best *what is going on here* expression.

She smiled brightly, and the force of it hit him in the solar plexus. "We're all getting to know each other."

"Wings?" Willow repeated, trying to get his attention. "Or sweet potato fries." Her voice lit up over the idea. "Oh, those sound awesome."

"Carbs in grease?" Dalia asked her, sounding slightly horrified.

"Match made in Heaven," Willow said, taking a swig of her martini.

"Anything's fine with me," Parker told her.

He was hungry enough to share in an appetizer. Plus, it was entertaining to watch Dalia go over to the dark side of cuisine. And he was curious enough about Hailey to hope she'd order another drink and start talking.

Willow came to her feet. "What do you want to drink?" she asked Parker.

He quickly rose. "I've got it. So, sweet potato fries for the table?" He glanced around at their glasses, but they all seemed relatively full.

Willow dropped back down. "You're a gentleman."

"Sure," he agreed with amusement. It was a whole twenty feet to the bar—hardly the most strenuous gentle-manly effort he'd ever put out.

Parker had learned earlier that the bartender's name was Badger. He seemed to be fortysomething, but still fit, with a weathered face and shaggy hair. Parker guessed he'd probably grown up in Alaska, maybe right here in Paradise.

"What can I get for you?" Badger asked as Parker approached the richly polished wooden bar.

It was coming up on six, and the restaurant was beginning to fill up with workers and a few families. Some of the guys had checked Parker out as he crossed the room, likely wondering what he was doing with three pretty women all to himself. The population here in Paradise definitely skewed male. If he had to guess, he'd say it was about fifteen or twenty to one.

"A beer," Parker answered. "Amber Ice if you've got it."

"We do."

"And a plate of sweet potato fries for the table."

"Coming right up." Badger turned for the glass-fronted fridge, extracting a bottle of Amber Ice. "Glass?" he called over his shoulder.

"I'm fine with the bottle."

When Badger set it down on the bar, Parker canted his head to the table of women. "How many rounds have they had?"

"Three. Except for Hailey. She's still on her second." Badger popped the cap off the beer.

"They do seem jovial."

"How's the room working out for you?" Badger asked, obviously referring to Parker's bed-and-breakfast room on the second floor of the building.

"It's fine. Bed's good. Water's hot. Wireless works." Paradise wasn't big enough to have a hotel. The Bear and Bar's three-room bed-and-breakfast or the Rapid Release rafting company's new cabins were the only rental options in town, and the cabins were full right now with the cast and crew of *Aurora Unleashed*.

"Good to hear," Badger said. "I'll get your fries going."

"Thanks, man." Parker tipped his bottle Badger's way as he headed back to the table.

Next to the window, Dalia and Willow were leaning toward each other, talking in earnest.

"You have to trust your equipment," Willow was saying.

Dalia looked amazed. "Just like that?" She made a flying motion with her hand. "Right over the edge of a cliff?"

Parker raised a quizzical brow to Hailey as he sat down, setting his beer on the table.

"Hang gliding," she said.

"Willow?" he asked, impressed.

"All adventure sports, all the time."

"Ever been?" he asked Hailey as the chatter carried on between Dalia and Willow.

"No thanks. I'm content with an airplane securely around me."

"Wise." Parker gave a nod and took a sip.

"Dalia told me about her article you read."

It took Parker a moment to understand what Hailey meant. "You mean the *Weekly Enterprise* thing? Wow. That was a long time ago." He was surprised the topic had come up. He and Dalia had been through a whole lot since way back then.

"How long have you been together?" Hailey asked conversationally.

"Coming up on five years."

"Did you change course then?" Hailey asked.

Parker didn't understand what she meant. He furrowed his brow in puzzlement.

"Your business," she elaborated. "Did bringing Dalia onboard change things for you?"

"You could say that." He might have been poised for growth when she joined up, but she'd absolutely had a hand in the relationships they'd built and the direction the company had taken. "She's a highly valued player in the company." He couldn't help but smile to himself at the understatement.

Dalia earned more than anyone else at PQH, with a generous salary plus a bonus structure. It had been the only way to lure her from an established company in Boston to what was then a risky start-up in Alaska. He hoped she'd stick with him for a long time to come, even though her bonus structure meant she could buy a mansion in Beacon Hill and retire anytime she wanted.

Luckily, she was a workaholic, so early retirement seemed unlikely. In fact, he'd often wondered why she insisted on earning so much money. She didn't have a lavish lifestyle. Nice clothes, sure, and she did have a taste for fine cuisine. But her apartment in Anchorage wasn't huge. She'd decorated it once and left it alone after that. He supposed she spent some money on her jewelry, but she wore the same quality pieces over and over again.

Maybe she *was* saving up for a mansion.

"I'm guessing her job is to help you buy other companies," Hailey said.

"What makes you guess that?" Not that she was wrong.

"The title of her article."

"What was the title of her article?" He couldn't remember it. All he remembered was that it had made sense, and she had made sense, and he knew he needed help if he wanted his business to grow—fast, to ensure his mother and sister's security and to keep his father from ever having influence over their lives again.

"Conglomerate Diversification in Supply Chain Management." Hailey bit off one of the olives in her martini. The move was sexy, so sexy.

Parker took a deep, cooling swallow of his beer.

"So?" Hailey prompted, stirring the remaining olives in what was left of her drink.

"So, what?" He fixated on her lips—full, pink, soft and

damp from the martini. They were the most kissable lips he'd ever seen.

"You hired her for the article, and?" If she'd meant to arouse him with the olive move, she was sure playing it cool with the question.

Parker didn't want to talk about Dalia. He was much more interested in Hailey. "How long have you lived in Paradise?"

She looked disappointed. Odd that she'd be disappointed in having the conversation switch to her. That hadn't been his past experience with women.

"Six years," she said.

"You grew up in Alaska?" He wondered where. He'd guess rural, maybe down the Kenai or toward the Canadian border.

"No. In Atlanta."

He wouldn't have guessed a metropolitan center, not in a million years, and he couldn't hold back a smile at the unlikely image. "The land of big hair, frothy skirts and mint juleps?"

She didn't miss a beat. "Those hoop skirts are *such* a problem in a small cockpit."

"I can imagine." He was imagining her in pretty pastels, a little lace and upswept hair. Makeup would make her eyes stand out even more, and the warm sun would put a blush in her cheeks. He liked the image a little too much and banished it. "So, what drew a Southern girl to Alaska?"

"What made you stay in Alaska?" she countered.

"I like it here."

She gestured to his suit and tie. "So, what's with the outfit then?"

"Ever been to Anchorage?"

"I have. And you're high-end even for Anchorage."

He cocked his head Dalia's way. "My image consultant."

"What's the image you're trying to project? Uptight and urbane?"

"Success and professionalism."

She twisted her glass by the stem and seemed to consider his answer—not in a good way. When she spoke, her tone said she didn't admire his choice. "You think that's what you're projecting?"

He did. "It's working for me so far."

"With whom?"

"The movers and shakers of Anchorage and beyond."

Her lips pursed. "Why do you care what they think?"

He bristled at what struck him as criticism. "I don't care what they *think*. I care what they *do*. I care about opening doors and building relationships as a key to business growth." He realized too late that he didn't have to explain himself to her, especially if she was going to be judgmental. He stopped talking and took a drink of his beer.

The expression in her eyes turned contemplative. "Exactly how big do you want to grow, Parker Hall?"

"Sky's the limit." He paused, holding her gaze while Badger set the platter of sweet potato fries on the table. "Especially if we keep finding nuggets the size of goose eggs."

HAILEY HAD SWITCHED TO SODA WHILE THEY MOVED through lighthearted topics and munched on a series of appetizers, but she had no intention of driving after two martinis. She could easily hitch a ride home with Badger or someone else. Eventually, they'd escorted a very jovial Dalia upstairs to her B and B room, and Parker offered to drive Willow back to her cabin.

The three of them piled into Parker's borrowed pickup and took Willow safely to her front door at Rapid Release. She was due on set in the morning, so Hailey went inside and made sure her alarm was properly set, then suggested she make it an early night. Hailey figured Willow would want time for coffee and a good breakfast before she jumped off a cliff or dove into the river, or whatever it was she had on her filming schedule for tomorrow.

Leaving, Hailey shut the cabin door to find Parker standing next to the pickup, gazing down the gentle slope to the river.

Hearing her footsteps across the screened-in porch, he turned her way. "I think someone's coming in."

Hailey opened the screen door, walked out and listened.

Coming up next to Parker, she heard the muted whine of an outboard motor from around the riverbend. "It must be Riley."

A flash of yellow and orange appeared on the water— the raft and the life jackets worn by the rafters. Their voices carried as they talked back and forth about the footage they'd shot on the trip. They seemed enthusiastic about their efforts.

Parker started for the shoreline, and Hailey followed along. She recognized some of the film crew beneath the white safety helmets. Another raft trailed behind the first, both loaded up with people and waterproof equipment cases.

"Hey, Hailey," Riley called to her as he shut down the outboard and tipped up the leg. He hopped easily from the stern of the raft, the water coming over his splash suit to his knees.

"Filming?" Hailey asked him, although it was obvious.

"Some B-roll of the falls and the gorge. I'm not sure it was wild enough for them." He walked onto the shore and braced the bow of the raft so the others could step out onto dry land.

Despite his business clothes, Parker stepped up to take the expensive equipment from the crew's hands as they moved forward. Riley gave him a nod of appreciation.

"Not wild enough for them?" Hailey was surprised to hear that. She'd rafted over the three waterfalls upriver and found them plenty wild.

They weren't the steepest ones in Riley's repertoire, but the rafts became airborne for a few seconds over the drops. It was where Mia's lawyer Marnie Anton had bounced out of the raft and had to be rescued from a whirlpool during the Finding Paradise matchmaking event. Exactly how much wilder did they want?

"We need more height for the drama shots," director Natasha Burton said as she took Parker's hand and stepped awkwardly out of the raft and onto the strip of soft sand in her splash suit and bulky life jacket. She removed her helmet and shook out her hair.

"I'll come up with some other options for you," Riley told her.

The second raft hit the shore, and Parker moved to hold the bow in place.

"Thanks, man," raft pilot Nicholas called out to him, since Parker had saved him from wading in from the stern.

"No problem," Parker answered as the passengers filed past him.

As the load lightened, Parker pulled the raft more securely onto the shore. Then he reached in to unstrap and remove the filming equipment.

Nicholas worked his way forward, handing waterproof cases to Parker.

"Looking to get on steady?" Riley joked, joining Parker in unloading.

Parker returned the friendly smile. "Looks like a nice setup you have here." He scanned the property then, the expanse of shaggy grass on the slope, a parking area up top, the Rapid Release office with Riley's living quarters, plus the five new cabins built over the past year.

"It's shaping up," Riley said.

"Been doing this for a while?" Parker asked.

"I started ten years ago with one raft and a dream."

"Built it all yourself?" Parker's question was casual, but Hailey's curiosity perked up.

She listened to him ask more about the business as the others stripped off their life jackets and trailed away toward the office and the parking lot.

"I'll grab a van," Nicholas called out, following the crowd.

Riley pulled the first raft farther onto the sandy shore. "We have four rafts now," he continued answering Parker's questions. "Generally, three of them are in service at any one time. Leaves us room for maintenance and repair, plus contingencies." He paused. "You need to be ready for contingencies."

"Do people come to Paradise specifically to run the river?" Parker hauled the second raft up onto the beach.

"They do now. Word started getting around on social media. It's a bit of a slow year now, but we'll make it up."

Parker gave a considered nod, looking around again. "The cabins must have set you back."

"They weren't cheap. Building materials are so bulky and heavy, the shipping costs kill you up here." Riley repacked the safety straps, coiled a rope and bailed some water from the floor of the raft.

On the second raft, Parker mirrored Riley's work. "Was it a risk for you to expand like that?"

Hearing Nicolas start up the van, Hailey moved the stray safety equipment clear of the access lane, giving him extra room to back up the raft trailer while she listened in on the men's conversation.

"Wilderness tourism is a growth sector," Riley said as they both finished the raft cleanup. "Thanks a lot, man. You're visiting?"

"Up from Anchorage for a few days," Parker answered vaguely.

Riley's gaze moved to Hailey, obviously assuming Parker was here to visit her. Riley gave her an encouraging smile. "You two have fun."

She wanted to set the record straight. "We're not—"

"I wouldn't mind taking a rafting trip while I'm here," Parker said.

"Sure," Riley answered easily. "Can you swing by tomorrow and we can check the schedule?"

"Absolutely."

Riley stood to the side while Nicolas backed the cargo van and trailer down the hill.

"Great to meet you," Parker said as he turned for his pickup truck.

Hailey fell into step beside him up the incline. "What was *that*?"

He acted like he didn't understand. "What was what?"

"You. All those questions."

"Just making conversation."

"You had a predatory gleam in your eyes."

"A *predatory* gleam?" He gave her a look that said she was delusional.

"Yes. You were calculating and plotting while you gave him the third degree."

Parker chuckled. "Calculating and plotting?"

"Can you not help yourself?"

"I was impressed with his business. He started with nothing, saw an opportunity and built it into something with big possibilities." He paused and looked thoughtfully around one more time. "There are some big possibilities in this."

"Are you branching out into tourism?"

"Hadn't thought of it until you mentioned it," he said on a teasing note.

They came to the passenger side and he opened the door.

She might have protested, but it seemed like such a natural thing for him to do that she knew it was a habit, not a statement.

She climbed in, but then turned back to him. "You should leave Riley alone."

He grinned as he pushed the door shut.

"I mean it," she said as he opened the driver's-side door.

"What do you think I'm going to do?"

"I don't know. Buy him out."

"I don't want to run a river rafting business." But Parker still looked thoughtful.

"See that?" she said, pointing to his expression. "You're thinking about it."

"You brought it up."

"I did not. You had it on your mind back there while you were quizzing him."

He shrugged as he turned the key to start the engine. "I guess I have the entrepreneurial gene."

"I've seen the entrepreneurial gene," she stated. She was lucky to have missed out on it herself. It was an insatiable monster.

Parker pulled the shifter into drive and started along the two tire tracks that served as a driveway in front of the cabins. "Seen it do what?"

"Destroy lives."

He glanced her way with an amused expression. "Seriously?"

"You can't win at it, nobody really wins."

"Oh, I have to disagree with you on that. You saw my new gold nugget. That was a win—likely one of many to come from that particular mining property."

"Temporary satisfaction. And you'll leave misery and destruction in your wake."

He frowned as they turned onto the main road, coming up to speed. "There's no destruction, only temporary disturbance. We reclaim everything. Replace the topsoil, replant the trees, seed a natural meadow. Moose and deer love the new habitat."

"I mean the people."

"What people?"

"Your success comes at the expense of others."

He frowned. "Business is not a zero-sum game, Hailey.

The people who work for me have good jobs, productive lives, for the most part doing something that interests them."

They passed by the buildings on the outskirts of Paradise.

"What about people like Riley?" she pressed.

"My business has nothing to do with Riley."

She wasn't buying that after what she'd just watched. "All those years, all that work, and a guy like you can just come along and buy it out from under him."

Parker's voice rose. "Well, there's a leap in logic."

Hailey lifted her brow, giving him a knowing look, staring until he glanced her way. "You were thinking about the possibilities of his business. For you."

"Thinking about the possibilities isn't the same as doing something about them. Maybe I was thinking about the possibilities for Riley."

"Uh-huh," she said skeptically.

"You can't read my mind."

The sun was dipping for the mountain peaks as they passed Yellow Road, the street that led off to the local school.

"I can read your expression. WSA housing is a right at Red Avenue. Or you can just drop me around the corner at the Bear and Bar."

"I'll take you home." He pulled around the corner. "Here?"

"Fifth unit down from the back of the café."

He angled up to the wooden sidewalk, rocking to a stop. "I dispute your claim that you can read my expression."

"Yeah?" She unbuckled her seat belt and turned her body to face him. "Go ahead. Think something."

He unbuckled and turned as well, propping his elbow on the steering wheel and looking amused. "Okay."

She studied his smug expression. "You're thinking I'll fail at this."

"That's a given." His expression softened a little, his gray eyes morphing from flint to smoke. His mouth softened around the edges, while his chin moved the slightest bit lower.

She didn't know what *he* was thinking, but *she* was thinking he looked like a poster guy for raw sexuality. If she didn't know better, she'd think he wanted to kiss her. But that couldn't be true, and it sure wasn't going to be her answer.

"You've stopped thinking about Riley and Rapid Release," she said.

His lips curved ever so slightly. "You're right about that."

"Point to me," she claimed.

He was silent for a moment, his smoldering look pulling hard on her emotions. "Point to you," he said softly.

She had to fight an urge to lean his way. She might have the advantage now with her guess about his thoughts, but that could change in a heartbeat. It was time to leave before she said or did something that turned the advantage Parker's way.

Chapter Four

PARKER SUPPOSED HE MUST HAVE THE ENTREPRE-neurial gene—whatever that was. While Hailey's accusations last night had gone further than his thoughts, they weren't completely off the mark. His brain had instinctively evaluated the opportunities for an operation like Riley's.

The guy had obviously spent a lot of money putting up the cabins. They were small but looked quite finely crafted, maybe eight hundred square feet. Glancing through the window, he'd seen they were open concept with a combined kitchen and living room, plus a bedroom, and a loft above. They each had a large covered and screened deck for a front porch, complete with cushioned furniture and a sweeping view of the river. Their peaked roofs gave a striking silhouette, and their honey-colored wood siding shone appealingly in the sunlight.

None of that came cheap. And with the slow season this year, it seemed likely Riley could be open to an investment. Parker had been honest when he'd told Hailey he didn't want to run a river rafting operation. But that didn't mean he wouldn't want to share in the profits. With three of his seven gold mines operating beyond expectations, and especially with the new potential at Lucky Breach, it was a good time to consider diversification.

A knock came on his B and B room door. His first thought was Hailey and how they'd left things between them last night. He'd really like to see her again. He'd especially like another lively conversation over morning coffee.

But he knew the odds weren't with him. She hadn't seemed to react to the sensual atmosphere in the pickup last night. It wasn't even clear she'd felt it.

He'd felt it clear as day. If she'd even come close to guessing what he was thinking there at the end, she'd have bolted from the truck.

Come to think of it, she pretty much had. Which gave him his answer.

The knock sounded again, and Parker shrugged into his suit jacket and crossed the room to answer.

Dalia paced through the open doorway, looking impressively fresh considering her martini binge last night.

"You don't have to say it," she told him, turning in the middle of the room next to the small sofa and round dining table.

He closed the door, surprised they weren't going directly down to breakfast. "Say what?"

"That I was unprofessional last night. I know, and I'm sorry." She stilled, looking contrite and uncertain in the light of the two windows bracketing the corner of his room. She was dressed smartly as ever, but her expression was one he'd never seen before.

"You were just having a little fun." He hoped she hadn't worried all night long about his reaction.

"I don't know what happened. The girls were a lot of fun, and we just kept drinking, and I just, I don't know—"

"So, you had a girls' night out." It was a completely normal thing to do.

"I was on the job," she countered.

"This is Alaska. This is Paradise. They like it when you let your hair down."

"I'm not a let-your-hair-down kind of woman."

"Really? I hadn't noticed."

She frowned. "Don't mock me."

That hadn't been his intent. Okay, maybe a little bit. But only because it was so rare for Dalia to get flustered.

"I've been thinking of diversifying," he said to move things along and let her off the hook, so she wouldn't stress about it.

She immediately snapped to attention, all business, back to normal except for the creases around her eyes that said she must have at least the remnants of a headache. "Yes. That's why we're here."

"I mean beyond mine support and supply chain."

"How so?"

"Tourism."

She frowned, looking even more like her usual self. "That's coming out of the left field. How long have you been leaning that way? You should tell me when you start thinking about new ideas."

"It's very recent."

She squinted, like she didn't believe him.

"You know the ground's looking excellent at Lucky Breach," he explained to give her context. "And the two Anchorage properties are beating projections first half of this year. That capital should be put to work."

"You expect me to argue that?"

"You look like you're warming up to disagree with me."

She lifted her brows. "Tourism?"

"Maybe. Maybe not. Wilderness tourism is up and coming."

She smiled at that, seeming like she was the one who was amused now. "We've been here three whole days, and you're a wilderness convert?"

"Hey, inspiration comes from where it comes."

"If you want to diversify, I can put some options together for you. Tourism, sure, but you should consider a few other sectors at the same time."

He suddenly realized how much work Dalia would undertake if he gave her the go-ahead. It hadn't been his intent to increase her load. "Too early for a full workup, I think."

"You sure?"

"I'm sure." He'd mull the idea a while longer before they took any major steps.

"Just give me the high sign if you want me to move on anything—" Dalia wrinkled her nose, her expression turning pinched. "Do you smell smoke?"

Parker moved to look through the window behind her, wondering if someone was burning brush nearby. At the same time, he noticed the odd odor. It wasn't woodsmoke. It smelled like burning grease.

"Breakfast gone awry?" he guessed.

A loud clanging suddenly engulfed the room.

Whatever had gone wrong in the kitchen had set off the fire alarm.

"Oh, that can't be good," Dalia called out, heading for the door.

"Don't—" Parker shouted, but he was too late.

She opened it and a cloud of smoke billowed through the doorway. The sprinklers kicked in, showering water, instantly soaking them.

Parker rushed her way, linking her arm with his as he checked the hallway. He could clearly see the fire exit door and urged her that way.

"My laptop," she called out as they passed the door to her room.

"It'll either survive or it won't," he said.

First priority was to get them both out of the building. He knew the third room on the floor was empty, so the others would be exiting from the ground floor. Presumably, the breakfast cooks had been in the kitchen when it had started and were the ones who pulled the alarm.

He pushed open the fire exit door, and they came out onto a small porch. The narrow metal staircase led to the ground on Red Avenue. A few people were already walking toward the cafe, having either heard the alarm or spotted the smoke.

Parker ushered Dalia down first, then they went around to the front to let everyone know the top floor was clear.

Mrs. France, owner of the Bear and Bar, was standing in the street, looking horrified as smoke billowed from the front windows. Breena had a comforting arm around her grandmother.

An aging red fire truck pulled up with Raven at the wheel. She and five men were dressed in turnout gear, and they piled out in a line next to Mrs. France, sizing up the building. Parker recognized Riley, Brodie and Mia's husband Silas.

He left Dalia, heading for Brodie, who seemed to be in charge.

"It started in the kitchen," Breena was telling Brodie. "When the fire extinguisher didn't put it out, we pulled the alarm and got out."

"That was the right thing to do," Brodie told her.

"The top floor is clear," Parker added. "Dalia and I were the only ones up there."

Mrs. France confirmed. "The other B and B room was empty."

A couple of the firefighters were unrolling the hose as another red truck pulled up. This one had a huge water tank on the back, and Parker realized Paradise didn't have any fire hydrants. The firefighters had to bring their own water to the scene.

"Riley, Silas," Brodie called out. "See if you can make it through to the kitchen." He looked over his shoulder. "Raven, with me. Let's check the propane tank." Then he raised his voice. "Everybody back up, stay on the other side of the street."

Parker might not have been geared up to fight the fire, but he could definitely help with crowd control. As he began ushering people to the opposite side of the road, his gaze caught on one of the firefighters, obviously a female. Though she was wearing a helmet and face shield, he recognized Hailey. His chest tightened with anxiety.

She opened a panel on the side of the water truck and hit a button. The truck's pump clattered to life. She and another firefighter hooked up and primed the hose, then stood poised, clearly waiting for a signal to spray down the building.

Smoke continued to billow out the front, a black cloud rising to the sky. Minutes later, Riley and Silas came back out the front door with their spent fire extinguishers.

Silas waved an arm and peeled off his oxygen mask. "We got it, it's under control."

Brodie and Raven appeared, returning from the back of the building.

"Xavier, Jackson," Silas called to the other firefighters. "Double check for flare-ups."

Two other firefighters donned their oxygen masks, hoisted their extinguishers and headed inside.

"Wow," Dalia said, exhaling next to Parker.

"That could have been a catastrophe," Parker said, thinking about the big propane tank used to fuel the kitchen stoves. They were lucky it hadn't gone up. His gaze sought out Hailey, impressed all over again with her capabilities. It seemed like she'd step up to almost anything.

Then he looked down the way to Mrs. France and Breena. This was a huge blow to the France family, a huge blow to the town as well. There were about fifty people in the crowd now, all looking distressed, many of them stopping to offer comforting words to Mrs. France.

"At least I have my phone," Dalia said.

Parker patted his own pocket, grateful he'd also been carrying his phone and wallet when they rushed out. It seemed unlikely their laptops had survived the smoke and water.

Willow appeared out of the crowd, stopping to stand next to Dalia. "Well, that's a huge mess."

"I hope they were insured," Dalia said.

"I expect they were," Willow responded. "But the town will rebuild the place in any event. Everyone loves that café."

Parker couldn't help but smile to himself thinking about small-town Alaska. Yeah, they'd rebuild. Probably right away. Everyone would just pick up, donate materials, use their time and skills and talents to make sure Mrs. France was up and running again as soon as possible.

He'd lend a hand so long as he was here. And he'd gladly donate to the rebuilding effort. Dalia would call that purchasing corporate goodwill. And he got that it might work that way. But it was also the right thing to do, and that was what he cared about.

Whether he invested in Galina or not, Lucky Breach was only forty minutes away by plane, so he was a neighbor now. Helping out after a disaster was just being a good neighbor.

AFTER CHANGING OUT OF HER FIREFIGHTING GEAR and helping put the trucks and equipment back into place with their supplies refreshed, Hailey headed for the Bear and Bar to see what needed doing first.

Raven had set up shop across the street with a lawn chair on the wooden sidewalk and a folding table in front of her. Tablet in hand, she was conferring with Breena and taking notes.

Hailey cut diagonally across the gravel street to get the latest.

The building had stopped smoking, and they'd confirmed the fire damage was confined to the kitchen. It would have to be rebuilt, and most of the equipment would need replacement, but the rest of the building had only smoke and water damage. It was relatively good news.

"Hailey?" The sound of Parker's voice sent a shiver of awareness along her spine as he came around the corner of the Bear and Bar.

She paused to wait for him. "Looks like you lost your accommodations in this." It was probably too much to hope that he'd fly on home to Anchorage and leave them all alone.

"Everything's smoke damaged but this suit and my cell phone and wallet."

"I'm sorry to hear that." She was sorry on a human level, even if she did hope it chased him out.

He gave a shrug of his broad shoulders. "Nothing that can't be cleaned or replaced. I didn't know you were a firefighter."

"Most of us took the training a couple of years ago."

"Good for you."

She gave him a critical look. "Would you be saying that if I was a guy?"

"No. I'd be expecting it," he admitted.

At least he was honest.

"You should get over that," she said.

"I'll try," he answered easily. "I guess I've been hanging out with a different kind of woman lately."

Hailey's attention shifted to Dalia and Willow, who were standing farther down the sidewalk talking. Talk about being on the opposite end of the spectrum from Hailey; Dalia was clearly the kind of woman Parker preferred. He might not be in a relationship with his business manager, but there were plenty of other sophisticated women in Anchorage.

"I guess I wouldn't expect Mia to take firefighter training," Hailey allowed. In her opinion, women should be whatever they wanted—firefighter, model, mother or engineer.

Parker grinned. "Can't see that myself."

"She'd fit in to your world though. Mia, I mean."

"Easily." He seemed to consider for a moment. "What brought her up here?"

"Silas."

"Sure." He waved a dismissive hand. "Love conquers all and everything. But seriously, love can't be that completely blind."

Hailey's gaze narrowed on him. "I don't know what you're saying."

"I'm saying relationships are about more than just the pitter-patter of your romantic heart. There's compatibility and lifestyle."

"Mia likes it here."

"Better than LA, Paris and Milan?"

"I assume so." Hailey had never flat-out asked Mia if she regretted leaving the bright lights of the international fashion world to be with Silas, but she seemed happy.

"What about you?" he asked.

"What about me?"

"Was there a guy in Paradise?" His expression turned pensive. "*Is* there a guy in Paradise?"

"Why does it have to be a guy?"

"So, that's a no."

"There are bush planes in Paradise." Hailey gave a decisive nod. "That's my first love."

"I like that," he said.

"Bush planes?"

"That you came here for your career."

Brodie called out from the Bear and Bar entrance. "We're clear to start the mop-up." He made a circle with his arm as a signal. "Park some pickups at the back by the door for a landfill brigade." Then he pointed to the Rapid Release van. "Riley's got tools, gloves and hard hats if you need them. We've got a couple of chainsaws, but we might need more."

"All hands on deck," Hailey said to Parker, pulling her leather work gloves from her back pocket and slipping them on as she walked toward the café.

He fell into step beside her.

She looked him over. "What are you doing?"

He seemed surprised by the question. "Same thing as you. Helping out."

She gestured to his suit and dress boots. "Not like that, you're not."

His brow furrowed.

She pressed her point. "You want to cover your three-thousand-dollar suit in ashes and soot?"

"Two," he said absently. But it was clear he got her point. "I'll find something else to wear."

"Bill's Hardware," she suggested. "And you need proper safety boots. Silas is about your size, maybe Riley too."

She didn't know why she was being so helpful. It was better all around if he took his ruined possessions, got on a plane and flew straight back to Anchorage. Then Paradise could get back to normal.

"I can buy my own clothes," he said with a frown.

She was surprised by his defensiveness. "I meant Bill's might not be open."

"Oh."

She left him there contemplating his options as she headed through the dining room and back to the kitchen, where the damage had been done.

Everything was blackened with smoke and soot—the walls, the ceiling, the counters and the stoves. The fryers were melted and misshapen, and the floor was still slippery with grease where they'd leaked.

Xavier was mopping it up, while Silas cut through sections of a long counter with his chainsaw to turn it into manageable pieces. The chainsaw spewed out exhaust and chain oil, but it wasn't like it could make the mess any worse. The back door was open, and the windows were blown out, so there was plenty of fresh air to offset the exhaust.

Cobra Stanford, WSA's tall, powerful Aircraft Maintenance Engineer, had disconnected one of the stoves from the wall and was muscling it toward a dolly.

"Hey, Hailey," he greeted her.

She and Cobra had been friends for years. Estranged from his own wealthy family, he'd left the Air Force and found a place he loved working at WSA.

"What a mess this is," she noted.

"It shouldn't take us too long," he said optimistically, looking around at the dozen people who'd already stepped up to help.

"Is Marnie back in town yet?" Hailey asked him.

Cobra's fiancée, Marnie Anton, was another romantic success story between LA and Paradise. Marnie was Mia's lawyer. She hadn't officially participated in the Finding Paradise matchmaking event, but that hadn't stopped her from falling for Cobra anyway.

They'd built a house down the river from Mia and Silas, managing a relationship where Marnie kept her job in LA part-time while Cobra carried on with his own career in Paradise. Hailey admired them for pulling it off.

"Not yet," Cobra answered. "She's got a big case going on right now."

"Forklift is on its way over from Galina," AJ, one of the Galina warehouse crew, confirmed through his company radio.

"ETA?" Brodie asked.

"Fifteen," AJ answered.

"We'll need a clear path for Cobra," Brodie called out. He pushed one end of a prep table to start a walkway for moving the stove.

Hailey started in on some of the smaller pieces of blackened debris, tossing them into a warped metal tray to be carried to one of the four pickups that would ferry the junk to the town landfill.

"Do we have any flights to worry about?" she asked Brodie while she worked.

"T and T-Two stayed at the strip with Shannon. Dean's out flying. They'll call if they need any help."

As Hailey nodded, she caught sight of Parker. He looked like a completely different man in work pants, a snug T-shirt, steel-toed boots and a hard hat, with a new pair of leather gloves covering his broad hands. Her chest gave an odd hitch at the sight of him looking so capable. She didn't know why. He looked exactly like the rest of the guys working in here— nothing remarkable.

He scanned the room and spotted Cobra struggling with the stove, immediately heading over to help.

"I can pivot it from this side," she heard him offer as he braced a corner of the big metal stove.

"Great," Cobra responded. "Watch the electrical. It's easy to get it tangled."

"Got it," Parker said. "Onto the dolly?"

"Yes. The forklift's too tall for the door."

Hailey cringed as she watched the two men lift the heavy stove, worried that one false move might injure one of them. But they got it safely positioned on the dolly just as the forklift's warning beacon sounded outside.

Everyone stood back to give them room, and when the forklift hoisted the stove in the back alleyway, there was a smattering of applause.

"Raven's already sourced some of the equipment out of Fairbanks," Brodie said to Hailey.

"That fast?" Even for Raven, it seemed impressive.

Brodie grinned. "This town runs on cinnamon buns."

Hailey didn't disagree with that. The Bear and Bar cinnamon buns were legendarily delicious and about the size of a dinner plate. She'd never successfully finished one, but she'd given it a good try a few times. Everyone would miss the Bear and Bar's bakery for as long as it was down.

As the forklift moved away, Parker approached.

"Thanks for helping us out," Brodie said to Parker as he took his leave to move a ladder.

"No problem," Parker answered. A sweat had broken out on his forehead, and a streak of soot marred one cheek. He should have looked unkempt, but he simply looked sexier.

"I see you found something to wear," she said.

"Bill was very generous. Just tossed me the keys and told me to help myself to whatever I wanted." Parker began gathering an armful of debris.

"He knows you're good for it." She went back to work.

"I sure hope someone else around here has faith in me." Arms full, they started for the door.

"Why?" she asked as they walked. "You need more new clothes? I don't think our local stores can meet your usual standards."

"Very funny," he said. "I meant I needed somewhere to stay. Willow's offered to share her cabin with Dalia."

Before the martini-fest, Hailey sure wouldn't have put those two together. But they'd seemed to get along surprisingly well.

"We might want to hide their martini glasses," she couldn't help but joke.

Parker smiled as they dumped the junk into the closest pickup box.

"WSA housing is full," Hailey said, taking his problem seriously. "Brodie didn't lay off staff during the downturn. We all just took fewer hours. But Galina should have empty—"

She stopped herself there, remembering she didn't want to make it easy for him to stay. Not only that, her suggestion would push Parker together with Galina and Raven. She knew she couldn't stop him from evaluating the company, but she didn't have to shove them into each other's arms.

"That's a good idea." Re-entering the buildings, he spotted Cobra disconnecting another stove, and quickly headed that direction. "Thanks, Hailey. I'll talk to Raven later."

"Terrific," Hailey muttered to his retreating back. "Well played, Hailey."

Her phone buzzed against her thigh.

Pulling off her sooty glove, she detoured for the quiet of the dining room and reached into her pants' pocket. T-Two might need help at the strip, or maybe Raven needed to arrange an airlift for some of the new equipment.

It was an unknown number. Her first thought was Parker, even though she'd just left him, and her chest gave a little hitch. She accepted the call and put it to her ear.

"Hello?"

"Seriously?" It was her sister Amber's voice. "When I use a burner, you pick up?"

Hailey could have kicked herself for being so careless. "You have a burner? Why do you have a burner?"

"Because it's the only way to get hold of you." Frustration was clear in Amber's voice.

"I was going to call you back." Hailey simply hadn't worked up the energy yet.

"Sure you were."

"We had a fire."

Fear replaced frustration in Amber's tone. "What? In a plane? Are you okay?"

"I'm fine. No, not in a plane. The café caught on fire this morning."

"Were you hurt?"

"No, I wasn't there. I'm on the fire department."

There was a silent pause. "You're a fireman?"

"A volunteer. Fire*fighter*, sister."

"Sure. Right. Of course. But you fight fires now?"

"They don't happen very often. It's a small town."

"I *know* that. I've seen it on the satellite photos."

The admission jolted Hailey. "Please tell me you didn't

commission them." Her family was wealthy enough to rent satellite time if they wanted, and potentially nosy enough to do just that.

"They're from a public mapping service. But they are pretty blurry. You know, now that you mention it, we—"

"Stop! I don't have time for this." Hailey looked back at the kitchen. "Any chance I can call you back?"

"No. None. We're talking right now."

Hailey heaved a sigh. Not that she could blame her sister. She wasn't the most reliable person in this instance.

"You need to come to the shareholders' meeting," Amber said.

Bangs and shouts came from the kitchen, and the chainsaw started up again, making Hailey anxious to get back to helping.

"I'll send you my proxy," she told Amber.

"It's more than just the usual issues."

"I trust you. Whatever you want is what I want too." Hailey couldn't imagine delving into the details of her family's business interests to come up with her own opinion on any particular motion.

Amber was in a much better position to decide for them both.

Amber's voice turned cajoling. "We miss you. *I* miss you."

Hailey softened her tone. "I miss you too. But you know what'll happen."

"I'll run interference with Dad."

"It's not just Dad." It was her mother too, and her brother, Kent. Her entire family would wheedlingly and relentlessly try to convince her to stay in Atlanta. She didn't have the energy to fight them all on their home turf.

"It can be a short trip," Amber said.

"Summer is WSA's busiest season. You know that." This year was quieter than usual, but Hailey wasn't going to mention that.

"You're the deciding vote," Amber said.

"No, *you're* the deciding vote."

"Mom's with me, and Dad's with Kent. It's a split."

"Then you and Mom will take my proxy and win." Hailey wasn't sure why this was a problem.

"*Hailey.*"

More shouts and crashes came from the Bear and Bar kitchen.

"Listen, Amber, the fire's barely out, and I really have to go help. Can I call you back tonight?"

"You won't."

"I will. I promise. I'll even video chat."

Amber's tone perked up at the offer. "You will?"

"Yes. Later."

"You *better* call."

"I will. Bye." Hailey ended the call before Amber could protest, then she turned to find Cobra coming her way.

He took in her expression and stopped short. "What? What happened?"

Hailey held up her phone. "My family."

His expression immediately turned sympathetic. "Something up?"

"The usual black sheep stuff. They need me, and I'm not there."

"What do they need you for?" Cobra asked, lowering his voice and moving closer.

The two of them had jokingly called themselves the Black Sheep Club for several years now, with blue-collar Cobra a disappointment to his high-achieving, professional family. Then when Marnie fell for Cobra, he and Hailey told her she could be an honorary member, since she was the white sheep of her criminal family.

"The annual shareholders' meeting." Hailey tucked her phone into her pocket. "Amber claims it's more than the usual decisions."

Cobra affectionately tapped on Hailey's helmet. "Don't let her get inside your head. If there're decisions, she can still make them for you."

"That's what *I* said."

"Hang in there, Black Sheep."

Hailey squared her shoulders. "I will. Thanks, brother."

He reached out to exchange their secret finger-grip handshake. It was a little thing, but it calmed her down to know she had at least one person who understood and was completely on her side.

Chapter Five

⟿

PARKER'S HEART FALTERED UNEXPECTEDLY AND HIS vision tunneled at seeing Hailey, who was sitting on a pickup tailgate across the alleyway, her legs dangling in the air and her hands braced behind her. Clearly exhausted, she had soot streaked across her face, and her hair was damp with sweat.

The evening was winding down, the bulk of the demolition work having been finished. Most had quit for the day, heading home both hungry and tired. He was starving too. If the café kitchen hadn't been demolished, he'd have ordered up a Super Bear Burger and a mound of fries.

In the end, dozens of people had stepped up, rotating through in shifts, making the work go faster than Parker could have imagined. The people of Paradise knew how to get things done.

Hailey had worked as hard as anyone, and he diverted to one of the coolers and pulled two bottles of beer from a pool of melting ice.

"Thirsty?" he asked as he approached, offering her one of the chilled bottles.

She gave a tired smile as she reached out to take it. "Thanks."

Wind from high in the mountains whistled across an open field between the café and the distant school, twisting around the end unit of the WSA housing that paralleled the back of the building.

"You look exhausted." He twisted the cap off his beer and propped his butt against the edge of the tailgate, turning his head to look at her.

"It was a long day."

Since she hadn't opened her own bottle, he reached over and gave the cap a twist, taking it off with a hiss.

She gave him a smile of thanks.

"You worked really hard." He couldn't help being impressed at the amount of work she'd accomplished alongside the men. He knew he shouldn't be amazed by that, but he didn't see it often in the city, and he was still getting used to it here.

Raven and Breena had helped too, but they'd been focused on phone calls and websites, searching for replacement kitchen equipment. The contractor for Riley's cabins was still in town, and he'd assessed the construction needs, giving a materials list to Raven.

"Everyone worked hard," Hailey said, then took a drink of the beer.

Parker drank too, realizing how thirsty he'd become. He'd pretty much pushed through nonstop since lunch.

Into the still quiet, a couple of German shepherd dogs trotted down Red Avenue toward Main Street, while the breeze picked up a notch, fluttering the leaves in the nearby birch trees, cooling Parker's damp neck and the roots of his hairline. A flock of birds chirped for a moment before lifting off to cross the field.

"Did you find out about Galina housing?" Hailey asked.

"Not yet." He paused, then gave in to the flirty joke that had popped into his head. "You want to make me a better offer?"

She rolled her eyes his way and paused to take another drink. "My room has a single bed."

"That would be cozy." He liked the thought of cuddling up close and personal with Hailey. He liked it a whole lot more than was good for him.

She looked him up and down. "I don't see how there'd be any room left for me."

"You could go on top."

"Ha-ha."

He was serious, but he wasn't about to let on. "So, where's everybody going to eat now?" It was hard for a one-restaurant town to lose its only dining establishment, even temporarily.

"The WSA cafeteria's still open." She nodded to the living complex behind the Bear and Bar. "The Galina housing people eat there, so you'd be welcome."

"I'll appreciate that," he said.

"And how will you feel about communal bathrooms?"

He'd done rustic before, not that it was his first choice. "Beggars can't be choosers."

"It'll be quite the comedown for you."

He slanted her a look. "Good thing you're not in marketing."

"I'm saying, compared to where you're used to living. I'm assuming you have something much more lavish in Anchorage."

"True," he agreed. He didn't live in luxury, but his house in Anchorage was a whole lot nicer than a fortyish-year-old barracks building.

They fell silent, both taking a drink.

"So, your other companies," she ventured conversationally. "They're mostly in Anchorage?"

"Most are. Some have opened facilities in Fairbanks. A

convenience, that." When an expensive piece of equipment broke down and brought operations to a halt, you wanted the repair facilities as close by as possible.

She squinted in curiosity. "I didn't know you had a mine near Fairbanks."

He wasn't sure why she'd expect to know that. "I do. And I have one near Paradise now."

She scoffed out a short laugh. "Paradise isn't Fairbanks or Anchorage."

"I'm not looking for a big urban center."

She turned her body, bending a knee and propping one work-booted foot on the tailgate. The interest in her eyes changed the tenor of the question. "What is it you're looking for, Parker?"

He could think of a dozen different ways to answer that question, starting with wanting her in his arms. "Same thing everyone else is, I suppose."

Her gaze narrowed with skepticism. "You think we're all looking for the same thing?"

"Yes."

"And what's that?"

"Peace, prosperity, friendship."

"Well, if you're going that high-level: life, liberty and the pursuit of happiness."

"Those things too," he said with a low chuckle.

She straightened, seeming more energized. "In my opinion, people want very different things out of life."

He wasn't sure he agreed with that. "I think it's all the same. They just see different ways to get there."

"Different ways of getting there *are* different things."

"They're different mechanisms of getting the *same* thing." He settled himself more comfortably on the tailgate, interested in hearing her philosophy.

She shook her head. "Some—like Mia, for example— want a luxurious mansion in Beverly Hills. While others— like Raven—want a rustic cabin in the woods."

"They're both looking for happiness."

"They're both looking for housing—very different kinds of housing." For some reason, Hailey smiled. Then she ducked her head as if she was trying to hide it.

"What?" he prompted, liking the way her expression had lit up with humor.

She scratched at the damp corner of her beer label while she looked back up. "Just a funny memory."

Now he was fascinated. "Do tell."

She took a beat as if she were making up her mind whether to share.

He waited, hoping she would.

"When Mia first moved here," she said, "Silas took her straight to Raven's cabin. It was just the two of them, and the place looked so dilapidated to Mia that she thought Silas was a serial killer and he'd taken her to his lair to do her in."

Parker smiled with amusement. "They got married after that?"

"Turns out he wasn't a serial killer."

"And she left her mansion for him." Parker liked the way the story stacked up for his side of the argument.

"In a way. But her husband had died, and it was his mansion."

"I think that proves my point," Parker said, and polished off his beer.

"I think it proves *my* point," Hailey countered.

"She found happiness without the mansion." That was his point.

"She didn't move into the rustic cabin."

He thought about that. Mia did still have a very nice house.

Hailey reached across the tailgate and touched her beer bottle to his with a clink. "Point to me."

Her self-satisfied grin sent a wave of warmth spiraling through him. It kept going while she tipped back the bottle for a drink.

He cleared his throat. "What about you, Hailey? What do you want?"

"Oh, I'm happy in my WSA room. We have private bathrooms over there."

"I didn't mean housing." He set down his empty bottle and rose to his feet, moving to stand in front of her as the sun dipped lower toward the mountains and the air cooled further around them. It had fallen completely quiet, with no one else left in sight. "I meant life."

"Life?" She turned to dangle both legs and gestured around herself. "I'm not here by accident. I'm a bush pilot, so I live in the bush."

"And your long-term plan?"

"This is my long-term plan."

"You still want to be a bush pilot when you're old?" He knew it was a tough job, a physically demanding job. Even the hardiest of robust men got tired of doing it after a while.

"I'm twenty-six."

"I'm thirty, so what?" He'd had his eye on the future since he was fifteen.

"So, I don't think I need to be planning my retirement just yet."

"There are a lot of things you can do between now and retirement. You want to move up in the company? Live somewhere else? Get married? Have kids?" He wasn't sure why he'd added those last two. Maybe because she was so desirable that he couldn't imagine her living life alone. There must be a lineup of guys looking to date her.

"Move up how at WSA? Brodie owns and runs the place, and Silas is his chief pilot. I'm already a captain."

Parker found himself easing closer, fascinated by such an unencumbered approach to the future. "You've never thought about what comes next?"

She tipped her head to stay focused on him, parting her lips, then stopping as if she was thinking through her answer.

He pulled up short to keep from kissing her.

Her hair was damp with sweat, messy and mostly pulled loose from the sad ponytail that had slipped down her neck. Soot had crept under the collar of her T-shirt and was sprinkled across the bridge of her nose. She was blotchy and messy, but all he could see were her beautiful eyes—her clear blue eyes and those soft pink lips that seemed to invite him in. It seemed like the most natural thing in the world to keep moving forward, slip a hand around her neck and then lean down—

"You look hungry," she said in an obvious attempt to avoid his question—not that he could remember his question.

"I am." He knew he meant something completely different than she did. He dipped his head a little closer, hoping she'd respond to the intimate gesture.

She didn't tell him no. But she didn't signal a yes either.

"You know what I'm thinking?" he pressed.

"That somebody better feed you?"

"That you're extraordinarily beautiful."

Her lips curved in an amused smile. "Oh man."

He didn't understand. "Oh man, what?"

"Oh man, you have strange taste in women, Parker Hall." She gestured with fluttering fingertips to her face and the clothes that were equally sooty. "This is not a pretty sight."

He brushed his index finger across the bottom of her chin. "I disagree."

"Parker." There was a warning in her tone.

He wasn't about to take maybe for an answer. He needed to hear one way or the other. "You know I want to kiss you."

"That's a bad idea."

"Is that a no?"

"It's an opinion, not a decision."

He couldn't help but smile at her verbal gymnastics. The woman knew how to keep a man on his toes.

"Can I kiss you?" He leaned closer still, tilting his head to one side.

She gave a sigh. "We should really think about this."

"For an unfettered woman, you're sure overthinking a kiss."

"For a methodical man, you're sure underthinking it."

He'd give her that. "Fair point."

"Thank you."

"I'm doing it anyway."

"Okay."

Her answer thrilled him, filling him with anticipation and desire. But he couldn't resist a final tease. "Unless, that is, you want to talk about it some more."

"No. I'm done talking. But I still think it's a bad idea." The last part came out in a whisper.

"Noted," he said, before leaning in.

Her lips were soft and malleable. Cool at first, but they warmed quickly, giving off a sweetness that filled his senses. The kiss carried on, and she shifted forward, lifting her hands to rest them lightly on his sides. He pushed his fingertips into her hair. It was soft, slightly damp with sweat and warm from the sunshine.

He deepened the kiss and it turned to a whole-body sensation, lighting his nerves, drawing him in like a magnet. He wrapped an arm around her waist and eased her close. She arched against him, kissing him back, her breasts brushing his chest and her thighs bracketing his legs.

He didn't want this to stop. He never wanted this to stop.

Then something clanked loudly in the distance, bringing him to his senses.

He drew away.

She blinked, her cheeks flushed, her eyes glassy and shaded green now, her lips swollen.

He gazed back, marveling that she'd grown even more beautiful in the past few seconds. Or maybe it had been minutes. He wanted it to be hours.

"Bad idea," she whispered in a husky voice.

"That was—" He was at a loss for words. How had a dusty little urchin impacted him like no woman before?

"I did warn you," she said.

"Did you feel it too?"

She gave a cocky grin and tipped her head sideways. "Are you asking me to grade your kiss?"

"No." But he wished she would. He wished she'd say something to indicate her world had been rocked the same as his.

She patted the flat of her hand on his chest then, scooting to one side and sliding off the tailgate. "They'll feed you at the cafeteria," she said, and started away as if the kiss hadn't surprised her in the least.

PARKER WAS A MASTER AT KISSING, JUST LIKE HE SEEMED to be a master at schmoozing. Even Dalia Volksberg with her Harvard MBA had been impressed by his business smarts.

Hailey knew Raven and Hugh didn't stand a chance.

She leaned back in the little armchair in her WSA room, closing her eyes in frustration and defeat. She could still feel Parker's fingertips in her hair, the pressure of his arm across her back, the tingle in the pit of her stomach. And she could still taste the sweet magic of his lips.

How was it possible for a kiss to be that good? How could it be so different from any other kiss?

Lips were lips. A kiss was a kiss.

Okay, some guys were sloppy. And if they'd eaten garlic or something, it sure sucked. And some guys were just too eager, too much pressure. It was a kiss, not a battle.

Parker was none of those, but that wasn't enough to explain the exquisite sensations that ran through her. They went beyond her lips, beyond his touch, through her skin to her very core. It was a sizzle, no, a current, no, a shiver or maybe a—

Her tablet chimed a melody, startling her eyes open.

She sat up straight. When she saw her sister's name on the video call, her stomach clenched in regret. She'd forgotten all about her promise to Amber. And it was late now, nearly two in the morning in Atlanta.

She quickly accepted the call, and Amber's face came up on the screen.

"I'm so sorry," Hailey said in a rush. "I forgot."

"*Sorry*? Sorry doesn't cut it. You blew me off, again!"

"I was . . ." Hailey's mind scrambled for an acceptable answer. "With a guy." She cringed as soon as the words were out. As excuses went, it was great. But Amber was going to have questions.

"Hello." Predictably, Amber's expression switched from annoyance to eager curiosity. "What guy? Where guy? What were you doing with the guy?"

"Here. In Paradise. He's just a guy who's in town for a few days."

"Ahh, a fling."

"No, not a fling. We didn't fling. We *won't* fling."

"So, what were you doing with him, then?"

Hailey realized she'd better dish something, or else her excuse of being with a guy wouldn't be any excuse at all. "Talking mostly, but we kissed too."

"Nice. But just kissed?"

"Just kissed." It was the mother of all kisses, but Amber didn't need to know that much.

"And you forgot all about me. Over a kiss?"

"It was a good kiss. Okay, a really good kiss." Hailey paused. "I mean, did you ever have a kiss that . . . pretty much . . ."

"Blew your socks off?"

"More than just my socks."

"Ahh." Amber paused. "Wait. And you stopped?"

"I don't really know him. And I'm not sure I like him. I mean, I think he's up to no good."

Amber frowned. "So, why'd you kiss him, then?"

That was a really good question. "It just sort of happened."

"What? Your lips accidentally bumped into his, and you thought what the hell?"

Hailey couldn't help but grin. "Close. I did see him coming though. I warned him it was a bad idea." And she stood by that opinion.

"But you did it anyway." Amber gave a heartfelt sigh. "Story of your life, little sister."

"Hey!"

"You moved to Alaska."

"*That* wasn't a bad idea."

"It was a terrible idea."

"I like it here, a lot better than there, a lot better than anywhere."

"You're acting like you're in college."

"No, I'm not. I have a good job. I'm a pilot. I take a lot of responsibility in my work."

"You're single and you live in a dorm."

Hailey could see where this was going—the same place every conversation with her family went. "I'm not coming home."

"You're abandoning me."

Hailey rolled her eyes at the melodrama. "I'm not abandoning you. Just vote my shares. Do whatever you want."

"Don't you even care what the fight's about?"

Hailey truly didn't. There were dozens of viable pathways to growing the family fortune. She wasn't spending any of it, so what did she care which pathway they took?

"Acquisition?" she guessed sarcastically. "Merger? We're divesting the jams and jellies division?"

"We don't have a jams and jellies division."

"We produce jams and jellies."

"It's the organic foods division, and it's beating second quarter projections."

"Bully for it. I don't need the details. I trust you. You're not going to make some huge mistake."

"There's a pivotal vote this year on the overarching organization and strategic direction of the corporation. There are nuances and future implications. We're not going to be the last generation of Barrosses, you know."

The turn of phrase took Hailey by surprise. "What does that mean? Is Sophie pregnant?" Her brother, Kent, and Sophie had been married for nearly three years.

"No."

"Are *you* pregnant?"

"I'm not even in a relationship. Not that you'd know if I was. Heck, I could have found a guy, gotten engaged and then married since we last talked."

"Plus, pregnant," Hailey couldn't help but point out.

"I'm not pregnant."

"None of those things really take very long."

"Oh, good grief."

"I'm just saying. You could meet a guy." A picture of Parker came up in Hailey's mind and she quickly shook it off. "Get engaged, get married and get pregnant in about a week if you put your mind to it."

"You are *really* good at distraction, you know that?"

Hailey hadn't intended to be distracting, but she went ahead and let Amber believe she'd wandered off topic on purpose. It was better than admitting her mind had wandered back to Parker by accident.

She gave her sister a saucy grin. "You don't want to talk about boys?"

"No, I don't want to talk about boys. I want to talk about business."

"Okay, here's one for you." Hailey decided to take advantage of the moment. "If you were looking to invest in a service company for a Barrosse industry—say, something in food transportation. Would you want it to be exclusive to Barrosse or share it with other food producers?"

"Why would we want to share?"

Hailey gave a nod. "That's what I thought you'd say."

"Why are we talking about this? We already own a trucking company."

"Pretend we needed another one."

"We'd expand the one we have. Why buy another?"

"Okay, warehousing, cold storage, maybe in a new region where an established company already has infrastructure that serves other grocery wholesalers." Hailey brought the theoretical question closer to the real question about Galina.

Amber shook her head. "Why would we share with our competition? It's a conflict."

"What would you do?"

"I don't know. Build our own warehouses?"

"What about buying the ones that are already there?"

Amber gave a little smirk. "Undercut the competition? Hailey, girl. Now you're thinking like a Barrosse."

"That's what I was worried about." Not that *she'd* think like a Barrosse, but that Parker would think like one.

"Come home, Hailey. Just for a couple of days."

Her sister's hopeful expression jolted Hailey with guilt. "I can't right now. But maybe soon." The minute the words were out, she wished she hadn't said them, wished she could call them back.

But Amber pounced. "For the meeting? We could probably push it for a couple of weeks if you were—"

"Maybe in the fall." Hailey bought herself some time.

Amber heaved an exaggerated sigh. "Will you? Will you really come home this time?"

"I will." Hailey knew she couldn't put it off forever. She'd have a few months to work her way up to it. She'd gird her emotions. She simply wouldn't let her parents' thinly veiled criticism get to her this time.

"Okay." Amber nodded. "Okay. I can live with that. You need to get to a lawyer though. The scanned one-page proxy form isn't going to work this time. We need an original signature, something that'll stand up to a challenge."

"I can do that." Hailey could take a day trip to Fairbanks or even Anchorage.

Amber was silent for a moment, looking wistful. "I miss you, sis."

"I miss you too."

Amber yawned. "I better get to bed."

"I'm sorry I forgot to call earlier."

"It's okay. I'll send you the lawyer stuff."

"Okay, bye." Hailey was oddly sad to sign off.

"Night." Amber reached out to the screen and disappeared.

AT A PICNIC TABLE IN THE WSA CAFETERIA, PARKER browsed the Rapid Release Whitewater Rafting Adventures website. Between bites of a delicious stack of fluffy hotcakes with maple syrup, he admired the action photos Riley had posted, and was more determined than ever to book himself a trip.

He'd invite Dalia along too, but he doubted she'd come. Adventure wasn't her thing. She'd also likely warn him about impulsive investments again, and she was entitled to voice her opinion. But it wasn't like he was planning to whip out his checkbook while flying over a waterfall. He was simply curious. And there was no harm in ground truthing the rafting experience.

Finishing his hotcakes, he downed the last of his coffee and spotted Brodie on the opposite side of the open rectangular room. The kitchen and the serving counter took up one end, with a self-serve coffee station off to the side. There was a lounge area at the opposite end with a game table, shuffleboard, comfortable chairs, and a big fireplace.

In between were two rows of five picnic tables, each with a different patterned, colorful plastic tablecloth that added to the cheerful, chaotic décor. On the walls, there were fishing and wildlife photos of local residents, along with some fantastic aerial shots of central Alaska. He was guessing someone on the WSA team was an avid photographer.

Parker deposited his tray and dishes in the collection stack, then refilled his white stoneware mug with some surprisingly good coffee and headed for Brodie. There were a couple of other guys at the table, but Brodie didn't seem to be in conversation with them.

"Morning," Parker said as he stood off the end of the picnic table.

Brodie glanced up from his omelet and orange juice. "Morning."

"Have you heard plans for the Bear and Bar today?" Parker was willing to help if something was going on. Otherwise, he'd head over to Galina and pick up where they'd left off in reviewing the business.

"Raven had a truck overnighting from Fairbanks," Brodie answered. "Depends on what's on it, I guess."

"I'll check with her. I'm heading for Galina now."

Brodie gazed at him with curiosity for a moment. It was clear he had questions he hesitated to ask.

"What?" Parker prompted.

"I'm just wondering about you being here."

"For breakfast?" Parker cocked his head. "I moved into the Galina barracks after the fire."

"In Paradise. Raven said you'd been in contact with Hugh."

"That's right."

Brodie waited, clearly expecting more information.

"You know it's been a tough year for them," Parker continued.

Brodie nodded at that. "It might be none of my business . . ."

"Ask away." Parker slipped onto the bench seat on the

opposite side of the table. "I'll tell you if it's none of your business."

"Why Galina?"

"Because of my new mine, Lucky Breach. The one over at the Broken Branch airstrip."

"You're moving into production?"

"I expect so."

"Galina services the entire area," Brodie said. "You'd be no different than any other customer."

"I know." Parker wasn't about to give away his business strategy. "I need certainty."

Brodie's expression began to close up. "Is there *un*certainty?"

"I don't know any more about that than you do." It was the truth. In fact, Brodie probably knew more than Parker about the likely future of Galina. "The two companies work closely together, don't they?"

Brodie's expression closed up even further. "Have for years."

"Listen, I know it's been a tough year all around in Alaska. I've come through it better than most, and I'm anxious for the economy to ramp up again, and I'm willing to invest in that."

Brodie took a moment to sip his coffee. "And what does investing look like?"

Parker gave a smile to take the bite out of his words. "That I won't disclose."

"Fair enough." More and more, Brodie struck Parker as a reasonable man. "But you should know Raven's important to this town."

"I can see that." Even if it hadn't been obvious to Parker before yesterday, it was crystal clear to him now. As he spoke, Parker caught sight of Hailey and rose to his feet. "Thanks."

"Don't know that we settled anything," Brodie said.

"We didn't make anything worse." Parker rapped his fingertips against the table and took his leave.

Hailey was at the serving counter with a tray on the slide in front of her. She was dressed in her usual work clothes, hair pulled back, face fresh and pretty, even in the utilitarian light of the cafeteria.

"Morning," he said, stopping beside her. He resisted an urge to brush his shoulder against hers. It was so tempting to touch her.

"Hi." Her greeting was short and impossible to interpret as she accepted a stack of hotcakes from one of the cooks—a tall, lean man with an angular clean-shaven face.

"Thanks, Fredo," she told him with a smile.

"Flying today?" Parker asked to keep the conversation going. He didn't know exactly what he wanted from her this morning. But after last night's astounding kiss, he wanted something.

She shook her head and started down the line. "Nothing on the books right now."

He walked with her. "Busy later?"

She cast a suspicious gaze his way as they came to the coffee station. "Why?"

He cleared his throat, oddly nervous now that he'd come up with a plan. "I thought you and I could—"

"I'm not going to date you, Parker." She poured a stream of maple syrup onto her hotcakes.

"I had the same thing," he said, buying himself a moment to regroup. "They're good."

"They're always good."

"Why not?" he asked, going back to the central question, ready to make his case. He couldn't bring himself to accept that their kiss was going to be a one-off.

To her credit, she didn't pretend to not understand. "Because I'm not who you think I am."

Her answer took him by surprise. "I think you're a fascinating woman whose kiss packs a significant punch."

She concentrated on pouring coffee. "You're in a small town. You're just a little bored."

"I'm not bored."

She set her coffee mug on the tray next to the hotcakes and lifted it. "You're here for what, a couple more days?"

He didn't know the answer to that. His time in Paradise had taken a few twists and turns, setting back his analysis of Galina. It might take longer than he'd expected. And he didn't mind that as much as he should have with Hailey here to keep him interested.

"That doesn't mean you can't get to know me," he pointed out.

She headed for a table of men that Parker recognized as pilots. "The answer is no."

"I didn't really ask you a question."

She halted, turning to face him. "You want to ask me a question?"

"Hang out with me later. Show me the town or give me a tour of the area. Take me up in a plane and fly me around."

"No."

"That's it, nothing but a no? No valid reason or explanation?" How was he supposed to argue against that?

With a grim smile that said the conversation was over, she pivoted and walked away.

"Morning, Hailey," one of the pilots greeted her as she sat down at the picnic table.

"Did you hear Xavier mowed down some poplar saplings at the cranberry strip last night?" another asked.

"He did?" Her tone was friendly and cheerful as she settled in.

"Turned the prop completely green," a third pilot added. "Cobra was fit to be tied when he saw it this morning."

"We were in there last year. It grew over that fast?" Hailey asked as Parker admitted defeat and headed for the exit.

"He was off center by about—"

The pilot's voice chopped off as Parker pushed open the door.

He paced along the wooden sidewalk, telling himself to shake it off. He *was* only in town for a few days. And maybe she hadn't been as into the kiss as he'd been.

Although she seemed like she was into the kiss.

While it was happening, she'd seemed very into the kiss.

Chapter Six

REMINDING HERSELF IT WAS ONLY A KISS AND ASSUR-
ing herself she'd made exactly the right decision in turning
Parker down, Hailey crossed Galina's expansive gravel
parking lot that stretched out in all direction around the big
warehouse complex. Employees' pickups and SUVs lined
the southern edge, nosed in against the trees, while a couple
of semitrailer trucks were backed into the western loading
dock. Another semi was pulling in now, its engine rum-
bling low as it lined up to back in and stirred up dust into
the still sunshine.

Hailey gave the big truck and its blaring backup alarm a
wide berth, entering through the door on the opposite side
of the loading dock. She knew to follow the marked pathway along the concrete wall, staying inside the red line for
safety as she made her way toward Raven's office.

A forklift beeped as it moved along an aisle beyond the
rows of shelving, its yellow beacon flashing against the
stacks of cardboard boxes. A couple of the workers shouted
instructions to each other in the reaches of the cavernous

building. AJ gave her a wave from where he was adding to a stack of pallets, his yellow hard hat and orange vest standing out against the boxes and crates.

A few steps later, she came to Raven's office. It was compact but efficient with a credenza and a small metal desk surrounded by several filing cabinets and a bookshelf overflowing with safety and procedure manuals. Raven was sitting at the desk, the tip of a pen between her teeth as she stared at a stack of papers in front of her.

"How's it going?" Hailey asked to announce her presence.

Raven looked up and blinked away her concentration. "Hey. How are you doing?"

"I'm good. Well, okay, I guess." Hailey entered the office and sat down in the battered leather guest chair. "That was some day yesterday."

Raven set down her pen and leaned back, bracing her hands behind her head. "*What* a mess."

"How are things looking on the repairs?" Hailey assumed that was Raven's most pressing problem and likely what had put a frown on her face.

"The construction crew can start work today," Raven said. "They'll rip out the fire-damaged wood and replace the studs and beams. We'll need a construction engineer to sign off when they're done. But that doesn't seem like a huge problem. We've got most of the cooking equipment on order. The fryers might be an issue. They're back-ordered out of Seattle."

"I'd be willing to take a Twin Otter down to Seattle and pick them up." The Twin Otters were WSA's largest planes, capable of carrying a significant amount of cargo.

Raven gave a grin at the suggestion. "I suppose it depends on how much Brodie likes his French fries."

"Sweet potato fries are his weakness," Hailey pointed out.

"Mine too," Raven agreed.

"Then we might just have to go on a fryer run."

"I'm in," Raven said with a laugh. Then she sobered. "I could use a few days away from all this."

"Yeah?" Hailey took a closer look at Raven, seeing dark shadows under her eyes and little lines at the corners. "You okay?"

"It's been a long year."

Hailey nodded to that. She was lucky not to need her regular paycheck. She could survive on what amounted to a third of her usual pay. And she always had the fail-safe of her family money. She preferred not to use the dividends when she wasn't participating in the running of the corporation, but it was sitting there in her bank account as a backup if she ever had a financial problem.

"I saw Parker this morning," she mentioned, hoping Raven would be open to talking about his plans.

"The fire sure messed up his day," Raven said. "He and Dalia were all set to go over the vehicular assets."

"How's that whole thing coming?"

"Slowly," Raven said. "Dalia in particular is highly detail oriented."

"Do you know what they want?"

Raven looked puzzled by the question.

"I mean, is Parker looking to make a minor investment or an outright purchase?"

Raven frowned, going silent for a moment. "I don't see Hugh selling the whole thing. Do you?"

"Not really. But have you asked him anything?"

"Not since the day Parker first arrived. I promised to show them around, and then—" She shrugged. "I guess it's going to be what it's going to be."

"Do you know anything about Parker and PQH?"

"Like what?"

"Well—" Hailey hesitated. She wanted to be a good friend, but she didn't want to overstep.

"*Is* there something about Parker and PQH?" Raven asked.

Hailey decided friendship trumped minding her own business. She shifted forward in her chair.

"You know my family has business interests back in Atlanta, right?" She didn't talk much about her family to her friends in Paradise, but she didn't keep them a secret either.

Raven nodded.

"Parker reminds me of them," Hailey said.

"In what way?"

"The cool approach. The calculating attitude. They might be my family, but I have to say the Barrosses are not the best business partners."

Raven's gaze narrowed, and Hailey knew she had to tread lightly.

"Feel free to ignore me," she quickly added. "And please don't take this the wrong way. But I really couldn't live with myself if I didn't warn you."

"Do you know something we don't?"

"Not about Parker specifically. There's not much publicly available about his companies."

"But you looked?"

"I looked," Hailey admitted with a nod. "It's that I've seen his type before. Methodically building his empire. I'm sure you've noticed he's a good talker, all suave and polished. He makes you feel like you're the most important person in the world, and that he likes you, and that his only goal is to be on your side. And you find yourself buying into it. But it's an act."

Hailey realized she was talking on a personal level now, but the same thing went for his business dealings.

"How do you know for sure it's an act?"

"Years and years of watching these things play out. Parker Hall's not altruistic. He's cunning and successful. Look how young he is compared to how much he's made."

"He does own some gold mines," Raven pointed out.

"Lots of people own gold mines. He's expanded to fuel,

repairs, machining. He's amassing an empire of everything he needs to service his own interests. And when he gets it, you can bet other people's interests fall by the wayside."

"I can't see Hugh giving up the controlling interest in Galina."

"There's a thin-edge-of-the-wedge approach that some people use. A guy gets in, doesn't have to be in a huge way. But then he's an owner, and he's also a customer. He starts wanting and needing things to support his own companies, and the pressure goes on for changes."

Raven sat silently, looking worried. "As in staffing changes?"

"*Any* kind of changes."

"But you're speculating, right?"

Hailey knew she'd pushed far enough. In fact, she'd pushed further than she'd intended.

"I'm speculating," she agreed. "But if you have a chance to talk to Hugh, you might suggest—"

"I don't see how I could do that. What if I pushed him the wrong way?"

"What if you kept quiet and he missed something important?"

"It's too risky."

"I get it." Hailey did get it.

And now she felt bad to have drawn Raven into it at all. It wasn't fair to throw her in the middle. "There's nothing you can do," she said. "There's nothing you should do. This is Hugh's decision. I'm sorry I said anything."

"Your family . . ."

Hailey waited.

"Are they really that bad?" Raven asked.

"They're not who I want to be, that's for sure." The Barrosses were hardworking and driven. They had many qualities that she could admire. But they were also ambitious and competitive. It had always been them against the world, and the world usually lost.

* * *

PARKER WAS IMPRESSED THE MOMENT HE ENTERED THE Rapid Release office. It reflected the same markers of success and attention to detail that Parker had seen in the rafts, the cargo vans and the cabins Riley had built for his clients.

"Chet says he wants to assess it personally." It was Willow's voice coming from behind a shelf of Rapid Release merchandise.

"That makes four of us plus all the gear," Riley answered her. "The raft's fine, but I don't see how we do it in an Islander. If we go bigger, it'll mean two pilots."

"For two planes?" Willow asked.

"Hello?" Parker called out to announce his presence.

Riley peered around the end of the shelf. "Hi, Parker."

"Am I interrupting?"

"Come on in."

Parker let the spring-loaded door shut behind him and moved toward the service counter at the back of the store. "I wanted to see about booking that raft trip. Hi, Willow."

Willow gave him a nod and a smile.

"We've hit a glitch with that," Riley said. "Nicholas is out on a five-day trip, and *Aurora Unleashed* needs to scout a new stunt location."

"I guess they have priority right now." Parker had been here long enough to appreciate the economic impact the film was having on the town.

"They do this summer," Riley said. "What about next week?"

Parker hadn't planned to stay in Paradise over the weekend. Although with the interruptions to his Galina assessment, he might need the extra time.

He wanted to stick around for another shot with Hailey, but he couldn't let his ego drive business decisions. As Dalia kept pointing out, there was work for him to do back in Anchorage.

"Unlikely," he said, being honest with both himself and Riley.

Willow's phone rang and she stepped away to take the call.

"That's too bad," Riley said. "But you never know, maybe you'll be back someday."

"You never know." If Parker did invest in Galina, he'd have a good excuse to come back and take a river trip among other things. If he was in town on a regular basis, Hailey lost her excuse for turning him down.

"I'd really like to show you around," Riley said.

"We'll make something work." Investment in Galina or not, there were good reasons to come back to Paradise.

Finished with her call, Willow returned. "Natasha says she'll give up the locations manager before she'll give up the stunt coordinator. They really don't have much faith in me, do they?"

"Remind me again how many times you've been a stunt-woman before now?" Riley drawled meaningfully.

"Very funny. I don't know how she'll break it to Chet. He seemed adamant that locations had to be part of the decision."

"We can bring him back stills from the trip," Riley said.

"I've got my helmet camera, I suppose. But that'll only show what's right in front of us."

"I take it the location scout is a river trip?" Parker asked, his mind putting the pieces together with what they'd been saying when he walked in on the conversation.

"Up to Tumbler Falls," Riley answered. "Natasha is looking for something, and I'm quoting here: 'breathtakingly spectacular to make audiences' spines tingle.'"

"I'm up for spine-tingling," Willow said with an enthusiastic grin.

"I doubt she's going to live past thirty," Riley said dryly.

"Where's Tumbler Falls?" Parker asked.

"North of Wildflower Lake Lodge."

Parker had heard of the luxury resort. It was famous across Alaska. And it gave him an idea.

"Maybe I could come along on the scout," he suggested. "Take the rafting trip with the rest of you. Two birds, one stone . . ."

Riley and Willow looked doubtfully at each other.

Parker was guessing at what he'd heard when he walked in. "What if I spring for a bigger plane? Then Chet—I'm assuming he's the locations guy—can come along too."

He knew he was going to extremes. But like the big gold nugget had earlier in the week, once something piqued his interest, he was impatient to learn the details. If he didn't, it would prey on his mind for weeks or months on end.

"That would work," Willow slowly said to Riley.

"We'd need a Twin Otter," Riley warned Parker.

Parker shrugged. That was fine with him.

"It's really a wild stretch of river," Riley continued, seeming to assess Parker.

Parker knew this was one time his businessman image probably wasn't working for him.

"I'm not easily scared." Then an even better idea popped into his head. A brilliant idea if he did say so himself. "Could we ask Hailey to fly us out there?"

As their pilot, she'd be forced to hang out with him some more. He struggled not to smile at his own resourcefulness. He loved it when a plan came together.

"She's our pilot," Willow said enthusiastically, her phone still in hand. "I'll let her know the new plan."

"Maybe you should go through Brodie to make it an official booking," Parker suggested.

He didn't much care about being official. But he didn't want to give Hailey the chance to avoid spending time with him. Let Brodie confirm the flight before Hailey knew Parker was part of the package.

"You sure you're ready for the costs?" Riley asked.

"It'll only be the difference between the two planes,"

Willow said, clearly in Parker's corner on this. "The production can pay Islander rates, and Parker can upgrade us."

Parker was content with that. "I'll upgrade us," he said to Riley.

"We'll need three villas," Willow added as she waited for the call to ring through. She looked at Parker. "Maybe four."

Riley spoke up. "You can crash in our loft or book a place of your own."

"I'll take a place of my own." It was getting hard not to bust out a huge grin. An overnight trip suited Parker better still.

HAILEY HAD NO IDEA HOW PARKER HAD ENDED UP IN the back of the Twin Otter with the film crew heading for Wildflower Lake Lodge. She was happy for any chance to fly the big airplane this year, but she was less excited about spending extra time with Parker.

Every time she'd caught him in her peripheral vision, she'd thought about their kiss, and the urge to do it again had roiled up inside her. It was beyond frustrating, but she had morals and standards. She couldn't bring herself to kiss Parker one minute, then diss and undermine him to Raven the next.

She had to keep her head on straight in this. Galina and Paradise were the priority, *not* her personal life.

It was an hour-long flight to Wildflower Lake, but soon they were short final for the narrow airstrip behind the lodge. As captain on this leg, Hailey was taking the landing. Her copilot, T-Two, would fly the left seat on the way home, evening things up.

It was a tricky strip nestled in a deep valley, but one she'd landed on many times before. She'd had to lose altitude between the mountains, then take a sharp right turn to line up with the center of the strip, going full flaps and touching down, bringing all that weight to a rolling halt in the shortest distance possible. It was a testament to a pilot's skill with the Otter and something they all tried for when they landed it.

"Nice," T-Two said through the radio as the wheels came down smoothly and they quickly slowed.

"Favorable headwind," she returned with a smile. But it had been a good landing, short to impress T-Two and smooth to please the passengers, just the way she liked to do it.

Then they hit a hidden bump on the strip, jolting the plane and tightening Hailey's shoulder straps.

"It's hard to be perfect all the time," T-Two said, flashing a teasing grin as she pressed on the brakes. He was a laid-back, good-humored pilot, tall and fit with blond good looks from his Norwegian heritage. He and his twin brother, Tristen, or "T," had arrived in Paradise four years ago and quickly settled into the community.

She brought the Otter to a full stop outside a small utility shed, which was the only infrastructure on the Wildflower Lake strip. They were about a mile from the lodge, but the shed held a few ATVs for transporting people and goods.

Hailey went through the shutdown process while T-Two headed back to open the door and lower the small staircase for the passengers. It was going to take an hour or so to unload all the rafting equipment and ferry it and the passengers to the lodge. They'd get settled and overnight, then do the river run tomorrow morning.

Despite everything—*everything* being Parker unexpectedly tagging along—Hailey was looking forward to the evening. As the only two women in the trip, she and Willow would share a villa and be able to chat into the night. They'd hit it off right away the first time Willow visited Paradise and had spent time together on every trip since. It was fun to have her in town for a good long stretch.

The plane rocked beneath her as people disembarked and started unloading the cargo. Hailey completed the shutdown and filled out the logbook. Then she stripped off her headset, hung it on the hook and pulled herself out of the seat to exit.

Under a blue sky dotted with fluffy clouds, the wind stirred up a little dust that blew in front of the shed's open overhead door. T-Two and Riley were inside organizing the ATVs, while Fernando and Parker unloaded the rafts and other cargo through the big double door at the rear of the aircraft.

Chet and Willow checked out the scenery, pointing and discussing what they saw. T-Two started up the multi-seat ATV, which had side-by-side seating for six. Riley mounted a standard four-wheeler with an attached cargo trailer.

Surrounded by various parts of the deflated and disassembled river raft, Parker balanced the outboard motor Fernando had handed down to him. He saw Riley approaching and waited to set the motor directly into the utility trailer.

Hailey's attention was caught and held by the definition of his muscles beneath the snug gray T-shirt. He was dressed like an Alaskan today. It was bad for her equilibrium that she liked that better than his business suits.

T-Two parked the multi-seat ATV facing the trail that led to the lodge. He did a scan and a head count, then strode toward the pile of equipment that the others were loading up.

"Who's coming on the first trip?" he asked, eyeing up the cargo, then hoisting some of the wooden frame into his arms. "This'll fit in the back seat. Willow? You and Chet want to hop in?"

"This is *amazing*," Willow said to no one in particular, her head still craned as she started toward the ATV. She took in the towering peaks all around them with rivers and waterfalls close enough to be visible to the naked eye.

"Hailey?" T-Two asked, canting his head to the ATV in a question.

Hailey preferred to hang back until the plane was completely unloaded and secured for the night. "Maybe Fernando wants to go first?" she suggested as he hopped down from the cargo door.

"Sure. I can head down with you," Fernando said to T-Two. He did a scan of the equipment and Parker and Riley, seeming satisfied they could load things up without him.

It wasn't until T-Two drove off with three of their party and Riley pulled away with the first load of equipment that Hailey realized she and Parker were being left behind on their own.

As Riley's motor faded down the trail, the quiet settled around them.

"So," she said, crossing her arms over her chest. "You're here."

"I'm here," he agreed, turning to face her.

They were six feet apart in the knee-high grass of the airstrip apron. The Otter's wing loomed above them, the remaining cargo piled beside.

"*Why* are you here?" She couldn't come up with a reason for him to have come along. Didn't he have better things to do in Paradise?

"I'm doing the rafting trip tomorrow," he answered, as if it made sense.

"Why come all the way here?" It wasn't like he couldn't take the trip from Paradise.

"I heard this one was going to be exciting."

"What about Galina?" Not that she wanted him to focus on Galina, not unless what he learned changed his mind about investing.

"Galina will still be there when I get back."

She frowned, not buying what he was so smoothly selling.

"Nicholas is out on a five-day raft trip," he said. "And Riley had to come here for the location scout."

"So, you dropped everything for a raft trip?"

"Not only for a raft trip." He took a step toward her. His expression shifted, turning attentive, alert and with definite purpose.

Apprehension prickled her skin like it had when he'd asked her on a date. "Oh no," she said, shaking her head.

"Oh no, what?" He took another step, and her pulse reacted, jumping to a faster rate.

"This isn't—" She pointed back and forth between them. "You're not thinking—"

A gleam came into his eyes. "I hear this place has a fantastic restaurant, very romantic."

"Is that a joke? That better be a joke."

"So, you're still a hard no on a date with me?"

"Parker." The man was exasperating.

"A person could change her mind."

"Not this mind. Not that fast."

He quirked an amused smile at that. "Relax, Hailey. I really am here for the raft trip. You were an afterthought."

An *afterthought*?

His grin went wide at that. "Now you look insulted."

"I'm not insulted." She wasn't. Why would she be insulted? She was the one who'd turned him down, not the other way around.

She was delighted. Yes, that was the word. She was *delighted* he wasn't using this trip as a ruse to try to spend time with her.

"I'm delighted," she stated her thoughts with conviction.

"Okay, now I'm the one who's insulted." He frowned. "What exactly is it that's wrong with me? And it's not that I don't live here. Nobody in a town the size of Paradise discounts anyone who doesn't live there."

The silence grew uncomfortable while he waited. But she couldn't tell him the truth. She couldn't tell him that dissuading Raven from his investment had put her in a conflict of interest.

She searched for a flaw she could use as an excuse, but it took a minute. "You're . . . fastidious."

His brow went up. "Fastidious?"

"Tidy." She gestured him up and down. "It's like you're all uptight about your appearance, which means you're uptight about other things. I don't like uptight."

"I'm wearing cargo pants and a T-shirt."

"It looks like you ironed them before putting them on." The pants were a crisp black, and the T-shirt had a whole lot of body to it. It was a nice color too, a powder blue, with a waffle texture, three buttons at the cowl neck and long, pushed-up sleeves. His tan boots weren't even scuffed with dirt yet.

"The outfit's brand-new. If you recall, my clothes were ruined in a fire."

"It's more than just that. Look at your hair." She leaned a little bit his way. "And that shave. Could it *be* any closer?"

"I have a very good razor."

"I bet you do."

"This is mostly Dalia."

Hailey saw the opening. "Dalia grooms you?"

"No, she doesn't—" He raked his hand through his short, neat hair. "*You* are tenacious."

"Are we discussing my flaws now?" Tenacity didn't sound like much of a flaw to her.

"That's only one of them," he said, sounding exasperated.

"Oh, do tell," she invited, crossing her arms over her chest.

"You're also judgmental."

"I can live with that." She had high standards. "What else you got?"

It was a moment before he responded. When he did, the frustration in his tone had turned to amusement. "A tendency toward gold fever."

The fight went out of her, and she accepted the change in mood. Truth was, she didn't really want to stand here bickering with him until the ATVs got back. "I did find a nice nugget out there."

She'd deserved to be excited about it. She'd pondered turning it into something, a necklace or maybe a bracelet. She'd taken to carrying it around in her pocket, pulling it out and looking at it, waiting for inspiration to strike.

He moved in closer, his tone cajoling now. "Admit it, you want to try panning again."

She remembered the swirling dirt in the pan, flakes twinkling at the bottom seam, the nugget emerging from the murk. She could see the appeal, and she would do it again given the chance.

"We can go back," he said. "Same deal as before."

Hailey hated that she was tempted. Worse, that she was tempted as much by Parker as she was by the gold. Dating him might be a hard no, but that didn't mean she could get their kiss out of her mind.

He was one captivating man—energizing, perceptive enough to keep her on her toes, with an underlying sense of humor that broke through her barriers way too often.

The danger of spending time with him was crystal clear. But still, gold panning wasn't dating. Who dug in the dirt and squatted beside a stream on a date? Nobody, that's who.

"Sure," she said before she could think it through any further. "I'll take some more of your gold."

PARKER SPENT THE EVENING HELPING RILEY REIN-flate and assemble the raft on the banks of the Paintbrush River. With a chance to ask questions, he learned more about Riley's approach to running his business. It was labor-intensive, which posed a challenge for profitability. But Parker also learned Alaskan river rafting was a unique and in-demand experience. There were significant barriers to entry because it took years to develop the skill set needed to help tourists safely experience the northern wilderness.

That meant the price point could be high, and that factor boded well for Riley's success.

The two men finished work and left the raft a few miles upriver, safely onshore and set for the morning trip. They returned to the lodge to join the others who'd met up on the restaurant deck framed against a spectacular view overlooking the lake. Sitting down at their table next to the rail, Parker ordered a bourbon and settled back in the comfortable chair.

Hailey was in his peripheral vision, across the table and two seats down. She was chatting with Willow seated next to her, using her hands to make her point and laughing at Willow's response. He really liked her laugh. He liked the flash of her smile and the blue-green tint to her eyes in the long rays of the late evening sun. That color reminded him of their kiss. It was hard not to stare and remember.

"That is definitely coming our way." T-Two pointed past Parker to the head of the valley.

Parker craned his neck to see a wall of steel-gray clouds billowing above a narrow valley and fanning across the lake. "That's ugly." He knew how fast storms could move in and that they'd be chased off the deck as soon as it hit.

"Good thing we're not flying anywhere tonight." T-Two checked the screen on his phone from his seat across the table. "It'll blow through fast. Should be clear by morning."

"That's a relief," Riley said. "We could do the river in the rain, but it wouldn't be nearly as much fun."

"Clear skies are pretty important for the vistas," Chet said.

"Does it rain here often?" Willow asked.

"It gets into patterns," Riley answered her. "And the systems keep moving. Not like down at the coast."

"They really get socked in," T-Two finished.

"How early do you think we'll be done tomorrow?" Hailey asked. She was also checking something on her phone.

Parker guessed it was aviation weather.

"Depends on Chet and Fernando," Riley said.

"We don't know what we'll see until we see it. I'm hoping there's plenty to stop for," Chet said.

"Depends on the hazards for me," Fernando said. Then he gave Willow a stern look. "I want contingency plans for our contingency plans."

Riley echoed Fernando's expression of concern, squinting down at Willow. "You listen to him."

"If anyone's going to keep me alive, it's Fernando," Willow joked, seeming to ignore Riley's dark look. "Anybody else hungry?"

"I could eat," Parker said. He and Riley had grabbed sandwiches before they took the ATVs up the river trail to assemble the raft, but that was hours ago.

"We might want to do it inside," T-Two suggested with another look at the sky.

Then Willow turned to Hailey. "Room service will bring pizza to our villa."

"I'm in for that," Hailey quickly agreed.

Parker felt cheated by an early breakup to the gathering. He hadn't seen Hailey since the airstrip.

"Pizza at Willow and Hailey's," Riley announced, interpreting Willow's suggestion quite differently than Parker had.

Parker was liking the man more and more. "On me," he offered as he polished off his bourbon.

Mist from the storm was crossing the deck now. It would soon turn into rain. The other parties at the outside tables began laughingly heading into the restaurant.

"We're in the mid creek villa," Willow said amicably. If she'd planned on having a girls' pizza party with Hailey, she didn't let on. "Third one up from the corner."

"I'll go inside and order," Parker said, rising. "Any preferences?"

"The more toppings the better," T-Two said.

"Loaded," Chet agreed.

Parker looked around, his gaze resting an extra second on Hailey. He wondered what she thought of the plan, but it was impossible to read her expression. "Do you have a preference?"

She shook her head, looking only fleetingly into his eyes.

"Alright. Loaded it is," he said and headed for the door.

His departure was followed by the sounds of scraping chairs and tapping feet as everyone else headed down the outside staircase to the wooden sidewalk that followed the ridge to the villas. A few raindrops plunked on the glass as he shut the door behind him.

He ordered three large pizzas and some beer and wine for good measure. While he waited, the sprinkles changed to rain and then turned to a full-on downpour. He hustled to the mid creek villa, stopping under the covered porch to rub his damp hair and shake the drops from his fingertips before going inside.

He came up short, nearly crashing into Hailey as she crossed the foyer.

"Hi," she said, stepping back and eyeing up his damp state.

"It's really coming down out there." He glanced around to see a villa very similar to his, although smaller and not as opulent. It had a large, high-ceilinged living room with a view of the lake through picture windows that went all the way to the peak of the ceiling. The kitchen and dining room were at the back, and a polished wood staircase led to a sleeping loft. Despite being larger, his villa only had one bedroom, while this looked to have two at opposite ends of the main floor.

"You should sit by the fire and dry off," she told him.

Parker saw that Riley was lighting a fire in the natural stone fireplace, using the stocked woodbox near the hearth and a basket of kindling and newspapers beside it. Orange flames flickered to life as Riley shut the glass doors.

"Have you noticed these places look like Silas and Mia's house?" Parker asked. He'd noticed the similarity in his own villa up the hill. But it was even more pronounced here.

"Mia really liked them," Hailey said. "So, Silas borrowed the plans and used the same builder. He made it bigger, especially in the kitchen. Plus, they added the garage."

"Have you ever thought about building something for yourself?" Parker couldn't imagine living in the Galina barracks year after year. Sure, WSA housing was a slight upgrade from Galina, but Hailey had lived there for six years.

"Every once in a while," she said, looking a bit wistful. "At first, I didn't know how long I'd stay working at WSA. And then I got settled. And then I didn't really want to—" She seemed to stop herself. "You thirsty? There are sodas in the fridge."

"I ordered beer and wine with the pizza. What were you going to say?"

"What?" She was clearly pretending to forget.

"You said you really didn't want to . . . ?" He waited.

"Oh, that." She smoothed back her ponytail. "It's really expensive to build in Paradise."

Parker could imagine it was. And he wasn't about to make her feel bad about not being able to afford the building costs. "Riley said transportation costs were a killer."

"They are. Mia can shrug it off, but I work for wages."

Parker saw a potential business opportunity for building construction in Paradise. A guy might build something on spec and underwrite mortgages for purchasers. It was interesting and likely doable. He couldn't help but smile at the thought of Dalia's reaction if he suggested real estate development on top of his other recent ideas.

"The fire looks warm," Hailey said as Riley rose from the hearth and dusted off his hands.

The hint was clear, but Parker didn't want to leave her.

"Are you coming on the raft trip tomorrow?" he asked instead.

"Me?" She seemed surprised by the question.

"Is there room for Hailey tomorrow?" Parker called out to Riley.

"Sure," Riley said, moving their way. "I've got room for six passengers."

"T-Two might want to—" Hailey started.

"He's welcome as well." Then Riley called back over his shoulder. "Hey, T-Two, going to come along on the rafting trip?"

T-Two looked interested. "Sure, yeah. Love to."

"There you go," Riley said to Hailey, sounding as if the decision was made. "We can all do it."

"Great," Parker said, and gave her shoulder a squeeze to seal the deal. He instantly realized his mistake as a tingle of awareness shot up his arm.

Hailey's gaze quickly swung his way, and their eyes met and held.

"I'll go grab the splash suits," Riley said to no one in particular. "We should have enough, but I want to check sizes."

Willow hopped up from an armchair. "I'll help."

"Did I say yes?" Hailey asked Parker.

"Yes to what?" He'd lost track of everything but her.

She blinked as the door shut behind Riley and Willow.

His hand still resting on her shoulder, he eased forward. Her T-shirt was thin, and his fingers pulsed against the heat of her skin.

"What?" she repeated, looking baffled.

"I don't remember," he admitted.

The murmur of Fernando's and Chet's voices seemed far away. Hailey's gaze was soft as moss beneath her thick lashes. The cute little freckles stood out on her cheekbones. As his gaze swept her soft lips, he was hit with the urge to kiss her.

He sucked a breath into his tight chest, easing closer still, even as he warned himself to stay back.

"What were we arguing about?" she asked in a bemused little voice.

"Were we arguing?" It didn't feel like they were arguing.

"We're always arguing," she said.

"We should stop."

"I don't see how. It comes so naturally."

"It's easy," he said. He slid his hand from her shoulder down her arm, taking her hand. "When I say something, don't automatically disagree."

"That's not easy." She was looking at their joined hands and clearly fighting a grin.

"Sure it is." He fought a new urge, the one to smooth a loose whisp of hair back from her forehead.

"Maybe if you were more honest," she said.

He frowned at that. He'd never been dishonest with her.

"I'm left guessing." She said it in a way that didn't sound critical.

He gave in to his impulse and smoothed the hair from her forehead. "You are honestly gorgeous."

"Flirting doesn't count."

"Who's flirting?"

"Seriously?" The lift of her eyebrows called him a liar.

"Right." He'd just said he'd be honest. "I'm flirting with you. Is it working?"

Instead of answering, she shook her head.

"Now who's being dishonest?"

She sidestepped his accusation. "Aaaand . . . we're still arguing."

Chet's voice rose from his chair beside the fire, gesticulating with both hands. "So, she wants *drama*, action, *excitement*."

Hailey seemed to realize how close she and Parker had

gotten to each other. She drew her hands from his and took a half step back.

"She wants safety too," Fernando countered. "Water-falls are tricky."

"The river trip," Hailey said, as if she'd just had an epiphany. "We were arguing about the river trip."

Chapter Seven

HAILEY WAS GLAD SHE'D TAGGED ALONG ON THE RIVER trip. It had been a spectacular ride from start to finish. They'd done it in multiple sections with stops in-between where Chet wanted reference shots or where Fernando wanted to consider the possibilities for the stunts requested by Natasha. Willow had strapped a camera to her helmet and Hailey couldn't wait to see the footage, especially the part where they'd gone over the waterfall. It was bigger than the waterfalls near Paradise. For a moment there, she'd expected them to all get dumped overboard. She didn't know how Riley had managed to keep the raft upright.

It was late in the day now, and they were all wet and tired as they finally cruised into Wildflower Lake, motoring up to the wharf in front of the lodge. Hailey disentangled her hands from the straps and got her feet under her on the unsteady floor of the raft. She took a step across and looked up to see Parker holding out a hand.

She took the help.

His grip was strong as he hoisted her up onto the dock.

Her legs were a little rubbery from bracing against the movement, and her life jacket rubbed into his before she steadied herself, grasping his upper arm. They were enveloped in splash suits and life jackets, their heads covered in helmets, but the arousal from last night rushed back anyway.

She sucked in a tight breath and her heart thudded deeply against her ribs. She told herself it was lingering exhilaration, but she knew it was Parker. The man had worked his way deep into her psyche.

She'd dreamed about him last night, sexy dreams where he held her in his arms and kissed his way from her lips to her neck to the tip of her bare shoulder and beyond.

It had only been a dream. He couldn't read her mind. Still, she'd felt ridiculously self-conscious eating her waffle across the table from him in the morning.

After that, he'd distracted her all day long, looking fit and rugged, making jokes and observations, pitching in like a pro while they launched and landed. She might be critical of his business approach, but she couldn't fault his participation in the raft trip. He'd been more than willing to help and seemed to know exactly what he was doing.

"Cold?" he asked her now as he peeled off his helmet.

"Cooling off fast," she said, doing the same. The breeze was chilly against her damp hair.

"You should head on up." He nodded toward the lodge above them on the hillside. "Get a hot drink and dry off."

"There's still work to do here." She wasn't about to bail while everyone else unloaded the raft.

"Plenty of us to help out."

"Including me."

Parker grimaced and gave a small shake of his head that said he was giving up on her. He turned his attention to Riley. "Can we break it all down tonight?"

"It'll be tiring," Riley answered from where he was setting carrying cases on the dock. "But it'll make the morning go smoothly."

The breeze freshened against Hailey's damp face, and she could smell the coming storm. She gazed down the valley to see clouds forming once again. "We're not flying anywhere before tomorrow," she added to the conversation.

"Agree with that," T-Two put in, looking in the same direction.

"I'm game if you want to get the gear loaded," Parker said to Riley.

Fernando and Chet were talking together, enthusiastically dissecting what they'd seen over the course of the day and the opportunities for the film. They seemed like smart guys, but they were smaller and slighter than the Alaskans, and didn't seem to consider breaking down the raft as part of their job.

Fair enough. It really wasn't.

Riley looked at T-Two, obviously asking for his opinion.

"I'm in," T-Two said, crouching down to release two paddles that were strapped inside the raft. "Let's get it done."

Hailey unzipped her life jacket, shrugged it off and looped it over her arm. She moved to take Chet's too, building an armful of gear to carry back to the villas. "You guys need any tools from up top?" she asked Riley, holding out her hand to Fernando for his helmet.

"A couple of wrenches," Riley answered. "And bring the green plastic case. It'll all be beside the dining table in our villa."

Parker's brow furrowed Hailey's way. "I can—"

Hailey shot him a *back off* look. "On it," she said to Riley.

Parker didn't look happy, but he didn't argue either.

She and Willow carried the helmets and life jackets up to Riley and T-Two's villa.

Hailey headed back with the tools, while Willow went to their villa for a shower.

Carrying the wrenches and dragging the wheeled plastic

case, she passed Fernando and Chet coming up the other way with armloads of splash suits. They nodded to her but were obviously still deep in discussion. Throughout the trip, they'd seemed jazzed by what they saw on the river and how it might play out in the film.

By the time Hailey got back, the raft was up on the dock and in a dozen pieces—the frame, the boards, the oars and safety equipment, and the inflatable tubes. While they finished the disassembly, she ferried two of the lodge's ATVs with their utility trailers from the garage to the edge of the lake.

It took numerous trips along the dock to get everything loaded into the trailers.

"They can sit by the garage overnight," Riley said, hopping onto one of the ATVs and starting the engine. "The rain won't hurt anything."

T-Two took the other, leaving Hailey and Parker to walk back together.

"You work too hard," he said as the other men trundled the ATVs carefully up the hillside, making sure their loads stayed in place.

"And you're too opinionated," she countered.

In answer, he paused and took her hand, lifted and turned it over to gaze pointedly at her palm. It was red from the cold water and scratched from the rough wood.

"Look at *this*," he said.

His reaction seemed overblown. It was nothing more than wear and tear from the day. Nothing had even gone wrong on the trip, no accidents, no emergencies. It wasn't anything like when Marnie bounced out of the raft and nearly drowned in the current before Cobra saved her life. Now *that* had been a serious rafting incident.

"You worked just as hard as me," she pointed out.

Parker had worked even harder, but if you did the math based on body frame and muscle mass, she figured they came out about even.

He held out his own palm, which was broad and calloused, apparently none the worse for wear.

"This isn't a contest."

He gave a cocky shrug. "Maybe not. But I win."

"I don't think there's an award for tough skin."

"My point is you should take it easier. Don't hurt yourself like that."

"It's barely a scratch. And why do you care how hard I work?"

Thunder rumbled in the distance, and Parker's expression sobered as the sun disappeared behind the dark clouds. He gazed at her hand like he was a palm reader.

"It reminds me of something," he finally said, his tone reflective and somber.

It was obviously something serious. "Of what?"

It was a moment before he answered. "My mom. And my sister." He paused then and inhaled. "Thing is, my dad was an absolute prick of a man. Sorry. I didn't mean for it to come out that way." He ran the pad of his thumb featherlight over her palm. "But he worked them *so* damn hard."

Hailey had no idea how to respond.

"Their hands seemed to get the worst of it," Parker continued. "They'd be cracked and bleeding at the end of some days."

A bleakness came into his eyes, and Hailey could hear the strained emotion in his voice.

"Eventually, I was able to help them," he said. "I got bigger and stronger and took more of the load." He paused and gently layered her hand between both of his. "But enough about that."

"It sounds terrible," she said, her sympathy going out to his mother and sister, and to Parker too. She wanted to ask more, like what had happened and where they were now. But that seemed intrusive and rude.

"What I meant to say is that you were great out there.

Really great out there." Thunder from above them seemed to punctuate his words. The wind suddenly gusted, and hailstones scattered around them. A couple hit her cheek, and they were big enough to sting. The hailstorm grew heavier, clattering loudly on a nearby shed roof.

Hailey shaded her eyes and glanced up to see that thick black clouds had converged above them, lightning strikes sparking deep in their gloom and sending rumbles of thunder through to her bones.

Parker put his hand on the small of her back, urging her forward. "Let's get away from the water."

The hailstones grew bigger still, bouncing off their heads as they dashed together for the shed at the edge of the deck.

"We should have kept the helmets," she called out as they ran.

He flung the shed door open, and they burst inside, halting among wooden racks, coiled ropes and hooks with life jackets. Paddles leaned in the corners, and workbenches were covered with tools and fishing equipment. The hailstones jangled on the tin roof above them, the sound increasing to a roaring din. A strong wind howled against the walls, shaking the little building.

"Now *that's* a storm," Hailey said on a laugh, glad to be out of it. "I'd sure hate to be up flying right now."

"Surely you wouldn't fly in this," Parker said, looking worried in the filtered daylight.

"I fly around squalls all the time. But I'd have to seriously reroute to avoid something this big. It's most definitely safer on the ground." As her voice died away, she realized how close they were clustered together between a workbench and a rack of life jackets.

The close stillness inside the shed rose around her, making the roar of the hailstones fade to the background. A musty smell of wood, plastic and motor oil permeated the stale air.

"Did the hailstones hurt you?" he asked and gently touched a spot on her cheek.

She shook her head, because nothing hurt right now. Quite the opposite. A shimmer of pleasurable awareness fanned out from his touch. It was followed closely by desire—a desire to lift herself up on her toes and kiss Parker deeply. She inhaled the scent of him: fresh, clean, slightly woodsy.

"You know this isn't a date," she muttered more to herself than to him.

He smiled at that but inched closer. "I sure hope it's not a date. I'd really be falling down on my game." Desire softened his smoky eyes.

"You should stop." She had to force out the words, because the last thing she wanted him to do was back off.

"Stop what?" he whispered.

"Looking at me . . . like that."

"Like what?"

"Like you are."

"You mean, like *you* are?"

He was right.

She could feel it. She was gazing back at him the same way—looking like a lovelorn teenager, thinking how incredibly hot he looked and sounded and smelled.

He dipped his head toward hers, tilting sideways, aligning their lips.

"Parker." She'd meant it as a warning, but it sounded much more like an invitation.

"You know it's going to be good," he whispered above the background din of hailstones.

She did know it was going to be good. And it wasn't like they hadn't kissed before. It wasn't like kissing him now would realign the planets or anything. Not when they'd already kissed each other.

"That's what I'm worried about," she admitted.

He smiled and cradled her cheek, bringing his lips down in slow motion.

The first brush ignited a heat that swelled her chest. She put her hand against his chest and let the sensations cascade through her.

His fingertips splayed into her hair while his free hand pressed the middle of her back, pulling her snug against him. His hand slowly lowered, increasing the intimacy of their embrace.

She arched her back and slanted her head, reveling in the kisses that were pulsing along her nerve endings. Her hands explored his chest and shoulders, the contours of him through the taut fabric of his T-shirt. She wanted to rip it off, to feel his skin on hers, to kiss her way across his pecs to his broad shoulders.

He braced his feet, steadying her while his kisses roamed. He pushed aside her collar, finding the bend of her neck over to her shoulder, his lips hot and moist. The back of his hand smoothed the side of her breast, down to the curve of her waist and the swell of her hips before moving around to pull her flush against his hardening body.

Lightning flashed in a smudged window. The hail surged in a fresh clatter, followed by a deep rumble of thunder that vibrated the earth beneath them. Something wrenched free outside, crashing into the wall and violently smashing a window.

Parker swiftly turned them, flattening Hailey protectively against the shield of his body as the glass clattered into the room and rained onto the floor.

Hailey felt the wind that whistled through the broken window.

"You okay?" Parker asked into her ear. "Anything hit you?"

"I'm fine," she said against the strength of his chest.

He drew back, holding her shoulders and checking her up and down, not seeming satisfied with her answer.

"I'm good," she assured him.

Beyond being good and beyond feeling safe, she was stunned by what had happened between them.

He seemed to steady himself as well, obviously recovered from the shock of the breaking window. But he also seemed to realize what they'd just—or just about—done.

She hadn't meant for things to get this far. But she hadn't done anything to stop it either.

"We should—" She gestured to the broken glass scattered across a workbench and down onto the floor.

"Report the damage."

"Yes." She pounced on the excuse. "So they can clean it up before somebody gets hurt."

"You're right," he agreed with a nod. He seemed as glad as she was for the interruption. He stepped back and let go of her arms as the hailstorm decreased and plunked to a halt, and the thunder rumbled farther in the distance.

THE STORM HAD ENDED HOURS AGO, BUT PARKER couldn't sleep.

A multicolored late-night sunset brought a glow to his villa bedroom. He could have pulled the blackout blinds, but he knew it wouldn't help. He was used to the endless summer days, so it wasn't the light that was keeping him awake.

He left the chalet and crossed the wooden walkway to a deck that overlooked the lake. There he plunked down on a bench and let his gaze go soft while thoughts of Hailey danced through his mind. He'd relived their kiss a hundred times already, wondering what had made her different from all the other women he'd ever kissed. Or if she really was different. Or if he was only obsessing about her because she kept backing off.

It had been a long time since a woman had turned him down. He'd grown jaded over the past few years with the endless attention of so many women. He wasn't a fool. They flirted with his bank balance more than they flirted with him.

The one thing they didn't say was no. Lately, he was the one backing off.

A pair of loons caught his attention, their haunting calls echoing as they glided over the still water. Then a flock of harlequin ducks lifted off from the shallows, fluttering high into the sky.

Although he couldn't settle down tonight, it was hard not to love the blend of tranquility and luxury here at Wildflower Lake. He'd heard about the resort many times, but the descriptions hadn't done it justice.

The pretty view blurred in front of him again as his thoughts turned inward.

Hailey had kissed him back. There was no doubt about it. She hadn't even tried to hide her enthusiasm. At least not at first. Afterward, well, he got the sense she preferred to pretend nothing had happened between them.

He didn't get her hard stance against dating him. Simply as a practical matter, if she eliminated anyone but the permanent residents of Paradise, she wouldn't have much of a social life.

Unless she was already dating someone. He considered the Paradise men he'd met so far.

It couldn't be Riley. He clearly had a thing for Willow. Parker would bet it wasn't Brodie, since he was her boss, and Parker had never sensed anything beyond professionalism between them. She'd also been all business with T-Two.

But there were plenty of other pilots at WSA, plus the guys on the Galina crew. But if she was already dating someone, would she really kiss Parker like that? If he were dating Hailey and she'd kissed another guy, he'd—

"Didn't think anyone else would be up." Her soft voice startled him. He hadn't even heard her footsteps on the walk.

"Couldn't sleep," he told her, turning as she made her

way to the bench. He wondered if he dared think she had the same problem for the same reason.

She was carrying an open bottle of wine. Her hair was knotted on the top of her head, mussed like she'd tried to sleep but couldn't. She was dressed in a pair of Wildflower Lake Lodge slippers and soft deep blue yoga pants that clung to her shapely legs, topped with a bulky pullover sweater. The sweater was a mosaic of pinks and purples. It was the most feminine outfit he'd ever seen her wear.

She sat down at the opposite end. "Me neither." Then she held out the half-full bottle.

He took it. "Please don't tell me you're halfway through this already."

She smiled at his joke. "Leftover from last night. Didn't think I'd need a glass."

He gazed at the bottle then looked back to her. "I've got glasses in my villa." And the villa was right behind them, maybe thirty yards away.

It seemed like she was tempted, and he waited.

"And if all I want is a glass?" she asked archly.

"All I'm offering is a glass."

She sat back then and shook her head. "I don't trust us."

Interesting answer. "Probably smart." He took a drink from the bottle. "We're not all that trustworthy."

A beat went by in silence, and then she shifted her body to face him, her expression turning more serious. "Have you ever been river rafting before?"

It was the last question he'd expected. "Never. Why?"

"You were good at it, like you knew what you were doing."

He handed back the bottle. "It wasn't hard to figure out—fast water, small boat, hang on tight. Chet and Fernando seemed happy with the outcome."

"They did. And Willow's *thrilled*."

"She sure loved the ride." He chuckled as he remembered her wide grin, her whoops of glee, and the exclamations about the footage she was getting on her helmet camera.

"That's our adventure girl." Hailey took another swig of the wine.

"How did that happen?" he asked. "I mean the whole movie thing."

"Scarlett Kensington came up summer before last with Willow and a bunch of other women from LA."

"On vacation?"

"On Raven and Mia's matchmaking adventure. Scarlett was a production assistant who always wanted to be a producer. Xavier liked Scarlett, and Willow wanted more adventure. Between them, they convinced Mia to finance a film. Two years later, voila." She spread her arms expansively, wine bottle and all.

"So, it's Scarlett's first movie?"

"As a producer, apparently so."

"Is it a really great script or something?" Parker asked, looking for the rationale for such a big investment on Mia's part.

He wasn't an expert by any means, but he knew very few independent films made money. And seeing the setup they had going at Mia and Silas's house, never mind the planned sequence on the Paintbrush River, this one had to have a big budget.

"I have no idea. I only know it's a female superhero northern adventure." Hailey passed back the bottle.

"Does Mia not mind losing money?" he asked before drinking. He couldn't imagine the incentive for investing in something so risky. And he was a gold miner.

"I think she must have a lot of money sitting around. Raven told me Mia thought it would be fun."

"Hundreds of thousands worth of *fun*?"

Hailey held her hands up in surrender. "Hey, I just fly the airplanes."

"There's no 'just' about it," he felt the need to point out.

"You know what I mean."

"I do. And you're good at it."

"You've flown with me exactly twice."

"Three times if you count both directions to Lucky Breach. I can tell you're good."

She reached over and whisked the bottle from his hand.

"Careful," he warned.

She looked at him with narrowed eyes. "Did that make you nervous?" She tossed the bottle from one hand to the other. "Huh? Did it?"

Her hands were too small to grip the bottle properly, plus she'd been drinking the wine. She tossed it between her hands another time.

"I think we've had enough broken glass for one day."

She paused then, her expression sobering, and he knew she had to be thinking about their kiss.

"Sorry," he said.

"For what?" She tossed it again.

"Stop doing that." He rose and went for the bottle.

But she moved it behind herself.

"Not funny," he said.

"Kind of funny." Her eyes were wide, her lips soft, her wispy hair shimmering in the dying rays of the sun.

"I feel like I totally misjudged you."

"Yeah?" She looked intrigued.

"I thought pilots were careful and cautious."

"Most are. But I'm a black sheep." She pointedly took a drink from the bottle.

"I don't believe that for a second."

"No? Just ask my parents."

He sat down on the bench beside her, his curiosity piqued. She'd barely mentioned her family before this.

"And if I did," he said. "What would they say?"

"That I lied to them."

It was hardly the revelation of the century. "That just means you were once a teenager."

She shook her head. "No, no. I was twenty."

"What did you lie about?" He still wasn't buying her black sheep claim.

"I told them I was going to Seattle on vacation, but instead I moved to Paradise."

He tried to imagine how that would happen. "So, a spur of the moment thing?"

"Not at all. I plotted, and I planned, and I lied to their faces, and then I disappeared." She waved the bottle. "I mean, I dropped them an email to say I was safe and sound. But it was a few weeks before I called and talked to anyone."

He tried to imagine her motivation for such an astounding decision. "Why didn't you call?"

"They'd have convinced me to come home."

He understood that. He'd left his father's mine without a word, hiding his mother and sister in a condo in Anchorage. It might have been overkill, but he'd feared his father would come after them and guilt them into coming back.

Hailey suddenly smacked her neck, obviously killing a mosquito. "I just couldn't do the big hair, frothy skirts and mint juleps." Her tone lightened the mood.

He smiled, remembering his own words. "Now *that* I can believe." He sure couldn't see her at balls and soirees.

She offered him the bottle and he took it.

"Not that you wouldn't look great in a frothy skirt with big hair." He was picturing it now. He'd intended the image to be amusing, but it wasn't. In his mind she looked incredibly beautiful.

"Honestly, it was the husband and three kids that really inspired me to escape."

He swallowed his mouthful of wine. "Husband?"

"Raven and Mia have nothing on my family where it comes to matchmaking."

"Husband?" Parker repeated.

She couldn't be married. *Could* she?

Hailey waved away another mosquito. "Every week, it was a new guy. Well, they had some favorites that kept showing up at dinners and dances—Walton, Holt . . . And somehow, I'd always end up catching a ride in their car, or eating at their table, or planning a charity auction with them and their families. It was beyond embarrassing."

"But you're not married." A mosquito bit him on the arm, and he smacked his hand on the little sting.

Another one buzzed his ear, and he waved it away. But it came back with friends, many, many friends.

Hailey jumped to her feet, her arms flailing. "Are they hatching somewhere?" she cried out.

Thousands of bugs suddenly swarmed them both, and he felt bites on his arms and his neck.

"Come *on*," he called, grasping her hand, breaking into a run for the door of his villa, just barely staying ahead of the insects.

SAFE INSIDE, HAILEY BRUSHED THE LINGERING MOSquitoes from her clothes and shook them out of her hair.

Parker clapped them between his hands as they tried to fly away.

"They must have been *starving*," Hailey said with a laugh, seeing the humor now that they weren't being eaten alive.

"And we looked delicious." Parker smiled back as he scanned the room for escapees.

"Wow," Hailey said as her heart rate settled and she took in their surroundings. "This is bigger than the other villas."

"It was the only one they had vacant. My other option was a bunk in Riley and T-Two's loft."

"Nice choice," Hailey said, stepping down to the gleaming hardwood floors of the sunken living area.

The fireplace in this villa was gas instead of wood, made

of white and gray marble with a golden thread running through it. There was a well-stocked bar against the back wall, with dozens of crystal glasses on feature shelves. Eight padded bar chairs were made of white leather, set in front of an inlaid wood bar.

She sat on one and spun around to take in three burgundy leather sofas that faced the fireplace, surrounding a square, glass-topped table with an ornate salmon carving in the middle. Pottery lamps decorated long tables behind the sofas.

She spotted a switch beside the fireplace and went over to give it a try. The flames popped to life, dancing around the fake logs behind the glass and reflecting off the reddish tinge of the polished wood floor.

Parker came up beside her, his tone gravelly and close to her ear. "So, you were saying . . ."

She thought back, not remembering anything of note. "What was I saying?"

"Your husband?"

The question confused her even more, and she turned. "Husband?"

"Atlanta. Your family's matchmaking. The husband and three kids."

"It never *worked*." She gave a small shudder at the very idea. "I got away."

"Good for you," he said with what sounded like sincerity.

"That's a first." It wasn't the answer she was used to getting.

Most people thought she should have snagged a rich, successful guy and proceeded to live the upscale dream. They questioned her sanity for leaving Atlanta for Paradise, for bailing on the family mansion in favor of a little room in WSA housing. Never mind giving up the glamour of party planning for delivering fuel barrels to exploration camps on cold autumn mornings.

"Good for you," he said more softly, and his smoke-gray gaze captured hers.

A pulse of desire restarted within her. The feelings she'd abandoned in the shed rushed back in full force. There was a reason she was wide awake at one in the morning. There was a reason every nerve in her body was pulsing with electricity.

The reason was Parker.

"We definitely can't be trusted," she said.

"I sure hope not."

He smoothed back her hair with a gentle palm, then cradled her head and kissed her lips.

Hailey's body started to liquefy. Luckily, Parker's arm slipped around her waist, bracing the small of her back, keeping her knees from buckling beneath her.

She kissed him back, tired of fighting her feelings, accepting this was going to happen one way or the other. They'd been dancing around their feelings for days—since the minute they'd laid eyes on each other, really. Logical or not, her emotions knew exactly what they wanted.

She wound her arms around his neck and gave herself up to the kiss.

It went on and on as her desire bloomed deep within her, growing from a glow to a blaze that soon overwhelmed her ability to reason. A moan caught in the back of her throat as he kissed her neck, her ear, her temple.

She leaned into the sensations, tasting the salty skin at the collar of his shirt. Hungry for more, she reached for his buttons, plunking them open one by one until she separated his shirt, revealing his smooth, muscular chest. She kissed that too, and he groaned, his hands convulsing on her hips.

Then he reached for the hem of her sweater.

She tipped back her head and raised her arms, and he peeled it off, revealing the worn T-shirt she'd been sleeping in—well, more like tossing and turning in. He went for that next, pulling it over her head, tossing it aside, then shrugging out of his own shirt.

He wrapped her fully in his arms, and she pressed against him, groaning inwardly at the sensation of skin on skin. He kissed her long and deep, then swooped her up into his arms and carried her into the bedroom, setting her down next to an opulent four-poster bed.

The air was cooler away from the fire. One window was open, bringing a fresh breeze in past the blinds. The sunset, or likely the sunrise at this point, streamed pink-toned light across the thick white comforter.

Parker pulled back the blanket, revealing crisp sheets.

Impatient to get on them, Hailey kicked off her shoes and stripped off her yoga pants. There was no point in being coy. They were way past that.

He joined her on the big bed, stretching out next to her, drawing her into his arms, their limbs becoming a naked tangle as their lips met once more.

He angled over her. "You are *so* beautiful."

"You are so sexy. How are you so sexy?"

He gave a self-conscious smile. "I have no idea."

She ran her hands over his shoulders, down his arms, memorizing the definition of his muscles. "Hard work," she ventured.

"Regular work," he said. Then he tugged her hair free and ran his fingers through it.

"You don't get this from regular work." Her fingertip tour moved to his pecs and washboard abs.

"Depends on the work."

"You work in an office."

He shrugged. "I still have mines."

The burning question tripped from her tongue. "What *are* you doing in Paradise, Parker Hall?"

He leaned in and she lost focus on his face. "Kissing you," he said, then proceeded to do just that.

His palms stroked up her sides, his caresses becoming more intimate. "Making love to you," he whispered, sending a haze of passion from her ear to the core of her body.

She gave herself up to the magic, touching and being touched, kissing and being kissed, and wrapped herself around him as their lovemaking grew bolder, faster, deeper.

She held on to the sensations as long as she could, but then lightning burst within her, carrying her on a wave of pleasure as she slowly floated back to earth.

Her first thought was *Uh-oh.* Her second was *Who cares?* They'd admitted to what they wanted. They'd done what they wanted. Maybe now her obsession with him would subside, and she could get back to doing what was best for the town.

Parker eased himself onto his side next to her.

They were both breathing fast and deep, and her heart was thudding hard against the wall of her chest.

The daylight was growing stronger outside, and birds chirped in the trees beyond the open window. A squirrel scolded something, and his call was answered by another farther away. The fresh pine-laden air filled Hailey's lungs. She couldn't remember the last time she'd felt this . . . content.

Parker traced a line with his fingertip along her arm, over her inner elbow and farther down to her wrist. Then he kissed the tip of her shoulder, heaving a big sigh. "That . . . was worth the wait."

She smiled. It was hard to argue with his logic. She couldn't remember any better sex than that. "It was."

He touched his forehead to her temple. "I'm glad you agree."

She gave herself another minute to revel, then she sat up.

"What?" He sounded surprised.

"I've got to get some sleep." She swung her legs over the edge of the bed, looking around for her underwear.

"Sleep here," he said.

She twisted her head to look at him. "Seriously? You think we should sleep together?"

"Why not?" he waved a hand over the bed. "We just—"

"Had sex." She paused for a moment to recall it. "Great sex. But it was just sex, Parker."

He sat up. "I'm not saying it was anything else. Doesn't mean you can't stay."

"Yeah, it does." She couldn't justify anything more than a quick fling.

Even now, she was feeling weird again about being intimate with a man she didn't completely trust. Not that she didn't trust him as a human being. She simply didn't trust him as a business mogul. And that mattered for the moment.

She located her panties and pulled them on, stepping into her yoga pants and shoes, wishing she'd brought her shirt into the bedroom. It seemed silly to cover her breasts with her arms, but a topless goodbye seemed awkward too.

She decided to brazen it out, walking around the bed to give Parker a final kiss.

His arms went around her, and the kiss lasted longer than she'd planned. A pulse of arousal reignited, surprising her. But she pulled back and gave him a smile. "I'll see you later."

He loosely held on to her arm, sliding to her hand, then let her fingertips slip from his as she walked away.

"Later," he said softly.

Back in the living room, she scooped her T-shirt and sweater from the floor where they'd dropped. She settled her clothes, ran her fingers through her messy hair, then stepped out into the silence of the sunrise. She guessed it was coming up on three. She was both satiated and sleepy. Too bad there wasn't much time left of the night.

Then again—she stretched her neck and arched the kinks out of her back—she supposed she wouldn't have gotten any sleep at all if she hadn't hopped into bed with Parker.

Chapter Eight

BACK ON THE GROUND IN PARADISE, WILLOW HOPPED into the passenger side of Hailey's truck, slamming the door behind her.

"What was that look?" she asked as Hailey started the engine.

"What look?" Hailey glanced out the side window and checked the mirror, but all she saw was Brodie talking to Cobra outside the hangar.

The Twin Otter was unloaded and shut down, and Riley was getting ready to drive away in his van.

"Parker's look. He was staring at you. He looked like he was dying to say something. Did you tick him off?"

Hailey laughed at the thought. "I don't think so."

"You sure?"

"I'm sure." Hailey backed up the truck from where it was nosed into the bush, swinging it around to face the parking lot exit and the road home. She was thinking about a nap.

"Then what's up?" Willow asked, sitting back and crossing one ankle over the opposite knee as they pulled forward.

"I had sex with him."

Willow grasped the armrest and sat up straight. "Say, what?"

"Last night. No big deal. One-time thing. For some reason, we couldn't seem to keep our hands off each other."

"So after the whitewater rafting." Willow gave a sage nod. "Adrenaline does weird things. You both must have been jazzed from the trip."

"Is that what happens to you? You get aroused from danger?"

Willow seemed to think about it. "Not exactly aroused, not sexually. Though I can see the adrenaline rush turning into something else. I don't usually have a guy and a bed handy right after."

"This was later," Hailey said, pondering the theory of exhilaration as an aphrodisiac.

It made sense. Not that she hadn't been attracted to Parker before the whitewater rafting. But maybe that's what had pushed her over the edge.

Dust billowed behind the tires as she came up to speed on the gravel road.

"Well, go you," Willow said as the trees flew by. "Maybe it was a lost puppy look."

"What?"

"Parker. Now that I think about it, maybe it was forlorn, not annoyed."

"Parker? Forlorn?" Hailey shook her head. She couldn't imagine that happening.

"Did you hurt his feelings?"

Hailey gaped at Willow along a straight stretch of road. "His *feelings*? He's a guy, an uberconfident, hard-nosed business shark." She gave her head a little shake and looked back at the road. "I didn't hurt his feelings. I gave him great sex."

Willow's tone turned even more interested. "Really good?"

"Really good," Hailey confirmed. "Like, the best I've ever had. And he seemed satisfied." She thought back to his expression, his tone, his gasping breaths.

Parker had seemed more than satisfied.

"So, what did you say?" Willow asked. "I mean after."

"That I needed some sleep. That I had a plane to fly."

"Anything else?"

"No."

"Like, were you tepid, subdued? Did you let him think he'd been just okay?"

"Your concern for Parker's ego is admirable. Surprising, but admirable."

"I always at least toss them a bone," Willow unrolled her window. "I mean, you don't have to say *the best I've ever had* or anything. But guys worry about that kind of thing."

"I don't think Parker worries about that kind of thing. And it was the best I've ever had. I think. I mean, it's the best I can remember." Hailey hadn't had that many lovers, but she sure didn't remember lovemaking being so . . . *consuming.*

"Did you tell him that?"

"No! I would have sounded trite, don't you think? Or fake. It would have sounded really fake."

"Guys believe that kind of thing. They want to, so they're willing to."

"I'm not going to get all gushy on him." Hailey shuddered at the thought. "It wasn't that kind of experience. I mean, we both went into it with our eyes wide open. We knew what we were doing, scratching an itch, you know."

"So, what now?"

"What do you mean?"

"With you and him?"

"Nothing now." Hailey wouldn't share that she was warning Raven about Parker's likely motives, since Galina's business was Galina's business. But nothing more was going to happen between her and Parker. "He'll be gone in a couple of days." And if Hailey had anything to say about it, he wouldn't be back.

PARKER HUNG BACK AT THE AIRSTRIP, WATCHING WHILE Silas taxied an Islander along the access road and into the parking lot. A Beaver had taken off several minutes ago with Tristen Erickson at the controls. WSA's Aircraft Maintenance Engineer, Cobra, was working in the hangar with another technician on the engine of a Caravan. And eight other airplanes were parked around the lot.

Parker had come to understand the pivotal role WSA played in servicing the local mines. He'd known there was a road into Paradise, making Galina's expediting possible. What he hadn't thought much about was the lack of roads out to the local projects.

Once goods arrived, they were landlocked. Except for the occasional barge in early summer when the rivers were high enough for navigation, nothing came or went without a WSA airplane.

Thinking about the possibilities of Rapid Release and the wilderness tourism sector was more a lark than anything. WSA on the other hand might represent a real opportunity. The pilots were having a slow season, Hailey had said so.

Hailey again.

Parker couldn't shake the image of her goodbye last night, nor the panic he'd felt when he realized she was serious. He'd wanted to haul her back onto the bed, to rekindle their passion, to hold her close and drift off to sleep with her wrapped tightly in his arms.

It was a cold splash of water to learn she preferred to leave—as if what had happened between them was no big deal. He didn't like what that might mean.

Silas climbed out of the cockpit, looking curiously at Parker as he approached in his flight suit and ball cap, his eyes covered with dark sunglasses.

"Parker," he said with a nod.

"Busy day?" Parker asked, hoping to engage him in conversation.

They'd only met once, that first day on the set of *Aurora Unleashed*. It hadn't exactly been an amicable meeting, but it hadn't been hostile either. And Silas's wife, Mia, and her cousin Raven seemed to have warmed up to Parker now. Hopefully, the two women had talked, and Silas understood Parker had good intentions.

"Not so busy," Silas said, glancing meaningfully at the parked planes. "You need something?"

"I just got back from Wildflower Lake. The film crew is looking at a location up there."

If Silas wondered or cared what the film crew scouting a location had to do with Parker, he didn't ask.

"I hear you're the chief pilot of the outfit," Parker continued.

Silas gave a nod. "You want to book a flight?"

"Maybe. In a day or so." Parker decided right then and there to arrange another gold-panning trip to Lucky Breach with Hailey.

It seemed the closest he could hope to come to a date—unless she somehow changed her mind and agreed to date him. His optimism flared up for a moment. Maybe he was reading too much into her abrupt departure last night. Maybe she'd simply been tired, just like she'd said.

Silas was giving him an odd look, obviously waiting for more information.

"Over to Broken Branch strip," Parker continued. "I've got a mine near there."

"I heard you found a kick-ass nugget."

Parker smiled at that, taking it as a friendly observation. "Biggest one I've ever seen."

"Are you talking motherload territory?"

"I wish. Might be an anomaly, but we'll sure keep looking. I saw Xavier leave just before you landed. Is the season picking up at all?"

"Spotty," Silas said. "Do you want me to put something on the books?" He gestured to the office door.

"Sure." Parker followed, deciding he might as well take a chance on Hailey's interest and availability. It took his eyes a moment to adjust to the change in light.

Silas walked around the battered counter and tapped on the keyboard. "Taking anything substantial for gear? Or just yourself?"

"Just me. Any chance Hailey's available to fly?"

Silas looked up, seeming surprised by the question.

"She took me in last time. I was impressed with her landing." Parker was being perfectly honest about that. It was a crappy little airstrip, and she'd done a great job.

"Hailey's busy tomorrow."

"Day after?"

"We try to spread the work around," Parker said with a frown. "I'm reluctant to bump others to put her on again."

"So, a client can't specify?" Parker asked. He wanted to keep this cordial, but he had no intention of flying to Lucky Breach without her.

"Sure," Silas said neutrally. "What time did you have in mind?"

The door opened behind Parker, and Silas looked past his shoulder.

"What's up?" Brodie asked conversationally.

"Just booking a trip for Parker," Silas said. To his credit, he didn't betray the slightest annoyance with Parker's special request.

Parker turned and gave Brodie a nod. "Nice to see you again, Brodie."

"How was Wildflower Lake?" Brodie asked.

"Top-notch."

Brodie grinned at that. "Cornelia knows how to give good service."

"The new summit villa was the only one available. It made me think she entertains royalty."

"She sometimes does."

"That explains the gold-plated faucets."

"Seriously?" Silas asked. "I'd heard they'd gone all-out on that new one, but . . ."

"Not literally made of gold," Parker admitted, making a half turn and stepping back to include them both in the conversation. "But it is off the charts opulent."

"I thought the regular villas were off the charts," Silas said.

Brodie jumped in. "Says the man who built his own."

"It's a solid floor plan and elevation for the north," Silas said.

"Your place seemed great," Parker said, meaning it.

"That's all Mia."

"It was a downgrade for Mia," Brodie said with a smirk.

Silas didn't miss a beat. "But I was an upgrade."

"Her last husband was dead."

The dark humor shocked Parker, but Silas just laughed. "That gave me a running start, for sure."

The phone on the counter jangled with a ring, and Silas picked it up. "West Slope Aviation."

Parker took a step back from Silas, approaching Brodie. "Spare a minute to talk?" he asked him.

"Sure." Brodie gestured to the group of three tables with mismatched chairs behind the counter. "Here okay?"

"It's fine," Parker said.

He followed Brodie to the back room, which opened out to an aging kitchen with a faded orange counter and a battered fridge. They took the table farthest back and sat down.

"What's up?" Brodie asked.

"It's a really nice place you've built up here," Parker opened.

Brodie glanced guardedly around the aging lounge and kitchen.

"I'm not being sarcastic," Parker assured him.

"We put the profits into planes, not into the building aesthetics."

"I applaud and agree with that."

Parker would usually do a soft segue into his pitch, but Brodie struck him as a no-nonsense kind of guy, so he dove right in. "You know I'm looking at an investment in Galina."

"So you said."

"You must also know they've had a tough year."

"What is Hugh saying?"

"We've only had the one serious conversation. I'm still assessing the opportunity."

"Did he actually say he was willing to sell?"

"Not sell necessarily. But he's open to looking at options for going forward."

"I'm surprised."

"Necessity is what it is."

"I suppose."

Parker relaxed his posture, trying to come across as laid-back and benign. "It got me to thinking."

Brodie's gaze narrowed, his expression hardening.

"About how closely intertwined Galina is with WSA," Parker added.

"One doesn't work without the other."

Parker nodded at that. "I'd like to talk to you about possibilities sometime." It was obvious from Brodie's reaction that this discussion couldn't be rushed.

Brodie's expression hardened further. "What possibilities?"

"I'm seriously looking to invest in Paradise. It seems likely Lucky Breach will become an ongoing concern, and that makes me interested in the long-term health and viability of the town."

Brodie shook his head. "Not interested."

The reaction didn't surprise Parker at all. "You've been running the show on your own for a long time."

"I have."

"You've got how many planes? Twelve?"

"Fourteen."

"You must have some debt servicing on the fleet."

Brodie didn't answer.

"I'm not here to hard-sell anything. I just want to let you know you might have options. If you want them." Parker set a business card down on the table and came to his feet. "I'll be in town a few more days if you have questions or want to talk."

Brodie's forehead furrowed and he went silent for a moment. "Exactly how far has it gone with Galina?"

Parker wouldn't normally answer a question like that, but he was looking to gain Brodie's trust here. "I'm reviewing the operation and assets, the financials, the customer base."

"And you're working with Raven on that?"

"I am."

Brodie paused. "I'm surprised Hugh let it get this far."

"He's looking for a mutual benefit."

Brodie gave a ghost of a smile at that. "I'm sure he is."

"I'll let you think it over," Parker said, and turned away and met Silas's tight expression where he watched them from the front office.

It was hard to tell how much he'd overheard. But it was easy to guess he'd heard enough. It was also obvious how he felt about the idea.

"THAT'S A TERRIBLE IDEA," HAILEY TOLD WILLOW.

"*Wolves*?" Dalia asked her at the same time.

"It'll set us apart, cinematically speaking," Scarlett said to them both.

The four women had settled on the porch of Willow's Rapid Release cabin, sipping wine, comfortable in padded wicker chairs. It was early evening and storm clouds gathered again at the head of the valley, the muggy air bringing out mosquitoes that tapped hopefully against the window screens.

"We're also planning an explosion," Scarlett added. "But I don't know the details yet. I don't think they've decided."

"You're blowing something up?" Hailey was intrigued by that idea.

Scarlett nodded emphatically. "Explosions sell tickets."

"Too bad you missed filming the café fire," Dalia said.

"I *know*," Willow put in. "I was thinking that at the time. I could have rushed out the front door, flames behind me, choking on the smoke." She covered her face with her hands. "See? Like that. You wouldn't have known it wasn't Hope. I'm sure they could have used the footage somewhere in the plot."

"Brodie wouldn't have let you go inside," Hailey noted.

"We didn't have cameras anyway," Scarlett said, sounding disappointed.

"Tell me about the wolves?" Hailey asked, wondering how they planned to get that on film.

"It won't be *actual* wolves chasing me." Willow sat forward and reached for the bottle of merlot on the low table between them. "We're borrowing a husky team from some guy down by the lake."

"Morty Green," Scarlett added while Willow topped up everyone's wineglasses.

"Huskies don't look anything like wolves," Hailey noted. "They're, like, a third of the size."

"They won't use huskies in the close-ups," Scarlett said. "They'll be like a blur in the background while they're chasing Willow."

"Well, you sure can't use real wolves in a close-up," Hailey pointed out, worried about how close they expected Willow to get to the wild animals.

"I really like that they added the Siberian angle," Dalia said. "It gives depth to Aurora's character."

All three women looked at Dalia in surprise.

"What?" Dalia asked them.

"I didn't take you for a fantasy–action movie type," Hailey said.

Dalia waved a dismissive hand. "I can appreciate the superhero universe. The stories are usually allegorical, social messages framed in the good fun of an action film."

Scarlett pointed at her. "That. What she said. *That's* why they work."

Hailey took in Dalia's burgundy blazer, black pants and silky blouse with its blue and white horizontal stripes. Her makeup and sleek black hair were perfect, and her bold midnight-blue glasses made her look ready for closing arguments.

Dalia's phone buzzed on the coffee table.

Hailey reflexively glanced toward the sound and saw Parker's name flash on the screen. Her breath momentarily hitched in her chest as she remembered their parting kiss at Wildflower Lake. In some ways, it seemed like a long time ago. In others, it felt like it had only been seconds.

She touched the tip of her tongue to her bottom lip, thinking she could still taste him.

"Natasha's got a line on an environmental research project," Scarlett said while Dalia reached for her phone. "They're observing a pack of wolves."

"Somewhere called the Lichen Plateau," Willow added.

"*Those* wolves?" Hailey straightened in alarm. "You don't want to get anywhere near those wolves."

A Colorado university team was studying a subspecies of the Mackenzie Valley wolves up in the Lichen Plateau. Dramatically white and silver-gray in color, they were specific to a three-hundred-mile range. They were beautiful, thought to be the largest wolves in the world, and reputedly fierce and territorial. They were highly intelligent pack hunters capable of bringing down moose and bison.

Hailey had seen them surround an adult bison from five hundred feet in the air, and she had no interest in getting any closer than that.

"I'm at Willow's right now," Dalia said into her phone.

Hailey tried to ignore the phone conversation, telling herself to stop thinking about Parker, stop remembering him and wanting him all over again. Making love was supposed to get him out of her system, not let him burrow even further inside.

"Fernando's very cautious," Willow was saying.

"Is it urgent?" Dalia asked, straightening up.

Hailey forced herself to focus on Willow. "At a full run, their strides are eight feet apart," she told her. "That's teeth and claws flying eight feet in the air and then chomping right down on your head."

"Dramatic, much?" Willow asked.

"Nobody's getting close enough to be chomped," Scarlett said.

"So, with Brodie?" Dalia asked, rising to her feet. "Sure. I can come along." She lifted her wineglass, gave the others a grin and took a swallow.

At the mention of Brodie's name, Hailey's attention shifted fully to Dalia.

"I can check online," Dalia said.

"Fernando won't let them eat me," Willow said to Hailey. "He'll get an expert . . ." Her voice faded away as Hailey focused on Dalia.

"You just can't help yourself, can you?" Dalia asked on a laugh.

"Hailey?" Willow's voice sounded hollow and far away.

Hailey blinked back to Willow but kept listening to Dalia.

"Okay. See you in a few minutes." Dalia ended the call.

"I said, Fernando won't let the wolves eat me," Willow repeated.

"He won't," Scarlett agreed.

"Listen to the biologist," Hailey warned, her antenna quivering over Parker's call. "Not to Fernando."

Willow gestured up and down her lean body. "I don't think I'd taste any good."

"Compared to a deer," Scarlett said with a nod.

"They eat moose," Hailey automatically noted, parsing her way through Dalia's side of the conversation and wondering what it meant.

"Still," Scarlett said.

"I have to meet up with Parker," Dalia told them all as she took a final sip of her wine and headed inside the cabin.

"Something up?" Willow asked, and Hailey was grateful for the woman's curiosity.

Hailey was dying to ask but didn't want to pry.

"Same old, same old," Dalia called over her shoulder. "He's like an opportunity radar system. The man never shuts it down."

Hailey knew he saw Rapid Release as an opportunity. But Dalia hadn't mentioned Riley. She'd mentioned Brodie. There was only one plausible reason for that.

Guilt and anxiety tightened her chest as she struggled to remember what she'd told Parker about WSA. He'd asked if WSA was busy this season. She'd been honest and told him they were slow. She'd told him other things too, one at a time, in seemingly unrelated conversations. He'd asked about their clients, their cargo, even Cobra's work maintaining the planes.

She was mortified to have given him ammunition against Brodie. It was even worse to think she might have been the one to pique his interest in the first place. Did Parker see WSA as another soft target? *Was* WSA another soft target?

A pickup sounded in the distance, then came into view,

bouncing over the two tire tracks that led over the grass and along the row of cabins.

The sight of Parker in the driver's seat brought visceral memories to Hailey's mind. The man pulled on her emotions like a magnet, turning her on even from this distance. She scooped up her wine and took a bracing drink, feeling like the worst traitor in the world.

He'd seen her as a source of business intel, that much was clear now. Smart move on his part. Diabolical move, but smart all the same. He'd cozied up to her to learn all he could about her employer, positioning himself to pounce.

And she'd foolishly fallen for his smooth, suave act. So much for thinking like a Barrosse. Her sister, Amber, would be appalled.

The pickup engine fell to silence. He got out and swung the cab door shut.

She kept her eyes averted as he rounded the hood, focusing on her anger to keep the attraction at bay.

"You want us to get out of the way?" Willow whispered to her as his footsteps swished through the grass.

"No," Hailey said sharply, way too sharply.

Scarlett overheard and sent a frown of curiosity.

Willow looked shocked. "You don't want to—"

"Just stay," Hailey told them both.

Dalia stepped back onto the porch and Parker paused at the bottom of the three stairs.

Hailey could feel his gaze on her, but she refused to look his way. All that sweet talk, the things they'd done, the way she'd felt. She was mortified at being duped.

"Hi, Willow," he said. "Scarlett."

The mere sound of his voice sent memories skittering along Hailey's spine. She hardened herself against them.

"Hi, Parker," both women answered.

"Hailey," he said. The effect of his deep voice was heightened when it rolled over her name.

Bracing herself, she glanced fleetingly his way, not

pausing long enough to focus. "Parker," she answered levelly.

"I'll catch you later," Dalia said to Willow, clearly oblivious to the undercurrent as she crossed the porch.

Parker stepped back to let her pass. He stayed still a minute longer, and Hailey could feel the heat of his gaze. She didn't look up until she heard both pickup doors slam shut.

"*What* was that?" Willow asked Hailey as the engine restarted.

"What did I miss?" Scarlett asked, looking back and forth between them.

"You heard what she said," Hailey answered.

It took Willow a moment to answer. "Who said what? You mean Dalia? I'm lost here."

"Tell me about it," Scarlett said to Willow.

"Yes, Dalia." Hailey might be late to the party, but there was enough Barrosse in her that she knew when she was right. "What she said over the phone."

"You mean to Parker. Just now," Willow confirmed.

"What did she say?" Scarlett asked, watching the truck turn and disappear behind the last cabin. "And why do you care? Wait. Are you into Parker?"

Willow lifted her brow, obviously wondering how much Hailey wanted to share with Scarlett.

"It's not about me," Hailey clarified. "They were discussing Brodie. And Brodie means WSA. And WSA means it was intel from me. And *that's* what Parker wanted all along. From me." She couldn't help ending on a bitter note.

She hated that she'd been so naïve.

Scarlett leaned closer to Willow and stage-whispered, "I've really missed something, haven't I."

Willow looked pointedly to Hailey.

"I slept with Parker," Hailey admitted.

"Hello?" Scarlett perked up. "Wait." Her tone changed to one of compassion. "Did he blow you off afterward?"

"It was the other way around." Willow paused. "Seriously, Hailey. You think Parker slept with you as some convoluted plan to get information on Brodie?"

"Well, given all the evidence . . ." What else was Hailey supposed to think?

"What evidence? That you're a hot woman, and he's a sexy guy?"

Hailey gestured to herself. "Hot? Seriously? He likes women like Dalia."

"It didn't look like there was anything between Parker and Dalia," Scarlett said.

"Not Dalia specifically," Hailey elaborated. "But women like her, glamorous women, sophisticated women. He's left his mining roots far behind. He's a big-city success now with an image to match. He's probably dripping with women back in Anchorage." Hailey didn't like the shot of jealousy that ran through her as she spoke. Knowing what she knew now, she shouldn't care anything about the women in Parker's life—just so long as she wasn't one of them.

"You're beautiful, Hailey," Willow said with sincerity. "You must have a mirror."

Scarlett emphatically nodded.

Hailey appreciated her friends' staunch support. But that wasn't the problem here. "He's still after Galina, and now he's after WSA too."

"You don't know that for sure," Willow said.

"I am sure. And I'll reconfirm as soon as I talk to Brodie. Parker is plotting something big for this town."

And Brodie needed to be warned.

Chapter Nine

PARKER WAS FLOORED TO LEARN THAT HAILEY HAD UN-
dermined him. One minute she was naked in his arms, the
next she was telling people he couldn't be trusted in business. He didn't know what had happened, but he was absolutely determined to find out.

He finally tracked her down on the film set at Silas and
Mia's. Willow and Buzz were doing a chase scene on foot
across the peaked roof of the house and garage. Everyone's
attention was on the action, giving Parker an opportunity
to approach Hailey.

She was slightly apart from the crew, between the river
and the catering tent. The surveyor's tape boundary was
behind her, but there wasn't much of an audience today.
The novelty of filming had apparently worn off.

He got close before she spotted him.

She didn't bolt as he marched forward. Instead, she
tucked her hair behind her ears and stiffened her spine. She
clearly knew the confrontation was inevitable.

"What the hell, Hailey?" he asked on a growling undertone as he came to a halt a couple of feet away.

She tossed her hair and turned her focus back to Willow. "What the hell what, Parker?"

"You're going to *pretend*?" he challenged in astonishment.

"Me pretend?" She gave a cold laugh at that. "That's a good one."

"*I* was operating in good faith." He had been open and honest about his intentions across the board.

Not so much Hailey, it seemed. She hadn't trusted him in the beginning and her tune hadn't changed even while their relationship did.

She crossed her arms over her chest, sarcasm clear in her tone. "Sure you were."

"Was this the plan all along?" he demanded.

She turned to him. "I don't know. Was it?"

"You *slept* with me." He couldn't believe she'd go that far. Had he completely misjudged her?

"*You* slept with *me*," she countered.

"I was attracted to you. I wanted to date you. What the hell were you doing?"

"Dating me?" She laughed again. "You were spying on me. You were spying on all of us."

He widened his stance, wondering if she was delusional or simply keeping up the ruse. "How so? I talked to Hugh before I came anywhere near Paradise. Then I came straight to Raven as soon as I hit town. I've been straight with everyone, *including you*, from the very beginning."

He'd thought she was being straight with him. He would have bet money on it. But no, she'd burrowed in like some sleeper agent. She'd played *just* hard enough to keep his interest.

"Straight?" she challenged.

He didn't get why she would ask that, because she knew the answer as well as he did. "Yes, straight."

"You've been vague. You've been obscure. You pretended all you wanted was a minor interest in Galina."

"That *was* what I wanted." He hadn't been vague or obscure about anything. Just as soon as WSA caught his interest, he'd let Brodie in on his thinking.

"*Ha*," she scoffed, as if she'd caught him in a lie.

He could see they weren't getting anywhere. She wasn't about to admit anything. All that was left was to salvage what he'd come for, if that was even possible.

"What did you tell them?" he asked.

A collective gasp came up from the film crew, and he caught sight of Willow taking a dive off the peak of the garage roof to land on an airbag below.

Hailey focused on the fall, then watched Willow bound up on the inflated blue and orange pad.

"And, cut," the director called through the loudspeaker while everyone broke out in applause.

"What did you tell them?" Parker repeated. He needed to know what he was up against.

She turned his way, looking like she was ready to do battle. "I merely pointed out your pattern."

"My pattern?" The answer baffled him.

"Yes."

He spread his hands. "What pattern? My pattern of what?"

"You don't think I know how this works?"

"How *what* works?"

Her eyes were hard jewels now, her anger focused on him like a laser beam. "How you build your empire."

"My *empire*?" That was a stretch. He'd had a pretty good run of it the past ten years, but it was hardly an empire.

"Gold mines, service companies, your own suppliers," she counted off on her fingers.

He was still lost.

"And what do you think happens to the people left behind?" she asked.

"*Who's* getting left behind?"

"Paradise."

"I'm not leaving Paradise behind." He had no idea where she'd gotten that idea. Him doing business in Paradise was only going to help them.

He tried to come up with a way to explain, to get her to understand. But her cold glare told him it was hopeless. He'd been charged, tried and convicted in her mind.

He steadied himself, knowing his emotions were messing with his logic. There was no going back with Hailey, only going forward for PQH.

"Hailey." He spoke levelly but firmly. "You need to butt out of my business."

"Butt *out*? Seriously? Raven is my friend. Brodie is my employer. What you're doing *is* my business."

"Not unless you own a piece of them."

"I'm allowed an opinion."

"And I'm allowed to sue you for restraint of trade." He wasn't sure if that was the right law, but Dalia wasn't here, and it was the first one he came up with off the top of his head.

She gave him a look and rolled her eyes. "No, you aren't. I'm not restraining your trade." She seemed sure about that, and she was probably right.

"Slander, then."

"I'd have to be lying for it to be slander."

"You *are* lying." Not that he knew exactly what she'd said. But whatever it was, it couldn't be true, because nothing he was doing should have made Raven and Brodie question his honesty the way they had.

She gave a satisfied smirk, saying without words that she thought she'd won.

"Take three," the director called through the loudspeaker.

He took a bracing breath, lowering his voice. "What did you tell them, Hailey?"

She tossed her hair again. "I told them what you're doing. Big guy needs an assurance of service from a little company. Big guy invests in little company. Little company doesn't please big guy, and big guy starts to flex his muscles."

He couldn't hold back any longer. "I'm not a demanding man."

Hailey's eyes went round and she choked on a laugh.

"Stop doing that. This isn't a joke." He'd been headed down a perfectly logical and profitable path here in Paradise when she'd suddenly thrown a stick of dynamite into the deal.

"Your self-concept is amusing," she said.

He waited for her to elaborate.

Applause burst out on set again.

"You refuse to take no for an answer," she said.

His thoughts shifted to their lovemaking. He might have been determined to spend time with her, but he hadn't pushed for anything more. She'd wanted sex as much as he had.

He frowned. "Are you accusing me of something?"

It seemed to take her a second to work out what he meant.

"No," she said quickly with a shake of her head. "Not that."

He was relieved. "Then what?"

"I'm accusing you of operating in your own interests."

"And what's wrong with *that*?" Who didn't operate in their own interests?

Hailey had operated in her own interests by leaving her family and living in Alaska.

"Nothing," she admitted.

He lifted his hands in the air, happy to have finally won the point.

But she wasn't finished. "I'm simply telling Hugh and Brodie to operate in theirs."

* * *

WITH TRUE NORTHERN GRIT, THE BEAR AND BAR OPENED
back up again in under two weeks. There was still a faint
whiff of charcoal in the air, but it wasn't enough to stop
anyone from ordering a cinnamon bun or a Super Bear
Burger.

Hailey and Willow were sharing a cinnamon bun.

"I never should have invited Dalia to stay at the cabin,"
Willow said, looking contrite as she tore off another piece
of the gooey spiral bun.

It was layered with cinnamon, butter and sugar and
slathered with cream cheese icing. As comfort food went,
it was tops.

Hailey knew she'd done the right thing warning Raven
and Brodie after Parker had shown his true colors. And she
was frustrated with herself for missing him. It wasn't like
they'd been friends. Hailey had plenty of friends, and none
of them were Parker.

And it wasn't the sex.

Still, she shifted in her chair just thinking about it.

Okay, the sex had been great. But she wasn't so shallow
as to pine away over sex alone. Who missed a one-night
stand?

She paused over that.

Was Parker a one-night stand?

"What are you thinking?" Willow asked. "You look like
you're in pain."

"I was wondering if Parker was a one-night stand."

Willow paused mid bite, looking surprised. "Are you
saying you might sleep with him again?"

"No! Not that." Hailey shifted again, getting twitchy
when she thought about the possibility of more sex with
Parker. She dug into the cinnamon bun for comfort. "I
meant it wasn't like we were dating."

"But you knew each other. So that's different." Willow

seemed to ponder for a moment. "It was more like a friends with benefits type situation."

"We're not friends." That much was crystal clear. "Maybe enemies. Or adversaries. I'd say we were at least adversaries, since he's out to hurt my real friends and I'm trying to mess up his business plans."

"Are you succeeding?"

"I don't know if Hugh or Brodie have made up their minds yet." Hailey's phone pinged with a text message.

"Maybe that's your answer," Willow said brightly.

Hailey checked the screen and saw it was from Amber. "My sister."

"How are things going with her?"

"Okay. She backed off on me coming home for the meeting."

"That's better than okay."

Hailey wiped her sticky fingertips and tapped to open the message. She'd promised herself she'd be more responsive to Amber's texts.

"Well, that's okay." She was relieved.

"What did she say?" Willow asked.

"Amber just needs me to go to Anchorage."

"Is she meeting you there?"

Hailey shook her head as she typed a quick response, asking for a deadline. "I need to see a lawyer and sign some papers to give her my proxy."

"I guess it's better than going all the way to Atlanta."

It was definitely better than going to Atlanta. But Hailey hoped she could put it off for a few more days. If she stayed here, she might be able to head off any of Parker's new tricks—like amped-up talk about a glorious future or sweetening the financial pot.

Her phone pinged again, with Amber telling her not to wait too long. She also included the name and number of the lawyer who'd drawn up the papers.

"Looks like the papers can wait a few days," Hailey told Willow.

"I wish I could come along," Willow said wistfully.

"Do you miss the big city?"

"Sometimes." Willow wiped off her fingers and thumb. "This is delicious, but I could go for a nice steakhouse right about now. And I wouldn't mind wandering through a shopping mall."

Hailey wasn't a big fan of shopping malls. She wasn't a shopper, more a dash into the store, grab what she needed and dash back out kind of person. "I'm hoping to get it done in and out in one day."

"Seriously? You're not taking advantage of a trip to the big city?"

"I don't need anything."

"You said you haven't been to Anchorage in almost a year. How can you not need anything?"

"I've been to Fairbanks. And Raven brings me in whatever I want."

"What about clothes and shoes? Jewelry? You have to try those things on before you decide."

Hailey glanced at her boots. She owned two styles of them, plus sneakers. She just kept ordering the same ones over and over. She hadn't worn heels in years. Which was yet another reason to stay away from Atlanta. The clothes in her closet back home were hopelessly outdated. She'd have to buy a whole new wardrobe to please her family.

"I'm not exactly fashion conscious."

"Maybe not here. But if you go somewhere nice." Willow leaned forward earnestly. "It feels amazing to get dressed up once in a while."

Hailey couldn't help but smile at the thought. "I haven't tried it in a while. I can't even imagine putting on makeup or wearing high heels."

Willow waved a hand. "It's like riding a bike. When the

film's done, you and I should do a girls' weekend—spa, shopping, makeovers."

Hailey shook her head. "Not my thing."

"Pampering? It's everybody's thing. Everyone loves a good massage and facial. Oh, and reflexology. You'll feel like a million bucks, I promise."

"That sounds very California."

Willow was undeterred—if anything, she was more excited. "Any chance I could get you to come to LA? The spas there are world-class."

"I'm sure they are."

"We should totally do it."

At this point, Hailey wasn't taking her seriously. "That's a long way to fly for a spa day."

"Not if we go straight from here."

"You want to fly private?" Now *that* would be an indulgence.

"Bad idea?" Willow asked.

"It would take three times as long, and there's no bathroom on board."

"But we could go direct, right?"

"Sure, if you don't count fuel and bathroom stops."

"Still." Willow took another piece of the cinnamon bun. "It'd be fun."

"It would be fun," Hailey conceded. A girls' weekend with Willow would probably be a blast. A solo weekend in a lawyer's office signing proxy paperwork, not so much.

Willow's phone rang, and she quickly wiped her fingers before picking it up from the table.

"Mia," she told Hailey before answering. "Hey, what's up."

Hailey took the opportunity to get back to the cinnamon bun. They were getting close to the center, the best part, where it got very soft, sweet and super tender. She was close to full, but a few more bites of comfort food wouldn't kill her.

"She *did*?" Willow asked, the tone of her voice piquing Hailey's curiosity. "She knows we'd use dynamite, right?"

Hailey stopped chewing and stared.

"Why *would* she?" Willow paused. "Well, sure, yeah, but—"

Hailey swallowed then stage-whispered, "What?"

"I can't believe she'd agree." Then Willow chuckled with delight. "She's right about that."

"Who?" Hailey asked, dying of curiosity now.

Willow covered the phone and whispered, "Raven." Then she listened to Mia again, looking shocked. "Is that safe?"

The answer hadn't helped Hailey's worry much.

"I guess Fernando knows what he's doing," Willow said.

Fernando. So, a film thing . . . involving Raven . . . and dynamite? Hailey tried to make some sense out of the conversation.

"I'm game," Willow said. She grinned and gave Hailey a wink. "Well, you people haven't killed me yet."

"*What* is going on?" Hailey rasped.

"Let me tell Hailey," Willow said, and pivoted the phone away from her mouth. "They're blowing up Raven's cabin."

Hailey's jaw dropped.

"She looks surprised," Willow said to Mia on a laugh.

Hailey found her voice. "Wait, what?"

"I'll touch base with Fernando." Willow paused. "She better." Another pause, and Willow turned serious. "I suppose. Yeah, I've been there. I've seen it."

Hailey couldn't wrap her head around the information. Sure, Raven's cabin was old and dilapidated. Hugh had once lived in it, and she'd inherited it when she took over running Galina. But Raven had lived there for years. She swore she loved it. And it wasn't like there were any extra houses in Paradise.

Raven was always adamant about not living in the

Galina barracks or in WSA staff housing. Hailey knew
Brodie had offered many times, once when her roof was
leaking in five places. But the leaks had been repaired, and
she'd updated her bathroom, even put in a wireless signal
booster so she could use her cell phone at home.

Willow ended the call.

"*Details*," Hailey immediately ordered.

"YOU MUST BE ABLE TO SEE HAILEY'S SIDE OF IT," DALIA
said from across the small table in Parker's room after
they'd moved back to the B and B.

Soot had been scrubbed from the walls, floor and fix-
tures, and new furniture had arrived at Galina's warehouse
just this morning. A faint scent of creosote lingered in the
air, but it was warm enough to keep the windows open and
the breeze circulating to dissipate the smell.

On his new laptop, Parker scrolled through a ten-year
graph of their accounts receivable, checking the detail on
some of the trends.

"Her *side*?" he asked Dalia. "There are no sides in right
and wrong."

Hailey had been wrong about him. What's more, he
hadn't given her a single reason to doubt his integrity,
not one.

"Have you checked the Atlanta Barrosses out at all?"
Dalia turned her screen so Parker could see it.

He barely glanced up. "Not interested."

Hailey was estranged from her family, so he didn't see
how they were relevant.

"We're talking intergenerational wealth," Dalia said.

"So?" He was surprised to learn Hailey was old money,
but it was still irrelevant to the situation—the situation being that he needed to work harder than ever to win Hugh's,
Raven's and Brodie's trust.

"That kind of wealth does something to a person." Dalia turned the tablet back her way.

Parker gave up on the numbers, since his brain was now fixated on Hailey. "What does it do?"

"Expectations, for one thing," Dalia said, still reading her screen and tapping something out, multitasking better than he could imagine.

"Hers or theirs?" He remembered what Hailey had said about her family trying to control her life.

Dalia looked puzzled. "Hers. You grow up cosseted and entitled, and you feel as though you can—"

"We're talking about Hailey here." Parker found himself rising to her defense. "She walked away from the family money. Being a bush pilot is hard work. And you've seen her—she lives a simple life."

Dalia blinked at him. "She undermined your business interests, stuck her opinion in where it didn't belong."

"She was worried about her friends."

"Why are you defending her?"

He didn't know. He truly didn't. "She's not rich and entitled is all I'm saying."

"She's audaciously meddlesome."

"Okay." He'd agree with that.

"That's a form of entitlement."

"You just can't say die, can you?"

"You have an emotional block when it comes to Hailey."

"I like her—*liked* her," he clarified.

"I know."

"I never thought she'd do what she did." The most upsetting part for him was that she hadn't even come to him. If she had suspicions about his motives, she could have asked straight-out. He could have reassured her.

"Well, look at that," Dalia said, frowning and clicking with her mouse.

"What?"

"Raven just canceled our meeting."

Parker raised his hands in frustration. "What *now*?"

"She says she has a schedule conflict."

"That's bullshit." Parker went for his phone, tapping Raven's number.

To her credit, she picked up. "Hi, Parker."

Parker took a beat to adjust his attitude. If she was going to be pleasant, he should return the favor. "Hi, Raven. Dalia says you have to cancel today."

"Sorry about that." Banging and clattering sounded in the background. "We're cleaning some things out here, and it's a hard deadline."

"I'm happy to come to you." He could talk to her around warehouse work if necessary.

"This one?" a faint voice said in the background.

Parker recognized it as Mia.

Raven's voice turned muffled. "Sure. I might as well keep it."

"You're at Mia's?" Parker asked. "I can meet you there if you like."

He and Dalia had come up with a concrete offer. He hoped seeing the dollar amount and considering the potential would win Raven over. It would be nice to have her on their side when they went to Hugh.

"I'm at home," she said.

Another background voice chimed in. "This one is nailed to the wall." It was Hailey.

"I really have to go, Parker," Raven said, sounding a bit breathless. "I'll try to reschedule." She ended the call.

"What was that?" Dalia asked.

"I have no idea." He set down his phone. "But Hailey was with her, and Mia was there. They sounded like they were cleaning out the garage or something."

"Raven doesn't have a garage." Dalia gave a little smile. "Raven barely has a house."

"Hailey's there with her," he repeated.

Dalia paused to take in his expression. "Oh, that's not good."

"Right?" Instead of Parker reassuring Raven, Hailey was filling her head with even more hyperbole and nonsense.

Making up his mind, he stood. "I'm going to Raven's."

Dalia looked skeptical. "Are you sure that's the right move?"

He knew standing back was the wrong move. If he had to duke it out with Hailey in front of Raven, so be it. "Maybe I can win them both over."

Dalia came to her feet, still looking skeptical. "Parker."

"I don't have a choice." The alternative was to leave the field open for Hailey, and he sure wasn't about to do that.

"This could backfire."

"So, stay here out of the fray."

"Are you kidding?" She went for the purse she'd dropped on the sofa. "Giving you good advice is my job. Watching you ignore it is entertaining."

Chapter Ten

⟜

AT THE END OF RAVEN'S DRIVEWAY, THE SECURITY guards tried to block Brodie from coming on the set.

Hailey saw the commotion and started his way, about to tell them to let him through. But Brodie barged past on his own, his expression daring anyone to try to stop him.

"Brodie," she called out as he marched toward the cabin.

He altered his course, his expression grim. "What's happening here?"

"Did Raven call you?"

"No. I was on my way from the airstrip, and I saw all the barricades." His darting gaze took in the pile of Raven's belongings in Hailey's pickup. "What the hell is going on?"

Raven appeared on the front porch then, and Brodie beelined for her before Hailey could explain.

"I can't say I expected *this*," Parker drawled from behind her.

"Spring cleaning?" Dalia asked as she sized up the disorganized jumble in the yard.

"The set's closed today." Hailey kept her voice even, disguising the contradictory surges of attraction and anger. "I'm surprised they let you in."

"Please," he said pityingly. "Like I couldn't talk my way past four local security guards."

"You really shouldn't be here." She didn't know what they wanted, but she wanted them gone—preferably back to Anchorage. "It's going to be dangerous."

Dalia darted a worried glance into the woods beside them, moving slightly closer to Parker. "The wolves?"

The question took Hailey by surprise. "The wolves aren't *here*."

"What wolves?" Parker asked.

"They're wandering around on the Lichen Plateau," Hailey said to Dalia.

"Thank goodness." She looked relieved.

"We're setting up for pyrotechnics." As Hailey spoke, a semi's diesel engine rumbled out on the road. They weren't moving the entire set to Raven's, but they needed cameras and sound equipment, plus the generators to run everything.

"What do they need with Raven?" Parker asked.

"You're here to see Raven." Hailey should have known.

"We had an appointment," Parker said.

Hailey looked him full-on for the first time. Their kisses came back in a rush. Their lovemaking came back. She should have seen it coming, but it still took her breath away.

His dark gaze was impossible to read, but there was a long pause before he spoke again. "I need to talk to her."

Hailey reached for the anger. "That's not going to happen right now."

"Is she inside?" He made a move in that direction.

"They're setting explosives," Hailey warned, stopping him. The demolitions team was already inside.

Cinematographer Vanessa Tracy wanted to set it off later in the evening.

Parker halted, brow furrowing. "You mean, they're blowing up—"

"—Raven's *cabin*?" Dalia finished on a note of awe.

"The place *is* falling apart," Hailey pointed out.

It had been a tough decision for Raven, but Mia had finally convinced her it was dangerous to keep living in such an old building. The foundation was rotting, and the roof trusses were suspect. Cosmetic repairs were one thing, but fixing the structure would cost more than building something completely new.

Raven was going to live with Mia and Silas while she did just that.

"Natasha says pyrotechnics sell tickets," Hailey continued talking to keep her emotions at bay. "An explosion of some kind was already in the script. It was Mia's idea to use Raven's place."

"How does Raven feel about it?" Parker asked.

Willow appeared then with Fernando, and Dalia quickly headed her way.

"As if you care," Hailey said to Parker, letting him know she wasn't buying his sensitive act.

"It's her home. She must have mixed emotions about blowing it up."

"She has feelings about it." Hailey couldn't keep the scorn from her voice. "Just like she has feelings about Galina."

The semitruck's back-up warning pierced the air as it backed slowly down the driveway.

"Was that a dig?" he asked.

"I'm not buying that you care about her feelings." Hailey took a few paces off the driveway onto a patch of scruffy grass where she wouldn't distract the semi driver.

Parker followed and faced her when he got there. His tone was terse, his shoulders square. "You think I'm that coldhearted."

Not about to be intimidated, Hailey crossed her arms and glared up at him. "I think you're blowing Galina out from under her without blinking an eye."

"I'm not—"

"So, yeah, *that* coldhearted."

He looked truly affronted now. "Blowing Galina *up*?"

"Metaphorically." Hailey clarified, even though it was obvious.

"I'm saving Galina."

"For your own ends."

"For everybody's ends. I'm providing a financial lifeline to a struggling company."

"They're not struggling that hard." Before Parker came along there had been no talk, none at all, about Galina being in financial trouble.

He lifted his brow. "I've seen their books."

"Like I'm going to trust your assessment."

He looked genuinely baffled by that—great acting on his part. "Why don't you trust me, Hailey?"

"Let me see . . . logic and clear judgment."

He scoffed out a laugh. "You've got nothing concrete, and you know it."

"This isn't a court of law. I don't need concrete. I know what I know, and what you're doing is greedy and wrong."

"It's a mutually beneficial arrangement."

"Ha!" She knew a whole lot better than that. "You're following a playbook." Her family's playbook.

"What would it take?" he asked.

"What would it take to what?" Hailey got distracted for a second as the workers opened up the back of the trailer.

"To convince you I'm trustworthy."

"In this instance?"

"Yes."

She zeroed in on him again. "You can't."

"Why not?"

"Because, eventually, you're going to move forward with your plan. You'll lull them into a sense of security. Then you'll amass influence and power within the company, and soon they'll have no choice but to do things your way."

She was obviously right, because he turned contemplative, gazing over the wild grass and scattered wildflowers, the fringe of trees and the dirt driveway and turnaround. "I like you, Hailey."

The statement took her completely by surprise. She didn't answer because she didn't know what it had to do with their argument.

"I like you a lot." He lifted his hand to grip the back of his neck, still staring into the distance. "I didn't expect it—coming up here to Paradise, meeting someone, feeling the way I do."

"Is this part of your game?" It felt like he was trying to co-opt her again.

"My feelings for you have nothing to do with business." He looked at her again.

She hated the faux sincerity in his eyes. It was realistic enough to make her question her own judgment. Logic told her he was playing her. But raw instinct told her to trust him.

He eased closer. "Don't you remember?" he asked her softly. "What it was like? You and me together?"

She remembered it all too well. It was like being lifted from the very face of the earth. Even now, the urge to lean into him was strong. She imagined his arms wrapping around her once again.

"What do you want?" she asked, hating the pleading note in her voice.

"I don't know," he said, easing closer still, forcing her world to narrow to him. "I thought I knew, but now I'm not so sure."

She didn't understand, and she gave her head a little shake to try to clear it.

His tone took on an entreating quality. "Is there anything, *anything* I can do that would let you trust me?"

Natasha's voice called something out above the semi's still-rumbling engine. But it was a vague distraction in the distance. There was one thing—one thing he could do that would earn Hailey's trust. But he'd never do it.

"Hailey?" Parker prompted.

"Walk away," she said.

He drew back with a frown. "From you?"

"From Galina, and from WSA. Walk away and leave them alone, and I'll believe you have integrity."

His gaze narrowed. "That's a big ask that has nothing to do with us."

She gave a shrug. It was what it was, and he'd asked what it would take.

"Wow," he said, exhaling. "We've been working on this thing for months."

"There are other deals, other businesses."

"There's nothing else near Lucky Breach."

"You can be their customer, Parker. Just not their partner." She didn't know why she bothered arguing against what was sure to be a definite no.

Parker opened his mouth. Then he closed it again, clamping his jaw.

She was surprised he was waiting this long to answer.

"Hey, Hailey?" Willow called from the side. She paced toward them, looking jazzed amid all the action and activity. "The guys say you better move your truck back from the explosion."

WATCHING SOMETHING BLOW UP SEEMED LIKE A FITting end to Parker's day.

He and Dalia were perched on a pickup tailgate parked against the trees. Fernando had cleared a perimeter of everyone but the camera operators and sound techs, who were behind shields. The town's fire and pumper trucks had been pulled into the yard, and four firefighters were on standby in their turnout gear.

"Are you nervous?" Dalia asked him. "I'm nervous. I like Willow a lot. I don't know why on earth she picked a profession like this."

Parker wasn't nervous. He'd worked around explosives on his mines in the past, and this demolitions crew seemed highly professional.

The thing that had him unsettled was Hailey asking him to walk away from the Paradise deals. With Willow's untimely interruption, he hadn't given an answer yet.

He knew it should have been a fast, hard no right then in the moment. Instead, he found himself mulling the implications, even considering agreeing, speculating that Hugh and Brodie would probably back out anyway. If Parker backed out himself, and did it first, he'd get points with Hailey. Maybe she'd see him again. Maybe she'd even agree to a date with him.

The director called for quiet on the set, and everyone settled.

When she called for action a few seconds later, Parker tensed up along with everyone else.

A small explosion went up at the back of the cabin, and Dalia startled. Then a bigger explosion rattled the ground and sent flames and smoke into the air.

He found himself gripping the edge of the tailgate waiting for Willow to run out the front door. Then, there she was, sprinting for all she was worth, diving forward facedown on the ground as a final explosion sent the cabin splintering and a fireball rolling into the air.

"She's on fire!" Dalia cried out, hopping down from the tailgate.

But the cameras kept rolling, and the firefighters didn't react. Parker guessed she was in a fire-retardant suit, and it was part of the stunt.

Willow rolled onto her back, snuffing the flames.

Natasha called cut, and the crew cheered and clapped. Parker joined them. It had been very impressive.

Fernando and a couple of crew members rushed to Willow's side to make sure she was okay and that the flames were completely extinguished. She nodded as they helped her to her feet, and Parker could see her broad smile from here.

Dalia hopped down from the tailgate to go see her.

Parker caught sight of Hailey nearby and was drawn her way. She was with Mia and Raven, who was staring in silence at her demolished home.

"I guess that settled it," Mia said, putting an arm around Raven and giving her a comforting squeeze.

"It was a spectacular send-off," Raven said, sounding a little shell-shocked.

"Couldn't ask for better than that," Hailey said.

"She was a great little cabin."

Mia gave her cousin a skeptical look. "She was an adequate little cabin."

"You're spoiled," Raven responded.

"And you're about to be spoiled too."

Hailey looked up and caught Parker staring.

He was embarrassed for eavesdropping and quickly glanced away, focusing instead on the firefighters who were checking out the perimeter of the burning building. It looked like they planned to let it burn to the ground to ease the cleanup.

When he glanced back at Hailey, she was coming his way. She slowed to a stop beside him.

"What's she going to do now?" he asked, referring to Raven, while they both watched the flames curl up from the debris, black smoke smearing the blue sky.

"Live with Mia and Silas while she builds something new. The property's great. It goes all the way to the river and Mia's just a ten-minute walk down the path."

"Nice to have family close by," he said.

Hailey scoffed a little at that. "Depends on the family."

"I suppose." There was family and there was family.

He lived about twenty minutes from his mother's condo. He'd be closer to his sister once she got married and moved into her husband's house. But he was content to stay far, far away from his father's property.

He and Hailey fell silent while the flames crackled, firefighters and crew called to one another, and Fernando helped Willow out of her messy fireproof suit.

"I know it wasn't a fair question," Hailey said.

"What wasn't fair?"

"Asking you to walk away from Galina and WSA."

He turned her way as hope surged within him. "You came up with something else?" He'd be willing to do almost anything to get back into her good graces.

"Not really."

His shoulders drooped. "Nothing?"

She shook her head.

He swore under his breath. There it was. Hailey or Galina. Or maybe neither if he guessed wrong. "You can't just give me a chance?"

"Too much risk in that. I've picked my side. My side is Paradise and my friends."

"What if you're wrong?"

"What if I'm right?"

He raked a hand through his hair, his stomach clenching, his anxiety completely out of proportion to the decision he was making. Of *course*, he should go ahead with the business deal. He couldn't let some pretty woman knock him completely off his game. Since when did he do that?

And what did he expect from Hailey anyway? Another date? Two? She was right to worry about the geography between them. His life was in Anchorage, and she clearly wasn't leaving Paradise.

Still, the knot in his stomach was pushing him to please her.

"What if I said yes?" he asked.

She stared at him in silence. "To . . ." She seemed afraid to ask.

"To walking away. What if I walked away?"

She backed up a step. "You wouldn't."

"I might." Against all odds, he was seriously thinking about it. He couldn't even imagine Dalia's reaction.

Hailey shook her head. "Stop messing with me, Parker."

"Why would I mess with you?"

"I don't know. You play mind games."

"No. You only think I play mind games. I don't."

She cocked her head to one side, skeptically sizing him up. "So . . . walk away then." She was obviously calling his bluff. "Pull your offer. Go back to Anchorage."

"Not without a commitment from you." Now that he was framing it up in his mind, he was seriously warming to the idea of having a shot with Hailey—if she was serious about him too.

Galina and WSA could provide expediting services to Lucky Breach without his ownership. He'd be a customer like everyone else. It might not be his first choice, but it was doable. Maybe he'd invest in something else.

Maybe he'd invest in Rapid Release or even Wildflower Lake. He'd loved it up there. He recognized that Hailey was part of what he'd loved about the lodge. But still . . . it was a possibility.

She was peering at him with increasing suspicion. "A commitment to *what*?" It was easy to see where her mind was going.

"Not *that*," he assured her. "Although, we've already done that, so I don't see—"

"We are *not* bartering for sex." But a flash of humor came into her eyes.

"Then what do I get?" he asked, matching her light-hearted tone. "For walking away from what could be the deal of the century, what do I get?"

Hailey scoffed. "The deal of the century? Please."

"It could be."

"Or they could turn you down flat, and you end up with nothing."

He could see her mind had gone to the same place as his, but he'd never admit to it. "I really don't see that happening."

"Okay." She tipped up her chin. "What *do* you see happening?"

He wasn't going to fall for her tactic. "I think the ball's in your court now."

It looked like she was thinking hard. "A date," she finally said.

He couldn't stop a smile.

But she wasn't finished making her offer. "You get in the plane with me tomorrow and go back to Anchorage for good, and I'll go out on a proper date with you."

The statement took him by surprise. "You're going to Anchorage tomorrow?"

"I have to see a lawyer."

"Are you in trouble?"

"No trouble. It's just some family business."

He held out his hand to shake, locking himself into the deal before reason could trump his emotions.

Chapter Eleven

⟜

SINCE PARKER NOW KNEW SHE'D BEEN OPERATING
against him, Hailey was a lot less conflicted about going on
a date with him. In Anchorage, she checked into the Blue
Lake Suites Hotel. It was close to the airport, updated and
comfortable.

The lawyer was more than accommodating, letting her
choose the meeting time and sending a car to bring Hailey
to his downtown office. It shouldn't have surprised her to
get the VIP treatment, since the firm was working in service of Magnolia Twenty Incorporated, and not for Hailey
herself. Still, it was nice.

The paperwork was straightforward, giving Amber the
power to vote Hailey's shares.

After signing about twenty pages, she left the law office
through the main floor lobby and spotted a clothing store
across the street. The window displays were attractive, and
she remembered what Willow had said about a shopping
spree in the city. Hailey was anything but an enthusiastic
shopper, but she did have a date tonight.

She smiled to herself as she headed for the crosswalk, a warm feeling blooming in her chest. She'd told Parker this wouldn't be about sex, but she couldn't help flirting with the idea.

He'd shocked her when he agreed to back off on Galina and WSA. She was still feeling skeptical the next morning, expecting him to back out, but he and Dalia had turned up at the airstrip to make good on his word.

Hailey entered the shop and gazed around, taking in the racks of colorful clothes.

She didn't want to go too girlie or formal. But it didn't take her long to find something that suited her—a cute teal-blue dress with a wide, snug waist and a skirt that landed several inches above her knees. It had a scoop neck and three-quarter sleeves with a gathered, pushed-up look. She put it over a pair of black leggings, then came across a pair of gray-blue high-heeled ankle boots that looked like they were made for the outfit.

On a roll, she picked out a pair of hoop earrings and some subtle shades of makeup—lipstick, mascara, blush. It had been years since she updated her makeup, so she figured she was due.

Back at the hotel, she had time for a shower and a blow-dry before dressing in the new outfit. With ten minutes to spare, she stopped in front of the full-length mirror. For a moment, she froze, drawing back in surprise. It looked like a stranger staring at her from the mirror.

The blow-dry had brought out the auburn in her hair, and it was longer and fuller than she remembered. Her eyes looked unnaturally big and bright with the dark mascara elongating her lashes. The dress flowed softly over her shoulders, highlighting her waist and showing off the leggings below. She loved the boots even more now than she had in the store.

A knock sounded on the door.

Parker was a few minutes early. Risky move, that, on a first date. But she was ready.

She hadn't thought about a purse, and there wasn't a pocket to be found on the outfit. So, she tucked her room key and a credit card into her boot and picked up her phone. Hopefully her hair lasted the night without the need for a comb.

She opened the door to find Parker looking casual by his standards in jeans, a blue speckled crew-neck shirt and a dark blazer. He wasn't freshly shaved tonight, which looked very sexy, but the informality surprised her.

He silently looked her up and down. "Who are you, and what have you done with my pilot?"

"Does Dalia know you left the house like this?" she asked in return.

He grinned, still drinking in her outfit with a warm, appreciative gaze.

"I haven't done this in a while," she said.

"You definitely haven't forgotten how. You ready?"

"I'm ready."

They left the hotel and headed for the driveway in a sleek, gunmetal-gray sedan that sparkled inside and out. Even the flooring was meticulously clean. The black leather seat beneath her was soft and smooth. The temperature was perfect, while low classical music played on the sound system.

"This is quite a change from my pickup," Hailey said as she gazed around.

They were traveling north, and the early evening sun was bright, but the gradual shading of the windshield made it easy on her eyes.

"I usually drive an SUV," he said. "It's a few years old and has seen plenty of gravel roads outside town. This one is good for business contacts, bankers and lawyers, people like that."

"And you thought I'd like it?" she couldn't help asking.

"I thought the change might be fun."

She stretched out her legs. "It's got comfort going for it, I'll give you that."

"Glad to hear it." He paused while he turned off the parkway, taking a left toward the shore. "I talked to Brodie this morning."

Hailey had believed Parker would keep his word, but a wave of relief passed through her just the same.

"He wasn't going to take me up on the offer anyway," Parker said.

"I'm not surprised."

He smirked. "Sure you are. Otherwise you wouldn't have been so uptight about it."

"I wasn't uptight."

He sent her a sidelong look that called her on her lie.

"Okay, a little uptight. But I'm not stunned he turned you down. Brodie's pretty independent."

"I got that. Still, when the chips are down, people make decisions they wouldn't otherwise consider."

Hailey agreed. The opinion was reinforced by her experience with her family's hardball tactics.

"And Hugh?" she asked.

"I'm meeting with him tomorrow morning. I think I owe it to him to have the conversation in person."

Hailey's worry returned. "You're not going to—"

"Date you tonight and betray you in the morning? Seriously? Is that still what you think of me?"

She opened her mouth to deny it.

"Of course that's what you still think of me." He gave a self-deprecating chuckle as he turned on the right signal light. "It's not like you've ever told me any different."

"I trust you," she said, realizing that she genuinely did.

That didn't mean she wouldn't be relieved when it was all over. She'd like it when everything was off the table, Raven's future was protected, and Paradise would stay just exactly as it was. But if she didn't trust Parker, she wouldn't be here now.

"Trust but verify?" he asked archly.

"Trust and *date*," she corrected him. "I got all dressed up before I verified anything."

He seemed to relax again. "And you look sensational."

"I look passable," she said. There were multiple levels of fashionable above her.

"Passable. Right. I'm about to watch every guy in the place stare at your *passable*."

"Where are we going?" she asked, realizing she had no idea where they were headed.

"The Brandywine Brewhouse."

"I've never been there."

"It's new. Woodsy décor, laid-back, nice view."

They parked in front of a two-story building and made their way along a brick pathway through an evergreen garden to a glass-fronted entry beneath a carved Brandywine Brewhouse sign.

The reception area was light and bustling, with a few parties waiting to be seated. The happy noise coming from the high-ceilinged dining room made its way back past a partial wall. A hostess checked their reservation, then led them up a sweeping staircase to the railed perimeter loft that made up the second floor.

Hailey was happy when the woman led them around to the front window overlooking the inlet.

"Did you bribe them for the view?" she asked as Parker took his seat across from her.

The hostess smiled at Hailey's joke. "Your waiter will be right with you."

The interior was done in polished wood with soaring cedar ceiling beams. The tables were inlaid wood in contrasting stripes, bare at the moment except for two woven placemats—no fancy centerpieces or extraneous china. Hailey liked that.

The tide was high slack and the blue ocean was calm, barely a breeze moving the trees along the waterfront pathway. A family rode past on bicycles, while an older couple walked their dog. A group of teenagers kicked a soccer ball around on a strip of grass at the edge of a small park. Another cyclist went by, and then another, and another.

"So many people," she commented.

"It's a big city."

And every one of them were strangers.

Hailey turned to gaze around the dining room. "It's been a long time since I've had any sense of anonymity."

He reached across the table and took her hand. "It's liberating."

She looked down at his strong fingers crossed over her own. "You mean I don't have to worry what all these people will think about me fraternizing with the big-city investor?"

"You don't have to worry about anything at all." He canted his head to the side. "For all they know, I run a hospital charity, and we've been in a relationship for five years."

"Donating to a hospital charity would be a nice thing to do."

"Who says I don't already?"

She held his gaze, trying to decide if he was being honest or deflecting. "Do you?"

"Yes."

She eyeballed his expression.

"You think I'd lie about that?" he asked with mock irritation.

"Trust but verify," she parroted his words.

"St. Marguerite's Women's. Do you want to see the tax receipts?"

Hailey fought a grin and shook her head. "It's enough that you offered."

"Too bad." He gave her hand a gentle squeeze. "They're

at my place. I could have taken you there after dessert and given you the tour."

PARKER DIDN'T WANT THE EVENING TO END.

After grilled halibut and maple-bourbon cake, he and Hailey had taken a walk along the shoreline path. As the sun dipped and the breeze came up, he shrugged out of his blazer and wrapped it around her shoulders. She hadn't seemed to mind the intimacy and slipped her arms into the sleeves.

He'd taken her hand then, walking in contented silence, listening to the waves on the shore while the seabirds called to one another, swooping low to see if he and Hailey were offering any breadcrumbs.

He caught a familiar white flash on the water and nudged her. "Take a look."

"What?"

He pointed. "Beluga whale."

She paused and turned, shading her eyes. "Nice. There's another one."

"They travel in pods."

"Do you see them often?"

"Occasionally. They move up and down the coast. There's a couple more. Look out to the left."

"I see them." She was quiet as she watched. "You know, I quite like the ocean."

"You didn't get that from growing up in Atlanta."

"True. We sometimes went to Charleston for a visit. But the appeal's not the surf and sand and sun."

The belugas swelled up again. There were at least six in the pod.

"I like this." She laughed. "The whales, the birds, those little crabs running around on the shore."

"The crabs are delicious. Well, the king crabs are, not these little guys. We should—" He stopped himself. If this had been someone other than Hailey, this would have been the moment he suggested a second date.

"Should what?" she asked, looking his way.

"I forgot you're heading home tomorrow."

She nodded. "Planes to fly. Fuel to deliver."

"Movies to make," he added.

"True. There's a location shoot coming up for the Lichen Plateau wolves."

"I hope they're filming them from the air."

"The Colorado university has a camp set up we can use as a base."

Parker didn't like the sound of that. "What do you mean, 'we'? And what do you mean, 'base'?"

"I'm their pilot."

"So, you'll stay with the plane?" He didn't like to think about anyone on the crew approaching the wolves on foot. But he particularly didn't like the idea of Hailey on the ground with a pack of wolves.

"I don't know the entire plan, but I told Willow to listen to the biologists. She shouldn't get anywhere near those things." Hailey gave a little shudder.

"That's good advice for both of you."

"Glad to have your approval," she said tartly. But her smile softened the reaction.

"I'm just saying, you should probably ask about safety precautions before you agree to anything."

She gazed at him with what looked like amusement. "Are you worried about me in the Alaskan wild?"

"Yes." He was. While he trusted professionals like Riley where it came to the dangers of white water, he didn't expect an LA safety crew to know what they needed to know about a Mackenzie Valley wolf pack.

"You think I might get eaten?" she teased.

He put a hand on her shoulder. "The packs up there are aggressive."

She covered his hand with hers. "I know. I'll be careful. I'm sure we'll all be very careful."

"Good."

"I've been flying in the bush for years, you know."

"I know that." He knew he shouldn't question her capabilities. But he didn't like the mental image of Hailey versus a Mackenzie wolf pack. "But stay with the plane, okay?" he couldn't seem to stop himself from muttering.

She smiled and shook her head at his worry.

The sun dipped lower as they watched the ocean, flaring pink across the scattered clouds above. It was getting late, but the last thing he wanted to do was end the date and take Hailey back to her hotel. He had no idea when he'd see her again.

She stifled a yawn.

"You're tired," he reluctantly said. He knew she had to fly in the morning.

"Getting there."

He put his arm around her shoulders. Then he drew her into a hug, stroking her hair and drawing her against his shoulder.

"I don't want to let you go," he whispered into her hair, tightening his embrace, as if that could make a difference.

She relaxed against him, and it felt *so* good. Then she tipped her head back. "Is a tour of your house still an option?"

He brightened. "Yeah?"

"Yeah."

"Absolutely." He tried to hold it back, but his mind leapt ahead to Hailey in his house, then in his bedroom, then naked in his arms.

He lived on the outskirts of Anchorage, up a hill overlooking the city, so it was a twenty-minute drive. He'd had the place built when he first started making good money. It wasn't huge, but it suited him, and he loved the view.

"Nice," Hailey said as they walked into an entryway above the living area.

It was a slate-floored foyer that stretched partway above the kitchen and held a couple of small armchairs, a closet, and a large leafy plant to soften the space. An open wood staircase led down to the high-ceilinged living room, which overlooked the city.

Parker slid his jacket from her shoulders and hung it in the closet. Then he gestured for her to head down the stairs, lingering for a moment to watch her against the backdrop of his home.

"That's some view," she said, her hand on the smooth rail as she descended the staircase, gazing across to the two stories of glass.

She looked spectacularly beautiful tonight, and he'd never get tired of the sight of her here. She came to the bottom and took in the long glass fireplace that ran between the living room and the kitchen. The dining room was in front of the kitchen overlooking the city.

"The hillside is steep here." He made his way down to stand beside her. "The bedrooms are another floor down."

She gazed around. "This isn't at all what I expected."

"What did you expect?"

"I don't know. Bigger, maybe. I know you're rich, so I thought you'd have a mansion."

"I live alone. I don't need a mansion. And Dalia says you're rich too. You don't live in a mansion."

"My family's rich, not me. And I grew up in one."

He couldn't help wondering what had happened to send her so far away from her family and her roots. He knew it had to be more than a fear of hoop skirts and big hair. But he didn't want to ask right now. The last thing he wanted to do was bring up something that might upset her.

"Ten bedrooms plus staff quarters over the garage," she continued. "They entertain a lot." She made her way to the glass wall. The sun was dipping farther now, the clouds turning a deeper pink. "I like this better."

"I don't know what I'd do with ten bedrooms." He moved to stand beside her. "I prefer to entertain elsewhere and keep my privacy."

She nodded, seeming to understand.

"Thirsty?" he asked.

She shook her head.

"Hungry?"

Another shake as she turned to face him, gently trailing her fingertips down his chest.

He smiled and bent his head to kiss her, wrapping his arms around her waist, drawing her close as the now familiar sensations of pleasure and desire washed through him. Her arms went around his neck as he kissed her over and over, drawing it out, wanting the moment to last forever.

When he came up for a breath, he smoothed her loose hair, gazing at her beauty, hardly believing she was here. "You're amazing," he whispered.

Her eyes were dusky with desire. "You're pretty amazing yourself."

He lifted her into his arms.

Her hand tightened on his shoulder. "Did you say the bedroom was downstairs?"

"I did." He started that way.

"Is it safe to carry me?"

"You hardly weigh a thing."

"Still—"

"You're scared of a staircase, bush-pilot wolf-lady?" He came to the landing.

She tightened her hold. "Don't you drop me."

He chuckled. "Like that's going to happen." He had the sexiest, most exciting and enchanting woman in the world willingly in his arms. The last thing he was going to do was screw it up.

The hall at the bottom of the stairs led to two bedrooms, one at each end of the house. It was dim down here, both ends of the hall lit only by high, narrow windows.

He turned to the right, pushing open the door to his room.

"Another wow," Hailey said, taking in the big bed and two armchairs, the wide bay window and the sliding glass doors that led onto a big balcony with a gas fireplace, furniture groupings and a hot tub.

He walked to the edge of the bed and set her on her feet. "The tour starts later," he said in a husky voice.

"Later," she agreed, moving easily into his arms.

Passion rising, he kissed the crease of her neck, sliding down the zipper at the back of the dress to reveal her shoulder so he could kiss that too.

She tugged up his shirt, pulling it over his head. Her fingertips traced a pattern on his bare chest, making him gasp at the sensation. Then she kissed him there, and he groaned, pushing her dress down her arms until it dropped to pool at her feet.

He released the catch of her bra, and they were skin to skin, their lips together, sharing sweet, exquisite kisses that pulsed desire all the way to his toes.

They fumbled and laughed over her tights and their shoes. But soon they were naked, tangled together on the bed. He wanted to explore, to take the whole night to learn every nuance of her body. But their time together was far too short. Their fire burned too hot. Much too soon they were making love.

He turned to put her on top, wanting to gaze at her alabaster skin, her swollen lips, her mussed hair, and the clear eyes that seemed to let him into her soul. He tried to focus, struggled to memorize her. But he failed.

Instead, his passion rose to a crescendo. They tumbled together into ecstasy, then lay gasping for breath in each other's arms.

* * *

HAILEY THOUGHT SHE'D PUT UP A GOOD FRONT, MAK-
ing idle chitchat while Parker drove her back to the hotel
this morning, telling her he was going to meet with Hugh
as soon as he could. She'd given him a quick kiss goodbye,
told him she'd make her own way to the airport and that
she'd see him again sometime.

Then she'd packed her small bag with her new dress,
boots and makeup.

Parker had offered breakfast at his place, but she hadn't
wanted to linger. Leaving was awkward enough as it was.
It was a two-night fling now. She'd never thought of herself
as a fling kind of person, but there was no denying that's
what she was with Parker.

She had breakfast at the hotel, then took a cab ride to the
private aircraft Fixed Base Operator at the airport. There,
she recognized the woman at the check-in desk—Bethany,
Hailey had learned from her name tag yesterday.

"Welcome back," Bethany said with a bright smile. "Off
to Paradise this morning?"

"I am."

"The fuel trucks are really backed up. You might want
to hang out in here until things clear a bit."

"Sure. Thanks." Hailey was grateful for the heads-up.

The Anchorage FBO was extraordinarily comfortable,
catering to a wide range of clients who flew in and out on
private aircraft. The lounge was quiet, empty right now,
meticulously clean with comfortable leather armchairs in
pristine condition. The kitchen offered a wide array of
snacks and beverages, and the bathroom facilities rivaled
most five-star hotels.

Hailey plunked down her shoulder bag and settled in
with her phone, opening up the mystery novel she hadn't
looked at in two weeks. She read the next paragraph and
became hopelessly confused about who was stalking

whom. So, she backed up a few pages to pick up the plot again.

Reminded then of the rogue cop and the TV news anchor who'd been framed by the mob and was on the run, she settled back into the story. The plot soared forward into action and danger.

"Hailey?"

Hailey looked up to find Bethany, surprised at how quickly time had flown past. She quickly tucked her phone into her pocket.

"There's a man here looking for you," Bethany said.

As she spoke, Hugh appeared in the lounge doorway.

"Hugh." Hailey was surprised to see him.

"I didn't think I'd catch you still here," he said, walking in.

"The fuel trucks are backed up. I'm just killing time." She waited, wondering if he'd share the news about Galina.

"I was hoping I could catch a lift?" he asked.

"Of course." It made sense he'd want to go to Paradise to talk to Raven and make new plans after hearing the news from Parker.

He nodded then, sitting down heavily as Bethany left the lounge. Hugh looked tired, his face creasing into a deepening frown.

A thread of unease passed through her.

"Everything okay?" she ventured.

"Not really," he said.

"Oh?" she prompted, hoping he wasn't upset about the deal falling through, then hoping it wasn't something worse.

Hugh swore bitterly, unusual for him.

"What happened?" she asked.

He dropped his head into his hands. "He pulled the deal. Parker changed his mind."

"About investing?" Hailey's stomach sank as she asked the question she already knew the answer to.

Hugh swore again.

She knew she should own up to her part in it, right now, right away. But she couldn't bring herself to confess. "It might be a blessing in disguise," she said instead.

He looked up, anger in his tone now. "It's a disaster, and there's no disguising it. My big plans . . ." His voice trailed off.

Hailey's sinking stomach turned sick. She struggled to find the silver lining, to excuse what she'd done. "It might turn out better in the end. I've seen this kind of thing before."

"You have, have you?"

"With my family. If you're not careful, a new investor can be a bad idea."

"You don't think I thought of that?" he asked sharply. "I assure you I weighed the risks and benefits extensively. It was an honest, solid deal for both of us. You don't come across that every day. You don't come across partners like Parker who don't want to micromanage, only to have the business succeed."

"I—" She realized she'd underestimated Hugh. She'd stepped in where she didn't belong, and regret flooded her system.

He ran a hand through his thick head of gray hair. "I'm sorry—I didn't mean to lash out like that. But we're all in a bind now."

She swallowed. "Hugh, I'm so sorry."

His eyes turned bleak, and a slight tremor came into his normally strong voice. "It's not your fault."

But it was her fault. And she had to tell him so. She needed to confess.

She opened her mouth, but no sound came out. She tried again, but the damning words still wouldn't come.

"What can I do? How can I help?" she offered instead, inwardly berating herself for her cowardice.

"Nothing," he said with a resigned shake of his head.

"I'll talk to him." She came to her feet.

Hugh didn't seem to have heard, gazing off in the distance instead. "I hate to have to tell Raven."

"I can try—"

But Hugh clearly wasn't listening, his voice low and introspective. "Without Parker Hall's investment, I have to lay off more staff. That means me working in Paradise again and Raven going back on the warehouse floor. If things do get better, we'll have to spend more time and more money training new staff. For now, we postpone capital projects and make do with aging equipment."

Hailey's throat went dry with remorse, and there was a tremor in her voice when she spoke up. "I'll get him back. I can talk to him and get him back."

Hugh shot her a flinty look.

"Let me try," she begged.

"It was a *very* firm no."

She drew a shaky breath. "Please, Hugh. Let me try to fix it." *Because it's my fault,* her mind cried out.

He clenched his jaw and stared at her for a long moment.

"If I fail, I fail," she offered. "You're no worse off than right now."

His shoulders dropped a notch and he sighed in resignation. "Fine," he said. "What can it hurt?"

Hailey nodded and lifted her bag. She slunk past Hugh, out of the lounge and out of the FBO. She had to track Parker down in person. She couldn't do this over the phone.

She took her best guess, looked up the address for PQH Holdings and took a cab back into downtown.

Catching sight of the Brandywine Brewhouse along the way, she got a lump in her throat, remembering the carefree romantic evening. Boy, had she come down hard from that.

Gazing out the cab window, she tried to formulate a speech to give to Parker, but she couldn't come up with anything to plausibly explain her about-face. Other than the truth. But the truth made her sound both reckless and naïve.

Which, she was. And it looked like her only choice now was to own it.

Far too soon, they stopped in front of a granite-faced high-rise office building with a glass-fronted lobby and rows of windows on the floors above.

She paid the cab and forced herself through the revolving door. She wanted to linger there in the lobby, but she pushed on, reading the directory, then taking the elevator to the twentieth floor.

The PQH Holdings office was far more cheerful than her mood. Bright and airy, it was done in pale wood tones and looked both professional and classy. A single receptionist sat out front behind a maple desk and next to a row of windows overlooking the street. Traffic buzzed below on the sunny day, and a few honking horns echoed between the buildings.

On the far side of the space, there were four reception chairs in an L-shape in a carpeted area dotted with green plants. A neat arrangement of magazines sat on a center table, and there was a water cooler in the corner.

"Can I help you?" the young woman asked with a welcoming smile.

Hailey took a few steps forward and the glass door swung silently shut behind her. "I was hoping to see Parker Hall."

"Can I give him your name?" the woman asked pleasantly.

"Hailey Barrosse."

She rose. "Please have a seat."

Hailey was surprised by the friendly reception. She'd expected to be told Parker was far too busy for a walk-in, and she needed an appointment. She'd been ready to plead her case just to get in to see him.

Instead, she perched on one of the comfortable chairs, her stomach growing jumpier by the second over backtracking and asking for his benevolence.

She closed her eyes and let the weight of her flight bag rest on the floor. She thought back to her distrust of the deal and how Hugh had made it crystal clear the benefits outweighed the risks.

Lesser of two evils? She quickly decided *that* wasn't a phrase she'd use with Parker.

Then again, it might not matter what she said. Both she and Parker knew full well what had happened, what she'd done, and how wrong she'd turned out to be. Had she really told him to kill the deal to show how serious he was about *her*? She wanted to melt into the floor at her utter idiocy.

He would probably send her packing. She wouldn't blame him if he did.

Parker appeared in the hallway behind the reception desk. "Hailey?" He looked more confused than pleased to see her.

Oh, this was going to sting.

She came to her feet. "Hi, Parker."

His forehead creased. "What happened? Is there something wrong with the plane?"

"No." She shook her head. "Nothing like that. I was hoping we could talk."

He paused for a moment, obviously trying to make sense of her appearance after their goodbye this morning. "Sure," he finally spoke and gestured to the hallway. "Come on back."

He let her go first but then came abreast while they walked before pushing open an office door and standing back to let her in.

His office was as classy as the reception area. Roomy, but not huge, with leafy plants blending nicely with the wood tones. Obviously set in a corner of the building, it had windows on two walls. There was a big desk, two guest chairs and a neatly arranged bookshelf, plus a meeting table with four chairs in the far corner.

"Have a seat." Parker turned one of the guest chairs to face the other and gestured for her to sit down. She briefly and appreciatively noted how he didn't sit behind the desk. It would've made what she was about to say even harder somehow.

While she sat, he turned the other, easing down to face her.

"What's up?" he asked, sitting forward, looking more concerned than surprised now, reaching out to take her hand.

"I made a mistake," she admitted, looking at their joined hands and feeling like she didn't deserve this level of intimacy. She wasn't here as the woman who'd dated him last night. She was here as the woman who'd messed with his business interests and made a huge mistake for him and everyone else in Paradise.

"A mistake flying?" His concern seemed to ramp up. "What happened? Are you okay?"

"Not flying." She shook her head even as she steeled herself. "I just talked to Hugh."

Parker nodded to that. "He and I met this morning."

"He's in trouble, Parker." Because she had no other choice, she took the plunge. "I messed it up by interfering."

Parker's face remained neutral. "I can't say I'm surprised."

"But you did it anyway."

"It was what you wanted."

She didn't have an answer for that.

He could have argued with her. He had argued with her. But she hadn't listened.

"I shouldn't have asked you to kill the deal."

"Are you saying you've changed your mind?"

"Yes." She didn't know if it was possible, but she absolutely had.

He cocked his head. "And you trust me now?"

"How I feel doesn't matter. Hugh's the one who counts."

"That's not an answer."

"I trust you more," she said honestly. "You seem like a really decent guy."

Parker crossed his arms, but there was a tiny uptick of his mouth. "You are one tough sell, Hailey Barrosse."

She pressed her luck. "Do you still think Galina is a good deal?"

"Yes."

"So, will you take it?"

He straightened and squared his shoulders, obviously considering his answer carefully. "I gave it up for a date with you."

"I know."

He raised his eyebrows. "And now you want backsies."

"I can't take back the date." Despite the tension in the room, her joke popped out.

"Very funny."

"Do you want me to pay for it?" she asked in mock innocence.

He cracked a smile. "No, I don't want you to pay for the date. And I sure don't want to take it back."

"So . . ." She dared to hope.

"I'll reinstate the offer to Hugh."

A lightness came over her shoulders, and she smiled wide with relief.

"There's a condition," he warned.

She braced herself. "Are we bartering?"

"We've always been bartering." He gave a self-satisfied smile. "It's the same condition I had last time."

She rolled the statement around in her head. "A date?"

"Not just one date. I'll work it out with Hugh. Then I'll come back to Paradise. And you—" He pointed toward her nose. "You will date me for as long as I'm there."

Her chest expanded in gratitude and relief. At the same

time, her pulse jumped in anticipation of dating Parker. "How long will you be there?"

He shook his head while his lips curved into a cunning smile. "Nope, no conditions for you. Yes or no."

"Yes," she said, wondering why she hadn't simply said that in the first place.

Chapter Twelve

PARKER NEEDED A FEW DAYS IN ANCHORAGE TO SETTLE things with Hugh and take care of other business, while Hailey had an appointment with a pack of wolves on the Lichen Plateau.

After kissing her goodbye and marveling at his good fortune in getting everything he wanted from his deal with her, he crossed the hall to Dalia's office to give her the news.

Typing on a keyboard, she looked up from her computer screen. "Hi, boss. We're now fully recovered from the sprinkler incident. Tech-Trident just delivered the upgraded laptops. They're loaded with our software packages, and I'm setting up the links now."

"There's been a development," he said, coming into her office, which was a mirror image of his with slightly fewer windows. He sat down in a guest chair.

She stopped typing and sat up straight. "What do you need?"

"The Galina deal is back on."

She leaned back in obvious surprise. "How did that happen?"

Dalia didn't know all the details, but she did know he'd backed off at Hailey's request.

When he first told her, she'd questioned his sanity for a full ten minutes but then accepted his decision with a little smirk that told him he was letting his heart rule his head. She was right about that, and he knew he was letting that happen all over again.

This deal was more about Hailey than anything else.

"Hailey changed her mind," he told Dalia.

Dalia's lips pursed, and he got the sense she was annoyed. Though he couldn't pinpoint why, since she'd been against canceling it in the first place.

"How'd you get her to do that?" Dalia asked in a disappointed tone.

"Why are you asking like *that*?"

"Because there's always been something off with this. Did you bribe her?"

"No." His instinct was to be offended. Then again, he'd have bribed her two days ago if he thought it would work. "The opposite. She bribed me."

Dalia tapped her temple. "Is this making sense inside your head?"

"It's making perfect sense."

"Well, it's losing something when you say it out loud."

He frowned at her joke. "Hugh needs the money. Hailey realized she was wrong. It's still a good deal for me. So—" He couldn't help feeling pleased with himself all over again. "The ball came back into my court."

Dalia's forehead furrowed and she leaned slightly forward. "Parker, what exactly did you do?"

"She agreed to go out with me—date me while we're in Paradise."

"Date you." Dalia was obviously waiting for more information.

"You know, drinks, dinner, things like that." He might even get her out gold panning again. One thing was for sure, Hailey was no ordinary date.

"And this dating thing was part of your deal?" Dalia asked.

"Yes."

"Parker, you can't bribe a woman to date you."

"I'm not bribing her. Like I said, *she* was bribing me." Maybe he really wasn't explaining this right.

"No." Dalia shook her head. "You're bribing her by reinstating the deal with Hugh."

"No, no." The tables were turned now. Hailey was the one who needed something from him.

"Where do you see this going?" Dalia challenged.

"Well, it's Paradise," he joked. "So probably the Bear and Bar."

"Don't mock me."

"I'm lightening the mood."

"You know I mean your relationship with Hailey."

"There's no relationship. We've had one date. Well, plus we went mining together, and then we—" He stopped himself before he could say they'd slept together at Wildflower Lake. That trip wasn't a date. It was . . . an experience, a fantastic experience.

"You're looking moony-eyed."

He blinked. "I am not."

"I'm just asking if you really like her."

"I do like her." There was no question of that.

"Then you might not want to start off by forcing her to go out with you. First you kill the deal to get to her, and now you're reinstating it to force her hand again."

"You had to be there," he said. And a person had to understand Hailey. She'd never let herself get backed into a corner.

"You're sure you want to do this?" Dalia asked.

There wasn't a doubt in his mind. "I'm positive. Which means we need to work out somewhere to stay in Paradise."

"Wait . . . *we*?"

"We'll wrap things up here, then operate remotely for a few weeks." He came to his feet. "I'll nail the details down with Hugh, and you can see what our options are."

"Can I have the option of staying here?"

"Funny. A couple of RVs or something. They make huge fifth wheels now, with pullouts, proper kitchens, and real furniture. You'll like them. They're much better than a B and B for long stays."

Dalia was looking a little shell-shocked. "We're going RVing in Paradise?"

"Someone else can drive them up for us. That road's pretty rough. There's likely a spot we can rent that has services. The Galina parking lot if nothing else."

"The Galina . . ." Dalia's voice faded away in stupefaction.

Parker didn't think it would come to that. There were likely nicer places than the busy, dusty Galina lot.

Energized, he pulled his phone from his pocket as he headed for the door, calling back over his shoulder. "Have someone check with Riley. Maybe we can park and hook up at his place."

As he entered his own office, Parker pulled up his contacts and pressed Hugh's number.

"Parker?" Hugh picked up, sounding surprised by the call.

"Hugh, hi. I've had a chance to do some more thinking on our deal."

There was silence on the other end.

Parker knew he'd been adamant, possibly slightly abrupt in their last conversation. But he'd felt guilty about stringing Hugh along and then walking away on a flimsy excuse. He felt like he hadn't operated in good faith with the man.

"Look, can we take another run at this?" he asked.

"What changed your mind?" Hugh asked cautiously.

"It's complicated. I was worried about how I'd fit into the town. I'd heard rumors—"

"You talked to Hailey."

Parker didn't know how much Hugh knew, so he was honest, if deliberately vague in his answer. "Hailey was part of it, yes. She helped me see a path forward. Could we meet? I'm at the office if you prefer, but maybe lunch?"

"Lunch sounds good." There was relief in Hugh's voice now.

Parker smiled to himself, unbelievably glad to have his Paradise plans back on track.

AN HOUR WEST OF PARADISE, COBRA HELD HIS SPREAD hand over a giant wolf track on the soft tundra. Hailey leaned down for a better look.

"I've sure never seen one that big," she said.

Cobra had come along on the trip as her co-pilot in the Twin Otter. It was an unusual role for him, but they were so far off the beaten track that Brodie had wanted an AME with them in case there were any mechanical problems.

"I'm thinking a hundred and forty, maybe a hundred and fifty pounds," he said.

"I'm still not crazy about this idea," she said, batting at a mosquito that buzzed around her head as she took in the endless horizon. It was early evening, and the sun was long past its northern zenith.

Emily Forge, one of the Colorado university biologists, had brought them to the team's observation post on the plateau. The caribou were migrating through right now and were a favorite prey of the resident wolf pack. She insisted their odds of seeing the wolves were very good at dusk. She also insisted the odds of getting eaten were quite remote.

Hailey had parked the plane a hundred yards back from

the lean-tos and camouflaged tents, avoiding the soft ground.

Behind them, Chet and Vanessa were listening to safety officer RJ Greene as they set up the photography equipment. Emily was advising the camera crew on how to stay hidden and avoid spooking the wolves.

Hailey had to admit, she was less concerned with them spooking the wolves than with the wolves spooking them. Like, say, if they decided the film crew was an easier target than the caribou.

"I really like the angle from here," Vanessa said, pointing off into the distance. "We'll get that peak in the background. With an extended magic hour, we're going to get just the right light for those gorgeous white wolves."

"Hopefully they'll show while the light is right," Emily said lightly.

"All we need is a little wolf luck," Vanessa said.

Rising from the wolf track, Hailey wasn't sure if she should hope for the wolves to show or hope for them to stay far away.

"Emily's done this before," Cobra said in a reassuring voice.

"I feel guilty hiding out in the plane."

"We're staying out of the way," he reminded her. "Plus, we can't fly home if they eat the pilot."

"Not funny." She scowled at him.

"A little bit funny."

There wasn't room for them in the small shelters even if they wanted to stay. So while the crew got everything settled, blending it into the landscape, Hailey and Cobra headed back to the plane and climbed inside, away from the bugs.

"So, how did it go with the lawyer in Anchorage?" he asked as they each cracked a bottle of water and settled into a couple of the passenger seats.

"Fine. Amber should be set to go."

Cobra knew about the shareholders' meeting and about the proxy. He understood frustrating families better than anyone else in Paradise and was always ready with sympathy and advice. "Sorry Marnie wasn't around to help."

Hailey shook her head. "It wouldn't have mattered. The law firm in Anchorage is affiliated with our corporate firm in Atlanta. My sister had it all set up when I got there."

"Do you think her plan will work?" He tipped his bottle and took a drink.

"I think she knows what she's doing."

"So, the meeting ought to be—"

Hailey cracked a grin. "Action-packed."

"Wish you could be a fly on the wall?"

"No, no, no." Hailey gave an adamant shake of her head. "I'd like to watch your dad's face when she whips out the affidavit."

"She does think he'll try something at the last minute."

"Gotta love family dynamics." Cobra sat up straight and peered out the side window. "Will you look at that." He reached for a pair of binoculars.

"You see something?" Hailey turned her head and squinted in the direction he was looking.

"I can't believe their luck."

"The wolves?" she asked.

"Vanessa and the camera crew. I count five, six . . . I'd say a dozen in total."

"Are they headed this way?"

"Coming down the hillside." He handed over the binoculars. "See the saddle and the three jagged rocks."

Hailey focused. "I see them."

"Scan to the west along the ridgeline."

"Oh yeah." The wolves came into view padding along the hillside in single file, making their way down to the plateau. She lowered the binoculars and looked at the little film encampment for a signal they were aware of the wolves' approach. "Do you think they're seeing this?"

"Vanessa seems like she's on the ball," Cobra said. "I can't imagine she's not scanning. And Emily's done this hundreds of times."

Hailey raised the binoculars again, watching in wonder as the detail of the wolves became clearer and clearer. At the bottom of the rise, they fanned out on the tundra and took up a trot.

"Looks like they're on a mission," she said, handing the binoculars back to Cobra. "Let's hope the mission's not us."

"I doubt they'll come near the plane." Cobra chuckled.

"I'm not worried about you and me." She was worried about the people huddled in the tents.

Cobra moved to the cockpit, where the view was more expansive.

"That explains it," he said, pointing out the front. "Caribou herd."

Hailey followed him to get a better look. The wolves' apparent route to the caribou herd would take them right past the encampment. They were growing closer now, maybe half a mile away.

"Should we open the door?" she asked, thinking the mosquitoes weren't the problem any longer. But the camera crew might want to dash for the plane if the wolves got too close.

"Let's sit tight. We don't want to mess anything up."

She watched the wolves growing steadily closer, but nobody made a dash for the safety of the plane.

Cobra rose and moved to the cargo area at the back of the plane, and Hailey saw he was taking out his rifle case.

"You don't really think we'll need to shoot at them." She might have a healthy fear of the wolves, but she hated the thought of killing one of them.

"I'll only scare them off. And only if the crew is in immediate danger." He opened the case and took the covers off the scope.

"I sure hope they're filming this," Hailey said. Despite her anxiety, she could see the footage would be amazing.

"I can't see it getting any better than this," Cobra agreed.

"I feel like we should be doing something."

"Nothing for us to do."

The wolves were taking a circuitous route, some of it around small ponds and mounds of earth, but also taking other twists and turns for reasons Hailey couldn't see.

Cobra settled himself near the door with his rifle.

"So, Marnie finally met your parents," Hailey opened while they watched. Cobra had taken a recent trip to LA that included a stopover in Seattle.

"She pretty much had to once I told my brother we were engaged."

"And how'd that go?"

"They loved her." He smiled. "Who wouldn't?"

"Agreed."

Marnie was fun and feisty, brilliant and successful. She'd been through a lot growing up but had landed on her feet as a successful lawyer.

"Safe bet they like her better than they like me."

"Perils of the Black Sheep Club," Hailey joked.

Her thoughts drifted to Parker, and to what her parents might make of him.

He wasn't from Atlanta, so that was a detraction. He was rich and successful. They'd like that. They'd also like that he was self-made and that he cared about success. And they'd like his single-minded focus on success. Their relationship—

She halted that thought in its tracks. She didn't have a relationship with Parker. Sex did not make a relationship. And he would never have a reason to meet her family.

"I went on a date with Parker in Anchorage," she casually mentioned, thinking she should soften the ground for when it next happened in Paradise.

Cobra gave her a sidelong look of surprise. "Where the hell did that come from?"

Hailey shrugged. "He asked me, and I said yes."

"Why would you date someone you don't like?"

"I don't dislike him. I mean, I didn't exactly trust him. At least, not at first since . . . you know. But he's personable and fun." She didn't add that he was also a fantastic lover. "And I'm starting to trust him. More than I did before, anyway."

"You're aware that you're rambling, right?"

She was rambling because the truth embarrassed her. But she'd always been able to talk to Cobra, and he'd always been a great sounding board. "To be honest, I made him a deal."

Cobra frowned before turning his gaze back to the advancing wolves. "What kind of a deal?"

"A date deal. He did something I wanted, and in exchange I said yes to the date."

Cobra's gaze narrowed on her. "Do I need to have a chat with this guy?"

"No." She quickly shook her head. "Ironically, I didn't end up wanting the thing I made the deal for, so I had to make a new deal." She laughed at herself. "New deal, new date, well dates plural this time. Do you think they're getting a little close?"

"They are," Cobra said, reaching for the handle on the plane's double doors to crack them open.

"Wait, they're turning," she said.

They both watched while the wolves made a ninety-degree turn.

"Well, how perfect is that?" Hailey asked. They'd come about as close as possible to the cameras without being a real danger, and now they were loping in front of the encampment like they were actors on cue.

As the last wolf headed off toward the caribou herd, Hailey breathed a happy sigh of relief.

"Seriously," Cobra said in a dark tone.

"Seriously, what?" The filming opportunity couldn't possibly have been better.

"Parker," Cobra said. "You need my help?"

The film crew cautiously emerged from their blinds, grinning and silently air-high-fiving one another.

"It's fine," she reassured Cobra. "He's . . . not what I thought." She pictured him on their date in Anchorage. "He's respectful and he's smart."

"And also coercive."

"It was more me pushing him this time. I thought he was bad for Hugh and Raven, but it turns out they want his investment."

"Brodie passed on that," Cobra said while the film crew chatted now and gesticulated outside.

Hailey wasn't shocked that Cobra knew about Parker's offer to Brodie. The two men were close friends.

"Did Brodie tell you why?" she asked.

"He doesn't know the guy, and he doesn't want to give up any control. He'd rather ride out the tough times on his own."

"But nothing specifically negative?"

"Not that he said. If you're hesitant about Parker—"

"Not about dating him," she was quick to say. "In business, he reminds me of my family, and that messes with my head."

"But your family's good at the business side."

"Too good."

"So, if you're both on the same side . . ."

Hailey considered it from that perspective. If she and Parker were on the same side, everything would be fine.

THINGS WERE COMING TOGETHER FOR PARKER.

He was content with his new living arrangements in Paradise. They'd set up two fifth wheel trailers at the outer edge of the Rapid Release parking lot behind Riley's office.

They'd situated them facing the river for the view, with the company vans and pickup trucks parked behind.

The view from the rear windows wasn't much to brag about, but the ground was firm and level beneath the units, they had power and water, and the vista out front was magnificent. Even Dalia had to admit the slide-outs made the living spaces roomy and comfortable. It might not be a five-star hotel suite, but they were bright, sparkling clean and comfortable.

Over at Lucky Breach, the miners continued to find nuggets, meaning he would have even more reason to spend time in Paradise in the future. It also made the investment into Galina that much more important to PQH Holdings. He was anxious now to finalize the paperwork with Hugh.

Colin had sent a couple of geologists into the area surrounding Lucky Breach. They'd tromped up mountains and along valleys trying to map out other promising ground. They'd come back with some solid theories on where to drill next, but their access was blocked because it crossed property owned by mining giant Halstead International.

Dalia was looking into the complication.

In the meantime, Parker had a date with Hailey. It might not be his dream date—a little crowded for his liking. It was an intimate gathering at Silas and Mia's for dinner with the director and stars of *Aurora Unleashed*. Since Riley's place was halfway between Paradise and Silas and Mia's house, Hailey had insisted on being the one to pick him up.

He'd worn a suit but skipped the tie. Then Hailey showed up in slim black jeans and a chunky turquoise sweater, and he worried he was overdressed.

But Silas also wore a jacket, and Mia was in an elegant dress. Stars Cash Monahan and Hope Martindale had gone fairly formal. Cash wore a tie while Hope wore a flashy purple sheath with shimmering appliqué. Brodie was in a dress shirt without a tie, while Raven and Willow had gone neutral like Hailey.

Parker realized it was impossible to be dressed wrong.

"Hailey," Mia called out to her as they arrived. "Come and tell us about the wolves."

Hailey gave Parker an apologetic look as she broke away. "Did you take a look at the raw footage?" she asked Mia.

"I did," Mia answered with enthusiasm. "Were they really that close?"

"Vanessa used zoom lenses."

Riley sauntered over to Parker. "How's the trailer setup working out for you?"

"Good, really good." Parker continued watching Hailey as she talked and gestured, sharing the excitement of filming the wolf pack.

She made the other women laugh, and the power of her smile hit him square in the solar plexus. It was a good hit, a hit that made him glad to be alive.

"Thanks for letting us set up there," Parker added, shifting his attention back to Riley.

"Not a problem."

"Any upswing in business?" Parker had decided against any immediate tourism investments now that Galina was moving forward, and they were looking into expanding around Lucky Breach. But he still wished Riley well.

"Things are pretty lean," Riley answered.

"I'm sorry to hear that."

"Is what it is." Riley took a sip of what looked like whisky.

"Are you keeping your head above water? Sorry, didn't mean for that to be a pun."

Riley's chuckle was half-hearted. "I wish it—"

Cash suddenly loomed up and clapped Riley on the shoulder. "Heard about your whitewater gig." The urbanely handsome man's voice was loud and hearty. Cash's jet-black hair combined with glacial pale blue eyes gave him an arresting appearance. "Can I catch a ride someday?"

Riley hesitated no more than a split second. "Sure. No problem."

Parker could guess the reason for the hesitation. Cash had only been in town for a couple of weeks, but already the rumors had circulated that he didn't expect to pay for anything.

Just what Riley needed, a financial drag on his business instead of a paying customer.

"I was looking to book a trip myself," Parker told Cash. "You're welcome to tag along."

Cash eyed Parker up, obviously trying to place him in the scheme of things, just as obviously considering the possibility Parker was a fan looking to get close to a movie star.

"Parker Hall." Parker offered his hand. "I'm here with Hailey."

"Oh yeah, Hailey. She's cool."

"I agree with that. What do you say?"

Cash still seemed to hesitate. "I don't—"

"That would work for me," Riley put in.

"Yeah? Sure, man. Cool," Cash said. He gave them a two-fingered salute and sauntered away.

"You didn't have to do that," Riley said while Cash joined Hope and Silas.

"He really is a freeloader," Parker observed.

"The whole town's stepping up to make sure he and Hope have a good experience."

Parker understood that. "The financial load shouldn't fall on you. Besides, it's the least I can do with you putting us up in your yard."

"That doesn't cost me anything."

"We'd be happy to pay rent," Parker said, wondering why he hadn't thought to offer before.

But Riley scoffed out a laugh. "The going rate for parking lot space in Paradise isn't worth the paperwork."

Parker chuckled in return.

His phone buzzed in his pocket, and he checked the screen. It was Dalia.

"Need to take that?" Riley asked.

"I'll just be a second."

Dalia knew he was at a party, and she wouldn't disturb him for no reason.

"Take your time," Riley said.

Parker put the phone to his ear as he stepped out to the sundeck. "What's up?"

The party noise softened behind him as he walked toward the rail. The twittering of chickadees came up as they swooped from tree to tree while the river burbled softly below.

"Sorry to bother you," Dalia opened.

"It's fine."

"Can you talk?"

"I stepped out on the deck, why?"

"The Halstead International property is in play."

Parker was heartened to hear that. "Good."

"No, not good," Dalia said. "They already have an offer on the table."

"From whom?"

"They won't say, and I can't figure it out. Offshore, most likely. The CEO was in Europe last week."

"Did you get a figure? Can we beat it?"

"Maybe . . . but . . ."

"But, what?" He put his hand on the rail, gazing down at the blue-green water slipping past. It was the color of Hailey's eyes, he thought—soft, slightly mossy, like when she was aroused.

"If we try to outbid them, we might give ourselves away."

Parker shook off the image of Hailey and forced himself to focus on the conversation. "Right." That would be a bad strategy.

If they looked eager, Halstead International might wonder why. And they might start looking into PQH Holdings and learn about their exploration. Worst-case scenario, Halstead could beat PQH to the punch on the new ground the geologists had identified.

"I think we should come at it with more attractive terms," Dalia said. "Instead of outbidding them, match the offer but leave them with an interest, maybe five percent."

He heard the glass door slide open behind him. "Why would I leave them with an interest in it? I'd end up with a partner I didn't want." He turned to see Hailey standing in the open doorway with a glass of red wine in her hand.

Her presence threw him for a second, but then he put on a welcoming smile.

"To sweeten the deal without sweetening the deal," Dalia said.

Hi, he mouthed to Hailey. "It wouldn't be my first choice," he answered Dalia.

"Maybe, but it's your best move."

He heaved a frustrated sigh. "I don't like the precedent it sets."

"Like it or not, I think it's your best play."

Parker knew that tone of voice. It meant Dalia was certain. And when she was certain, she was generally right.

"Clock's ticking," she said.

"Make the deal," he answered.

"Roger, that." She ended the call.

He pocketed his phone and walked Hailey's way. "Hi, there."

"Everything okay?" she asked.

"All good." He said, moving toward her.

She still looked quizzical.

"That was Dalia. Just some business stuff."

Hailey cocked her head. "Paradise business?"

"Mining business," he said easily. "They're finding more nuggets at Lucky Breach, by the way."

She watched him closely, like she was debating something inside her head. "Big ones?"

"Big enough." He kept the conversational thread going in the new direction. "Nowhere near the size of the monster nugget. Any thoughts on what I should do with that one?"

"Sell it and buy a house?" Sounding like she was joking, she turned to head back inside the house.

"There's an idea," he joked back, following her into the dining room.

Cobra was just inside the door, and Hailey gave the big man a friendly hug.

"You made it," she said, sounding happy.

He gave a broad grin as he drew away. "With Marnie in tow. She's over there talking to Mia."

Mia was talking with a compact, auburn-haired woman in a short black dress with leggings and high heels. In a second, Hailey was off to meet them.

"Evening, Cobra," Parker greeted the man as she walked away. He'd met him when they cleaned up after the fire and seen him a few times since.

"I hear you're dating Hailey," Cobra said.

"I am." Parker couldn't help but be pleased Hailey would share that with Cobra. He knew the two were close.

"She said it was some kind of a bargain." Cobra's expression turned grim, his eyes narrowing.

Parker wasn't looking for a fight, so he kept his tone even. "What did she tell you?"

"Why don't *you* tell me."

"Tell you what?"

"The truth."

"Whatever Hailey told you is the truth," Parker said.

Cobra widened his stance. "You know how bad that sounds, right?"

"You're fishing, and I'm not going to bite."

"She said you made a deal, that she wanted something from you, and you coerced her into dating you."

"It wasn't coercion." It had been a game more than anything. She'd wanted to say yes all along, that much was obvious to Parker.

"Yeah?" Cobra pressed. "Tell me what it was."

"You don't have to protect her."

Cobra coughed out a laugh. "As if."

"Then what is this?" Parker didn't appreciate Cobra trying to intimidate him. Not that it would work. He also resented the implication that Hailey was Cobra's responsibility to protect.

"Just a guy talking to another guy," Cobra said.

"Telling him what?"

"To treat Hailey with respect."

"I do."

"She deserves it."

"I know." Parker inhaled deeply. "You don't need to do this."

"You sure?"

"We're dating because we like each other." Parker paused, considering his feelings for her. "I like her. I respect her. And my intentions are purely . . . honorable sounds so—"

"They better be honorable." But Cobra looked more amused now than annoyed.

"Sure. In the context of the twenty-first century, they're perfectly honorable."

"That's what I wanted to hear."

Parker's gaze drifted back to Hailey, who was chatting with Mia and Marnie. The faint sound of her laugher put a warmth in his chest, and he listened for a moment.

"I haven't met your fiancée," he said to Cobra.

"She's been down in LA."

Hailey had mentioned Cobra and Marnie's long-distance arrangement.

"How does that work for you?" Parker asked.

"Fine. She's got her dreams. I've got mine. We spend as much time together as we can."

"Does the culture shock get to you?" Parker could feel the difference coming back from Anchorage to Paradise. He could only imagine what it must be like to switch back and forth with LA.

"Every switch takes a couple of days. You thirsty?" Cobra made a move to a silver tub of iced beer on a side table.

"Sounds good." Parker accepted a damp bottle. "I've been ten years in Anchorage."

"Where are you from?" Cobra twisted off his beer cap.

"Porcupine Mine, unincorporated."

Cobra squinted for a second. "Alaska?"

"Northeast of Anchorage."

"I would not have guessed that." Cobra tipped back his bottle to drink.

"Dalia would be happy to hear you say so. She's my business manager. She's big into image. Wants me to look businessman, not miner."

Cobra glanced down at Parker's hands, obviously checking for strength and calluses.

Though he thought it was a little much, Parker held open a palm.

"You know how to work," Cobra said with approval.

"I can when I need to."

"That's all that counts."

Parker pressed his palm against his dress slacks for a second, feeling the divergence between his two worlds.

Chapter Thirteen

PARKER'S HAND RESTED LOOSELY ON HAILEY'S SHOULder. Cozy and relaxed, she leaned back against the sofa sipping her third, maybe even fourth glass of wine. It had been a while since dinner, and Silas kept topping it up.

People had gradually said their goodbyes and left the dinner party until only Mia and Silas, Cobra and Marnie, and Hailey and Parker were left.

"Scarlett's been fielding calls from established writers and even some from production companies," Marnie said. "Turns out, Alaska is a hot location right now."

"She's *ours*," Mia said staunchly. "We're not going to share her."

"You can't be thinking about another film already," Silas said to his wife.

"Why not?" Mia asked. "What would stop us?"

"You should wait to see if this one makes any money," Hailey pointed out merely as a practical matter.

"And lose momentum?" Mia asked.

"I've got to go with Mia on that," Parker said. "If other

people want in already, it means you've got a good thing going."

"That's a stretch," Hailey told him.

"Uh-oh," Cobra muttered.

"Uh-oh, what?" Marnie asked him.

"Trouble in Paradise."

"I assume that's a joke of some kind."

"Those two are dating." Cobra lifted his glass in their direction.

Mia's, Silas's and Marnie's gazes all swung to Hailey. "You are?" they asked as one.

"We are," Hailey said. She leaned sideways, resting her cheek against Parker's shoulder, and he settled his arm around her.

"When did that happen?" Marnie asked.

"Does Raven know?" Mia asked.

"How did *you* know?" Marnie asked Cobra.

"I talk to people," he said with mock defensiveness. "They tell me things."

"Since when are you the town gossip?" Silas asked Cobra.

"See?" Marnie said to Mia in a triumphant voice. "I keep telling you he's chatty."

"It was Raven who claimed he was quiet," Mia said.

"Oh, sure," Silas drawled. "Throw Raven under the bus."

"She's not here," Mia said with a shrug. Then she looked to Hailey. "So, how long has this been going on?"

"Not long," Parker said.

It all felt so natural to Hailey—natural and quite wonderful to tell people about their relationship. She liked sitting here cuddled up to Parker among the other town couples, sipping wine and enjoying the evening.

"Is it serious?" Mia asked.

"Mia," Silas cautioned.

"What?" she asked her husband. "I can't be curious?"

"You're being nosy."

"Not serious," Hailey said. "We're just getting to know each other. You guys all know how that goes."

The two other couples nodded.

"We should back off," Marnie said. "Let them work through it themselves."

"Parker knows where I stand," Cobra said with a meaningful look in Parker's direction.

Hailey craned her neck to look up at Parker. "How's that?"

"If I disrespect you, he plans to crush me like a bug."

Silas burst out laughing.

"You don't think I could?" Cobra asked Silas.

"I'd put up a fight," Parker said. "But the question's academic. It's not going to happen."

"More wine?" Silas asked around as he rose from his chair.

"Me, please," Mia said, waggling her glass.

"Sure," Marnie said. "Missing Alastair's wine cellar isn't so bad when I come here."

"This is from his cellar," Mia said. "Hannah sends me care packages."

"I *knew* this was a great bottle."

"Hailey?" Silas asked as he poured for Mia.

"Please." Hailey might be already glowing from the alcohol, but she was enjoying the feeling and didn't want it to ebb.

"That's the spirit," Silas said as he came her way.

"You do know you're not driving," Parker rumbled in her ear.

"I know," she easily agreed. She'd passed the *not driving* point quite some time ago. But Paradise was such a small place, there were always options.

"Anything for you?" Silas asked Parker.

Parker shook his head. "I'm good." He tipped back his highball glass and finished his bourbon.

"Are they all pitching Alaskan settings?" Mia asked Marnie.

Marnie nodded as she sipped her wine. "Natasha Burton's already known as an up-and-comer. That's rubbed off on Scarlett, who's now considered the Alaskan connection."

"Not bad for a long weekend," Mia said.

Hailey smiled to herself. What had started off as a zany matchmaking scheme for the men of Paradise had paid dividends in unexpected ways to both the town and the women who participated. Marnie was the lawyer on the project and met Cobra. Willow got her first gig as a stunt-woman out of the long weekend. And Scarlett's film producer career got a huge boost.

"I was skeptical about the wolves," Hailey put in. "But they cooperated very nicely. I think Scarlett has a magic touch."

"That's what I'm thinking," Mia said. "We need to lock that woman down to a second film."

"*Aurora Unleashed, the Sequel*?" Silas teased.

"I'm in favor," Cobra said. "Anything that gives Marnie more work to do in Paradise."

"We'll commission a script," Mia said with a flourish, picking her phone up from a side table.

Silas gently removed it from her hand. "You're over the legal limit for script commissioning," he told her.

"Party pooper," she said with an amused smile.

"We should head home," Cobra said.

Cobra and Marnie had built their own house just down the river from Mia and Silas, so it was only a short walk for them along a well-cleared trail.

"Agreed." Marnie rolled to her feet. "The last thing I want to do is give legal advice while under the influence. But, man, that's good wine."

"Come back tomorrow and give me legal advice," Mia said.

Hailey's eyelids grew heavy as Cobra and Marnie made their way to the door. She knew she'd overindulged, but she couldn't bring herself to care.

"I should get her home," Parker said, sounding like he was a long way off.

"Guest room's right down the hall," Silas said.

"That'll be easiest," Mia added.

Hailey was up for that. She loved Mia's guest room. It had one of the most comfortable beds in town. Not that she'd have any problem getting to sleep tonight. She was already halfway there.

"You want to stay?" Parker asked her.

"Sure," she managed, although the word sounded a little bit slurred to her ears.

The next thing she knew, she was scooped up into Parker's arms.

She closed her eyes to keep the room from swaying while he walked.

"I sure hope you don't feel too bad tomorrow," he said as he closed the bedroom door behind them.

The room was dusk, the sun briefly dipping behind the mountains and only a dim night-light shining from the en suite.

Parker pulled back the covers and sat her down on the sheets, tugging off her shoes and snapping the button on her jeans.

"Now we're getting somewhere," she muttered, anticipating being pulled into his arms.

He chuckled low. "We're not getting anywhere. Not with you like this."

"Like what?" she asked. "A little tipsy?" She still wanted to make love with him.

He lifted her legs and gently swung them onto the bed.

She lay back onto the sinfully comfortable mattress with its soft sheets and cloudlike pillow, just the right plumpness and softness.

She patted the other pillow, her voice going singsong. "Come and check this out."

"Maybe another time," he said from where he'd crouched

at the edge of the bed. He smoothed her hair from her forehead.

"They won't care if you stay," she said, closing her eyes. "They already know. Everybody already knows."

"I'm not worried about them," he said, and she felt the whisper of a kiss on the forehead.

"What are you worried about?"

"Sleep," he said.

"I'm not that tired." She wished he'd crawl in beside her. It would be so amazing to drift off in his arms and sleep there all night long.

IT HAD BEEN ALL PARKER COULD DO LAST NIGHT TO walk away while Hailey asked him to stay. But he didn't want anything to happen when she wasn't sober. And she'd been right earlier when she told everyone they were just getting to know each other.

Their relationship was brand-new, and it had started in an unconventional way. It wasn't right for him to assume he could crawl into bed and cuddle while she slept off four glasses of wine. He could only guess what Silas would have thought of him if he had.

He shook his head now as he pulled up to Galina, wondering how she was feeling this morning. He hoped she could take the rest of the day off to recover. But for him, there was work to do.

His phone rang as he swung into a parking spot against the trees that lined the gravel lot. It was Dalia, the call he was waiting for.

He accepted it. "Tell me it's good news."

"It's good and bad," she said.

"Can it never be straight good?" he asked with mock frustration.

She laughed lightly. "No. No, Parker. With you, it can never be straight good news."

"You're saying it's my fault?"

"I'm saying there are always too many moving parts with your deals for everything to come together at once."

"What's the good news, then?" He wanted to start the day off on a high note.

"Halstead International is open to the deal retaining five percent."

"So, somewhat good news." He'd still rather buy their property outright.

"It's a minor interest. Buck up."

She was right. Parker could live with losing five percent of the profits. It wasn't like Halstead International could influence his decisions.

"And the bad news?" he asked.

"There's a water-license issue."

Parker stilled over that. "What kind of an issue?" Water license problems could stop a mining project in its tracks.

"To keep the existing permit, you have to set up a new downstream field laboratory."

That didn't sound too serious. It sounded like the regular course of business. Parker had no problem protecting water quality.

"By the end of the month." It was clear from her tone that the timeline was a problem.

"Is that doable?"

"I'm in talks with Six Stone Labs out of Seattle. It'll be tricky."

"What do they need from us?"

"I've put them in touch with Colin. They're itemizing an equipment list and looking for techs who want adventure."

"I'm outside Galina right now. I'll talk to Raven about transport for the equipment."

"If you want the contracts drawn up, I should go back to Anchorage and work with Simon."

Parker gave a grin. "That must be your favorite part of the whole deal."

Dalia had been itching for an excuse to go back to Anchorage. But she was right. Looping in their lawyer Simon Gallio was the obvious next step.

"So, sue me. Priority on Halstead International, the Galina deal after that?"

"Let's get it done." Parker opened the door to the aging pickup, thinking he should probably buy himself a vehicle to leave here in Paradise. He planned to be back—often.

"I'll call you from Anchorage," she said.

Parker signed off and started for the warehouse. He skirted the loading dock, came in through a side door and made his way along the marked walkway at the edge of the clanking, cavernous space until he was at Raven's office.

She had her head down typing on her laptop.

He opened his mouth to announce himself when her radio crackled.

"Raven? AJ here."

She keyed the microphone that was clipped to her shirt pocket. "Go, AJ." Her brows went up questioningly as she spotted Parker.

"We've got another one of those labeling problems," AJ said.

"A serious one?"

"The acetylene tanks for Viking Mine."

"Viking again? What is *with* their suppliers?"

"Sorry, boss."

She came to her feet. "Not your fault. I'll be right out."

"Thanks. AJ, out."

"Hi, Parker," she said as she rounded the end of the desk. "Something more I can get for you?" Her tone was brisk, and even as she asked the question, she was brushing past him on her way out.

"Yes," he answered, pivoting to follow.

"Shoot," she responded over her shoulder, grabbing a white hard hat from a shelf.

He did the same, settling it on his head. "I need to organize a delivery to Lucky Breach."

"No problem."

"It's time sensitive," he said. They turned down a wider aisle and he pulled up beside her.

She glanced his way. "I can throw it on a truck in a day or two. Out of Fairbanks or Anchorage?"

"The equipment's in Seattle."

"Oh. Well, that's a little harder."

They came to the loading dock to see AJ and Kenneth standing inside a semitrailer.

"Viking needs them yesterday," AJ said as they entered, his flashlight beam wobbling and his voice bouncing back inside the mostly empty trailer.

"Can we relabel them ourselves?" Raven stepped into the trailer, looking down at the flashlight beam to study the sticker on one of the four tanks.

"Not without an inspector to sign off," AJ answered. "Closest one is in Fairbanks."

"We have to bring someone in from Fairbanks?" Her question was incredulous.

"Either that or send the tanks back out."

"If they're mislabeled," Parker ventured, drawing everyone's gaze his way. "Can you transport them at all?"

"So long as we don't take them off the truck."

"Truck's going back to Anchorage now." A burly man Parker presumed to be the driver walked in behind them.

"We unload them, they're stuck here waiting on the inspector," AJ said.

A deafening crash reverberated behind them.

Parker reflexively lunged, dragging Raven to the floor, twisting and covering her with his body.

When the noise stopped, he looked back to see a cloud of dust rising inside the warehouse, the yellow beacon of a forklift flashing within it.

"You okay?" he asked Raven, drawing his weight away from her.

She gave a rapid nod. "Fine. Good."

AJ hopped to his feet. "Leon!" he shouted, rushing to the crash site. "You okay, man?"

A coughing sound came from the dust cloud as Parker hopped to his feet, reaching back to grasp Raven's hand and pull her up.

She adjusted her hard hat.

"I'm okay," Leon called out, his voice sounding hoarse, followed by coughing.

Raven hustled toward the debris.

Leon was backing away from the forklift, which had obviously caught the corner of a shelf, tipped the whole thing over and sent boxes of what looked like wine crashing to the floor.

"Please tell me that wasn't the Wildflower Lake order," Raven said dryly as she stopped in front of the mess.

Three staff members arrived at a trot from other parts of the warehouse.

"I'll get a shovel and a broom," one of them said.

"We'll need a mini loader." AJ hit a button to open the bay door to the parking lot.

The other two workers positioned themselves on opposite ends of the shelving unit. "I think we can right it by hand," one of them said.

Leon quickly stepped up to help.

"Watch yourself," Parker said to Raven, who was standing close. It looked like the boxes were all piled on one another and not on the shelves, but he worried something might slide around.

"Watch out yourself," she said to him. "I've got steel toes."

Parker was in a suit and dress boots, so they both stepped back and let the men wearing proper gear take care of righting the shelf.

It clattered back into place, while a couple of precariously balanced boxes shifted in the pile. But they didn't seem to add anything to the breakage.

"So," Raven said, dusting off her hands and looking to Parker. "What was it you needed?"

"Scientific supplies and equipment from Seattle."

"Right. And you're in a hurry."

"Yes, please." He knew the clock was ticking on the water license.

She blew out a breath. "Just what I needed this week."

"Problem?" he asked.

"No. No. We'll get it done for you. Give me the supplier names and your purchase order."

"Thanks, Raven."

"Sure," she said, while a river of wine flowed toward them. "Not like there's anything else going on around here."

HAILEY DIDN'T LIKE WHAT RAVEN'S STORY SAID ABOUT Parker's character.

She'd arrived back from a flight to the Mile High Research camp just as Raven and T-Two finished loading a grocery order into a Beaver for his run to Wildflower Lake. The two women had sat down in the pilots' lounge behind the WSA office.

"Was he a jerk about it?" Hailey asked, hoping she'd misunderstood, and Parker hadn't been insistent on Raven dropping everything to meet his needs.

"Not a jerk," Raven said, laying her leather work gloves on the table and flexing her hands. "He was perfectly polite. But what was I supposed to say? We're already slammed this week. Would you mind very much waiting your turn?"

"You can only do what you can do."

Raven coughed out a laugh. "Sure, but in a couple of weeks, he'll be my new boss."

"Hugh will still have controlling interest, right?" Hailey hoped that was the case. She didn't know the particulars of the deal, just that they'd come to an agreement and the lawyers were drafting the paperwork.

"Hugh retains fifty-five percent."

"Only that?" Hailey asked.

On the one hand, 55 percent was clear controlling interest. On the other hand, 45 percent was a significant share of a business for somebody who wanted to push other people around.

"So they tell me."

"Beer?" Hailey asked, rising to go to the fridge. "Soda?"

"A soda would be great." Raven slumped back in her chair, looking tired.

It was coming up on five o'clock. In the regular world, it was quitting time. But Paradise wasn't the regular world. Hailey knew Raven worked fourteen-hour days in the summer, and it sounded like it was worse than usual right now.

"Long day?" Hailey opened the fridge that held mostly beverages and located a couple of colas.

"And it's not over yet. I still have to open an account for PQH Holdings, contact Parker's vendors in Seattle, fill out an accident report, and—"

"Accident?" Hailey looked back, feeling a shaft of unease.

"Forklift versus wine. The wine lost."

"I hope nobody was hurt." Hailey was guessing Raven would have led with that if there'd been an injury. She sat back down and slid one of the cans of cola across the table.

"Minor dent in the forklift, but that was all." Raven pulled the tab and popped the can open with a hiss.

Hailey had to ask the important question. "Not Wildflower Lake wine."

Raven grinned and gestured with her can. "That's what *I* asked. No. It wasn't the good stuff."

"Relieved to hear that."

They both fell silent for a moment sipping their drinks. The air compressor in the hangar was a muffled rattle through the wall, while radio operator Shannon's voice was indistinct in the back room.

"Mia says you're dating Parker." Raven reopened the conversation.

"I am."

"So . . ." Raven raised a quizzical brow.

Hailey could guess what she was thinking. Given how convinced Hailey had been that Parker wasn't trustworthy, what was she doing dating him now?

"It's complicated." Hailey didn't even know where to start.

"Hot but complicated? You're not the first woman with that problem."

"I didn't admit it to Hugh," Hailey said. "But I asked Parker to walk away from the deal."

"That doesn't surprise me."

"I figured he was pulling a fast one, and there was no way he'd let his mark off the hook."

"So, you called his bluff."

"It wasn't a bluff. He walked away to prove his good intentions." Hailey paused. "If I'd realized how bad things were at Galina . . ."

"I didn't realize it either. Hugh didn't tell me everything. But you fixed it. That's what counts in the end."

"And here we are." Hailey was grateful for Raven's understanding.

"Here we are." Raven leaned in and flashed a curious, conspiratorial grin. "*Dating* means . . . what, exactly?"

Hailey rested her elbows on the table. "Are you asking about my sex life?"

Raven leaned farther forward. "Absolutely. How's your sex life?"

"It's good."

Raven's grin went wide. "That's what I like to hear."

"How's yours?"

"Nonexistent."

The office door opened, and Brodie walked in.

"Hi, Hailey." His gaze shifted to Raven then, warming as it rested there for a moment.

Brodie and Raven tried to keep things between them all business, but their mutual attraction was hard to hide. It was obvious to everyone.

"Speaking of which . . ." Hailey muttered under her breath.

Raven kicked her under the table.

"Everything go well on the flight?" he asked Hailey.

"All good. I gave Cobra the logbook. The Islander's coming up on a fifty-hour service."

"Thanks. How are things at Galina?" he asked Raven.

"Lost a few cases of wine today."

He frowned. "Missing, lost?"

"Broken lost. Nothing we can't handle. And don't worry, it wasn't the Wildflower Lake order."

Brodie grinned and shook his head at that.

The office door opened again. This time it was Parker. Brodie turned to greet him, while Hailey's heart skipped a beat at the sight.

Parker seemed surprised to see her.

"Well, your day's looking up," Raven said.

"I don't think he's here for me."

A split second later, Parker gave her a warm smile.

"He looks happy to see you," Raven said.

"He does." At least he did now. But there'd been something in his expression for just a moment there that made her radar tingle.

She determinedly shook off the feeling. Her paranoia had caused enough problems already. She wasn't some super sleuth. She was a bush pilot who'd been out of the entrepreneurial game for years now.

She smiled back.

Parker's eyes sparkled and he waggled his brow. Then he turned his attention to Brodie. "Can I get a delivery to Broken Branch strip?"

"You bet," Brodie said.

"Well, that was hot," Raven said.

"He is hot." Hailey had not one doubt about that.

"It's like the world disappeared around you."

"Not quite." That hadn't been Hailey's impression at all. She got the sense that Parker always knew exactly what was going on around him.

Brodie made his way behind the counter and brought up the computer screen. "What's the cargo?"

"Were you with him last night?" Raven asked Hailey in an undertone.

"I've got a crate in the back of my pickup," Parker told Brodie. "Three feet by two by six, two hundred pounds."

"I was," Hailey answered Raven.

"And?"

"I fell asleep after too much wine."

"Any hazardous materials?" Brodie asked.

"No. Just hardware."

"Bad planning on your part," Raven said.

"It was at Mia's." Hailey defended her wine consumption.

"Oh, well, okay then."

"Not a problem," Brodie said to Parker. "Silas is doing a run to Viking Mine in the morning. We can loop back and drop it off."

"Perfect." Parker looked past Brodie and into the lounge, but he zeroed in on Raven instead of Hailey. "Raven, what would it take to get me an SUV?"

"Is this a rush too?" she asked.

He didn't seem to hear the edge of humor in her voice and played it straight. "As soon as possible, if you don't mind."

"Sure." Raven answered with resignation. "Whatever

you need. We don't have a car carrier scheduled. But we can probably find room for it inside a trailer. Is it out of Fairbanks or Anchorage?"

"Whatever's easiest."

"Your choice."

Hailey understood why Raven wasn't pushing back on Parker. She could also tell that Parker didn't mean to cause her grief. He wanted what he wanted, and he was used to getting it. It was only business.

"I know a guy at a dealership in Anchorage," Parker said, moving their way. "I'll give him a call and let you know."

"Whenever you're ready," Raven said.

Parker's attention moved to Hailey as he walked. His gaze softened, and his lips curved into a smile. "Sleep well?"

"You left," she said accusingly. She was sure she'd asked him to stay.

"Hello?" Raven glanced back and forth between them, clearly sensing more to the story than Hailey had already told her.

"I'm a gentleman," he said.

"I didn't drink that much wine." When she woke up this morning, she'd wished he'd stayed. But now she'd admit she was glad he'd left. It had been the chivalrous thing to do.

"Enough to put you to sleep." He took a vacant chair between them and took her hand. "I was going to call you."

"I was in the air."

"Are you done for the day now?"

She nodded.

Raven's chair scraped the floor as she pushed it back. "You two are entertaining, but I have to get back."

"Don't go." Hailey realized they were being rude.

"My work is never done," Raven said as she rose, taking her soda with her.

"Can I catch a ride?" Brodie asked her.

"You bet."

Hailey watched the two fall into step together.

"Are they a thing?" Parker asked her as the door closed behind them.

"It's complicated."

He squeezed her hand. "I understand complicated."

She gazed at their hands then looked up to his face. "Business and romance . . ." She let the thought trail away.

He raised her fingertips to his lips for a light kiss. "I missed you last night."

She fought a smile. "I didn't really notice you were gone."

He put his free hand to his chest. "Ouch."

"Sorry I drank so much."

"I'm not. You were having fun."

"I was," she agreed, remembering the warm fuzzy feeling of cuddling up to him while her friends talked and joked.

"What are you doing now?" he asked, glancing around at the empty office.

"*Right* now?" She couldn't help thinking about Shannon still in the back room operating the radio.

"Not *here*," he said with a laugh. "My place. The trailer's nicer than you'd expect."

She liked the idea of seeing where he was living. "Yeah?"

"Roomy bed." He slid his hand to the back of her neck and urged her forward for a kiss. "Plenty roomy."

She sighed. "Sounds good."

Chapter Fourteen

PARKER FINALLY FELT SUBLIMELY SATISFIED—LIKE HE'D just spent the perfect night with Hailey. They'd made love until late, slept in each other's arms, then rekindled their passion in the early morning.

But Hailey had a morning flight, and Parker needed to buy himself an SUV, review the Halstead International contract, and finalize the laboratory plans with Colin and Six Stone Labs to ensure they met the water license deadline.

As he lathered up in the shower, his thoughts wandered back to waking up next to Hailey. He relived their romantic morning, their quick breakfast of grainy Bear and Bar bagels with peanut butter and jam, joking and laughing with her over coffee. Then he hummed a little as he rinsed off, trying to remember the last time he'd started a day with this much optimism about life.

Dried and dressed, he settled in at one of the chairs around the dining room table. The slide-outs in the fifth wheel trailer meant there was room for a proper sofa, two armchairs, a decorative gas fireplace and a wooden dining table for four.

Renting the RVs had proved to be a great decision. He'd be comfortable here for as long as he wanted to stay. Well, maybe not in midwinter. He couldn't imagine they'd take the snow load, and the walls weren't insulated for twenty below.

He pulled up the Anchorage car dealership website to browse their in-stock vehicles and call his friend Sammy.

A brisk rap sounded on his door.

"Come in," he called out, clicking on a likely-looking gunmetal-gray SUV with an upgraded suspension package and deep-treaded tires.

It was Riley who came up the two steps and into the small entry area. "Morning."

"Hey, Riley. What's up?"

"Not much. It's a quiet morning."

"Come on in. Coffee?" Parker nodded to the coffee maker on one of three counters in the decent-size kitchen.

Riley was closer, so he moved to help himself, easily spotting a mug through the glass door of the cupboard. "Thanks."

"Need anything in it?" Parker took his black. So, it turned out, did Hailey. Yet another thing he liked about her.

"It's fine like this." Riley pulled up a chair. "Working?"

"Shopping. I expect to be back and forth to Paradise in the future, so I'm shipping up an SUV. You be okay if I stored it here?" Parker came up with the idea on the fly.

"No problem. We've got plenty of room."

"Thanks." Parker spun his laptop. "What do you think of this one? It's the end of the model year, and they're discounting their demo models."

Riley leaned in. "That's got all the bells and whistles."

"Leather interior." Parker liked that.

"Off-road suspension package and undercoat protection."

"I'll need that here." There wasn't a single paved road in Paradise. "Surround sound, Bluetooth, heads-up display."

Riley chuckled. "Overkill, maybe?"

"Nothing wrong with a good trim package."

"Sounds like a steal."

Parker took in Riley's expression, thinking the man seemed distracted. "Something up?"

Riley turned his cup. "Had some disappointing news this morning."

Parker closed his laptop and straightened. "What happened?"

"I'd made a deal to sell some of my property. The survey was done, the parcel subdivided off. It's prime land down by the river, just this side of Cobra and Marnie's place."

"The deal fell apart?" Parker guessed.

Riley nodded. "The guy was looking at expanding his rotary-wing operation, Panther Flight, out of Fairbanks."

"I've used them before," Parker said. He was surprised to learn they were looking at Paradise. Then again, maybe he shouldn't have been surprised. After all, he'd seen the potential in Paradise; others must see it too.

"They've put the expansion plans on hold."

"You were counting on the money," Parker guessed.

Riley nodded. "When we first met . . ." He paused. "I got the feeling you might be sizing up Rapid Release."

"I was," Parker admitted.

"But?"

"I decided the tourism business was too far out of my wheelhouse for now."

Riley looked disappointed but took it in stride.

"However," Parker added, thinking things through on the fly and feeling like something important had just dropped into his lap, "tell me more about the property you have for sale."

Riley perked up. "Yeah?"

"I might be in the market. What's it zoned?"

Riley grinned. "It's zoned Paradise. That means you can do anything you want on it. Are you thinking about an office?"

"I don't know yet." Parker gazed around the trailer. "I mean, once I've got a vehicle for Paradise."

"You'll need a place to park it," Riley added with good humor.

"I can't see living in this once the snow flies."

"You'd freeze your ass off."

"I would. Is it subdividable?"

"I just subdivided it without a problem. There's no minimum lot size, only what the market will bear."

"River frontage." Parker's mind was ticking along now.

If the owner of Panther Flight was thinking the same thing Parker was thinking about Paradise's future, then an early investment into real estate here was sure to pay off. As central Alaska opened up, investment and infrastructure were sure to follow.

"Plenty of it." Riley polished off his coffee. "You should come take a walk with me. There's a particular building site up on the bluff. The view's to die for."

"I'd like that." Parker was already dressed casually, so he followed Riley out the door, and they took a trail that led from the edge of the parking lot north above the river.

While they walked, Riley pointed out the features of the land and the approximate boundaries of the parcel.

"How much are you keeping for yourself?" Parker asked.

"Just a few acres. I need enough to run the business, expand the cabins in the future and keep my access to the river."

They stopped at the top of the bluff, and Parker gazed around. There was plenty of space for a house, and an office, and still leave the potential to sell part of it off in the future.

If the mining ground proved out the way he hoped it

would, things were going to open up in the region, and
Paradise was the natural jumping-off point. He was liking
the future potential for both Galina and WSA.

In fact, he had an idea to get Galina an even bigger piece
of the pie.

"I'll take it," he said to Riley.

Riley drew back in obvious shock. "You haven't even
asked the price."

"Were you happy with the deal you made with Panther
Flight?"

"I was."

"I'll go for the same. I'm sure it was fair."

"You're serious." Riley looked like he was waiting for
the punch line.

"I'm serious. When I see something I want, I know I
want it."

A grin spread across Riley's face. "That's fantastic."

"Draft me up a bill of sale. I think I'll hang out up here
for a while, pull my thoughts together."

"You bet," Riley said. He inhaled the fresh air and gazed
with Parker at the meadow on the bluff, the forest on either
side, the river snaking through the valley below and the
green-tinged glacier that stretched its fingers up to the
snow-dusted peaks in the distance.

Riley reached out his hand to shake. "Thanks for this,
Parker."

"Thank you. Do you mind keeping this under the radar
for now?" Parker was putting the pieces of a puzzle together, and he didn't want to show his whole hand to anyone just yet.

"You bet. I'll leave you to it." With a final grin and a
disbelieving shake of his head, Riley turned for the path
back.

Parker stared straight ahead, his vision going soft on the
vista. He could see the path forward so clearly, and he
couldn't wait to get started.

He drew his phone from his pocket and tapped Hugh's number.

"Parker," Hugh answered, sounding happy to hear from him.

Parker walked farther along the bluff, too energized to stand still. "How are things in Anchorage?"

"They're good. I'm busy planning a winter getaway with Elaine. She was thinking Maui."

"Maui's nice."

"A little house on the beach, barefoot mai tais, fresh-caught fish."

"Sounds terrific."

"Thanks to you. It's nice to have the financial worries lifted."

"I'm glad to hear that. Listen, Hugh, has Galina ever thought about investing in infrastructure?"

Hugh paused. "You mean the warehouse?"

"Beyond Paradise. I was thinking about the Broken Branch airstrip."

Hugh was silent for a moment. "Uh, you want us to buy an airstrip?"

"Buy it and upgrade it."

Skepticism was clear in Hugh's tone. "What would be the return on that?"

"Little right now," Parker admitted. "But central Alaska is poised. Paradise is poised. We could get it for a song, pump some money into lengthening and resurfacing it—"

"Whoa. Hang on. Resurfacing something that far off the beaten track gets really expensive really fast."

"It's an investment." Parker preferred not to tip his hand to Hugh right away, so he stayed vague. "When things open up—"

"You mean *if* things open up. I've been operating in that area for decades, Parker. The boom times are always *just around the corner*. You can't trust them to arrive."

"They are just around the corner this time, Hugh."

"I'm sorry Parker, but I can't agree to this."

"I understand. I'll use the discretionary spending clause." Parker had written a clause into the contract that gave him sole discretion over a portion of his investment.

Hugh was silent for a moment. Then his tone went flat. "I thought we'd talk about how that money was spent."

"This is important to me," Parker said.

"I guess I have no choice."

Parker knew he was disappointed. But he also knew Hugh would be happy once the whole picture came to light. "There's still plenty left for your priorities," he said to try to soften the blow.

"I understand." Hugh drew a deep breath.

"Don't worry."

"Sure."

"It's all going to work," Parker said reassuringly, hoping to keep Hugh from fretting over the details. "Talk again soon?"

"Okay. Bye for now."

Optimism pumping through him, Parker ended the call and gazed off at the distant mountains.

HAILEY LEANED AGAINST THE FRONT OF RAVEN'S five-ton truck parked at the turnaround at the top of Myers Mountain Road watching the film crew set up their equipment in the wide spot. Willow and Buzz had been dropped by helicopter far up on the cliff and were positioning their hang gliders.

The scenery was rugged, with sheer rock faces, rivers and waterfalls, altitude-stunted trees and shady crevices lined with moss and lichen. Willow was a red flash and yellow dot in the distance. Buzz's glider was dark green with a black pattern, somewhat menacing looking—which was the point.

"Are you *sure* about that?" Raven's voice rose from

around the side of the truck, where she was on a call with Hugh. "Because that's really hard to believe." She fell silent for a few moments.

"Does it change anything?" she asked. "*Can* it change anything?"

Hailey wondered if she should walk away and give Raven some privacy.

But Raven was returning. It was clear she could see Hailey, and she didn't seem to care she was being overheard. "No, not crippling, but definitely disappointing."

Raven shook her head as she walked, making Hailey curious about the conversation.

"Right. It is what it is." She thumped back against the grill next to Hailey. "Yeah. Okay. Bye." She ended the call.

Hailey focused on Scarlett, who seemed busy checking and double-checking details with the film crew members. If Raven didn't want to talk, Hailey wasn't going to pry.

"Well, that sucks," Raven said, opening the conversation.

"What happened?"

"It's Parker."

Hailey's attention perked up and she moved her gaze from Scarlett to Raven.

"He wants Galina to buy the Broken Branch airstrip."

The statement made no sense to Hailey. "I don't understand."

Raven's voice rose. "Neither does Hugh."

"Why would he do that?" Broken Branch was a crappy little airstrip in the middle of nowhere.

"It gets worse," Raven said.

"We're ready to synchronize up here," Fernando's voice crackled over the walkie-talkies.

"You ready, Vanessa?" Natasha called out to the cinematographer.

"All set," Vanessa answered, giving a thumbs-up. Three cameras were focused on different altitudes, obviously ready to catch all the action as the gliders swooped down from the cliff.

The whole crew stilled waiting for Natasha's call.

"And . . . action." Natasha set the shot in motion.

Hailey straightened away from the truck and looked up into the sky, her eyes shaded from the bright sun by her WSA ball cap.

Willow jumped first, the yellow flash of her glider bright against the blue sky. She was followed by Buzz's green and black rig, then by the cameraman following them to get in-the-air footage as Buzz pretended to chase Willow.

The three rigs settled into some turns and glides.

"How does it get worse?" Hailey prompted Raven as they watched the action sequence unfold.

"Parker wants to improve the strip."

"That's—"

"Expensive." Raven's tone was flat.

"And unnecessary." It took a confident pilot, but the Beaver and the Islander could land easily. It was wide enough that even the Twin Otter could make it in and out if necessary. "All that we service up there are—" The answer hit Hailey square in the eyes. She slumped back, swamped with foreboding.

Raven looked her way. "What?"

"Lucky Breach."

"What about it?"

"They're ramping up development and looking to go into serious production."

"We knew that."

"Parker's using Galina to pay for the upgrades to directly benefit the Lucky Breach mine."

"But that's . . ."

"*Exactly* how the game works." Hailey had let her guard down, thinking that Parker wouldn't push his own interests. "Hugh shouldn't go for it."

Raven shook her head. "He doesn't have a choice."

"He owns fifty-five percent, that gives him control."

"There's this clause in the contract we didn't think too much about. But it gives Parker sole discretion over a percentage of his investment."

"The innocuous-looking contract clause." Hailey knew all about those.

"Hugh expected to have input." Raven looked back up to the sky, watching Willow and the others' progress.

"But it turns out you don't."

"Apparently not."

Hailey felt obligated to point out Galina's options. "You know the deal's not finalized," she said in an undertone. "You could still get out."

"Hugh says it's not enough of a reason to back out. It's just *really bloody* disappointing. I had plans . . . and . . . well, I guess I don't have quite as many plans now."

"I know what you mean," Hailey said, feeling deflated by what the news revealed about Parker.

"You had plans, too." There was sympathy in Raven's tone. She reached out to give Hailey a squeeze on the shoulder.

"Not long-term ones."

"But plans all the same."

"Plans for the next few weeks, anyway."

Just when Parker seemed too good to be true, Hailey learned that he was. Like Hugh and Raven, she could back out of the relationship . . . *if* that was what she wanted.

A gasp went up from the crew, and she quickly looked up at Willow.

"That's fast," Raven marveled as Willow and Buzz seemed to be rocketing toward the earth.

The hang gliding cameraman had backed off now, circling above them so the cameras on the ground could get wide view of the action.

"That woman has nerves of steel," Hailey said.

"I don't know whether to be impressed or horrified."

"Give me a propeller and a solid fuselage any day of the week." Hailey cringed as Willow swooped low over the treetops.

"Nice," someone on the crew said as Willow executed a tight turn, staying just ahead of Buzz.

Then she caught an air current, rose about twenty feet, came their way and brought herself down gently onto the road.

Buzz landed slightly in front of her, and they both whooped with delight as they peeled out of their helmets and harnesses. Some of the crew members rushed forward to help them with the gear.

Hailey was thrilled by her friend's success, reminded that good things were happening all around her in Paradise, even if her own happiness had just shriveled a notch.

SOMETHING WAS BOTHERING HAILEY.

Parker couldn't put his finger on it. She was talking and smiling, relaying Willow's adventure in hang gliding and Scarlett's excitement about the footage from the stunt over a casual dinner out on the Bear and Bar sundeck. But there was something missing—in her tone or maybe in her eyes.

"It seems like there's a lot of action in the film," he said, watching her closely from across the table. Clouds were gathering in the distance again this evening, but it would take a while for the rain to reach them. They'd have time to finish their burgers.

"Fight to chase to fight to chase from what I can tell." She gave a little laugh that didn't quite ring true before she popped a sweet potato fry into her mouth.

"Action in an action film," he said. "Makes sense."

"What about you?" she asked, picking up another fry. "Anything interesting in your day?"

"The usual. They're finding more gold at Lucky Breach.

Dalia's frustrated with our lawyer. The lawyer's frustrated with the accountant. On it goes."

"Lucky Breach?" she prompted, stilling while she waited for his answer.

"What about them?"

"Is something up over there?"

"Why?" He tried to lighten the mood. "You want to go gold panning again?"

She waited a moment longer. "Sure."

"We can, you know, anytime you like." He wanted her to be happy, and she'd definitely been happy while they panned for gold.

Her phone pinged where it was sitting out on the table. She glanced down.

"Need to read that?" he asked.

"It's Amber." She picked the phone up and tapped to open the message. Her lips compressed as she read.

"Everything okay?"

"The board meeting was today."

He suddenly realized why she seemed preoccupied and wondered why she hadn't mentioned it was happening today. "Any glitches?"

She shook her head. "Dad was Dad, but there was nothing he could do against a flawlessly executed affidavit and proxy agreement. The reorganization motion passed." She typed in a message. "I'm telling her congratulations."

"Should we celebrate?" he asked. "Champagne?"

Hailey frowned. "That would be overkill."

"Maybe, but it's still a good excuse for champagne." Parker was feeling celebratory himself.

He'd soon own property here in Paradise. He'd even given in to temptation this afternoon and checked out some housing plans. And Hugh might not know it yet, but the Broken Branch airstrip was going to be a profitable investment.

"You think the Bear and Bar stocks champagne?" There was an edge of sarcasm to her question.

"We could raid Mia's stash." From what Parker had seen, Mia loved nothing better than sharing her wine collection. And he would love to hear the pop of a cork tonight, even if he couldn't yet share the details.

Hailey pursed her lips, but the glint of humor was back in her eyes. "You think we should break into Mia's house and steal champagne?"

"I don't think they lock the doors." He kept the joke going.

"There are a hundred witnesses camped out in her yard."

"Even better," he said. "We'll blend with the crowd." He reached out to take Hailey's hand. "What do you say?"

"I say we're *not* stealing Mia's champagne."

"What about a nice Cabernet Sauvignon?"

"I'm not embarking on a life of crime."

"I meant I've got a bottle back at my trailer."

"So, this is a ploy to get me to your place?"

"Yes," he admitted. Forget the champagne, he wanted to hold Hailey in his arms, make love to her or not. It didn't matter. What he really needed was assurance that everything was good between them.

She looked like she was making up her mind.

"We could go gold panning in the morning," he offered to sweeten the deal. "Unless you have to do a flight."

"Tomorrow's my day off."

He perked up at that, lifting her hand to brush his lips against her knuckles. "So, we can drink wine tonight and find gold tomorrow? What did you do with your last nugget?"

Discomfort flashed over her expression.

"What?" he prompted, curious about her reaction. "Did you sell it off?"

"No."

"You look guilty," he teased.

"I don't feel guilty."

"So, where's the nugget?"

She sat back. Then she unzipped a little pocket on the side of her cargo pants. Opening her palm, she showed him the nugget sheepishly. "It's been my good-luck charm."

He was oddly touched that she'd carried it around. It hadn't exactly been a gift from him, since she'd found it herself.

Still, he was touched. He lifted it from her palm and turned it, checking out the shape and texture. "It really is a pretty one."

"I was thinking a bracelet or maybe a necklace."

"They make nice rings."

She spread her bare fingers. "I'm not a ring person."

"Are you a necklace person?" He'd only ever seen her wear earrings that night they went out in Anchorage. He remembered the teal-blue dress now, her gorgeous legs, and how sublimely happy he'd felt sitting across the table from her in the Brandywine Brewhouse.

"A necklace is a possibility. I sure can't wear it as an earring." She cocked her head to one side. "I'd look like a pirate."

He grinned at the image. "Maybe we'll find another one tomorrow." He wanted to nail down their plans.

"What are the odds we'll find a match?" she asked, taking back the nugget and slipping it into her pocket.

"You never know. We might."

She scoffed a laugh. "There's optimists, and then there's fantasists."

"I'm an optimist, definitely an optimist." He took her hand again, stroking it between his fingers.

A raindrop splattered on the table beside them as thunder rumbled in the distance.

"See that?" he said with satisfaction. "That's fate telling us to go home and open the Cabernet Sauvignon."

"Now *that's* an optimistic outlook," she stated as more fat raindrops splatted on the wooden table.

A couple of waitresses rushed through the door heading for the occupied tables.

"You two want a table inside?" one of them asked as she efficiently picked up their dishes.

"Just the check," Parker said.

He kept Hailey's hand as they rose, her sexy smile telling him she was on board for the wine at his place.

IN THE MORNING, HAILEY WANDERED OUT OF THE SUR-prisingly roomy bathroom in Parker's RV. She'd borrowed one of his dress shirts as a robe and twisted her hair up in a towel. Her doubts about him had evaporated last night while they chatted over wine, made love in his bed, and then slept in each other's arms.

He might not be perfect. But nobody was. Everyone had their own interests. One selfish expenditure didn't mean Parker wasn't still saving Galina.

The bedroom was empty, so she took the short staircase down to the kitchen and living area. The carpet was soft under her feet. Sunlight streamed in through the big front windows that overlooked the river.

"Parker?" she called softly, glancing around the empty space, surprised he'd left and wondering why.

Their wineglasses and the empty bottle were still sitting on the counter from last night alongside the plate they'd used to snack on grapes and berries. She ran some water into the sink, poured in a dollop of soap to wash the few dishes. Then she rinsed the wine bottle for recycling and wiped down the counters, all the while thinking the kitchen was set up very conveniently. The stove was next to the fridge, the sink under the window, and a length of bare, useful counter between the kitchen and the dining table.

She heard Parker's voice, indistinct out back. She couldn't see him since the shade was drawn on the window there. When Riley answered, she realized it was just as well the shade was drawn, since Parker's white shirt was only a thin covering over her naked body.

Parker's day was obviously underway.

She hadn't expected he was serious about flying to Lucky Breach and panning for gold. But she had hoped they could hang out for the morning. Maybe cook breakfast and linger over coffee.

She opened the fridge, checking for breakfast possibilities.

"I thought we could skip the cost of the lawyers," Parker said, his voice clearer now, the two men's footfalls sounding on the gravel. "You and I just sign off on the contract as-is."

Hailey straightened from the fridge. *Contract?*

"Fine by me," Riley responded with a chuckle. "It's about as standard as it gets."

She closed the door, drawn closer to the window.

"I really appreciate this," Riley said in a lowered tone. "Cash flow was about to go critical."

"Dalia can arrange the funds transfer today," Parker said. "Do you have her number? She'll need your banking details for the accountant."

"I've got the number," Riley said, and their voices began to fade again as they moved toward the back of the RV. "I'll call her right away."

"Great doing business with you," Parker said. He added something else, but Hailey couldn't make it out.

She leaned back against the counter, wondering how long this deal had been cooking.

It had to have been a while, since they'd obviously settled on all the terms. She wondered why Parker hadn't mentioned it. Then she wondered if Riley should get a lawyer. Then she hated herself for doubting Parker all over again.

His footstep sounded outside the door, and she quickly scooted back up to the bedroom, not wanting him to know she'd overheard.

She unwound the towel from her hair and tossed it into the bathroom.

"Hailey?" Parker called, clicking the door shut behind him.

"Upstairs," she called back, although that had to be obvious. There was nowhere else for her to be. "I'm getting dressed."

"I'll put on the coffee," he answered, while her mind processed the new information.

She combed out her damp hair, changed into her clothes from yesterday and came downstairs to a steaming cup of coffee on the dining table. Parker was already seated and halfway through a cup.

"Morning," he said with a warm smile.

"Morning," she answered, slipping into the chair, struck again by his rugged good looks and wanting desperately for him to have integrity to go along with them.

He took her hand. "I'm so glad you stayed. You're beautiful in the morning."

"You're not so bad yourself."

He gave her hand a parting squeeze.

"You were outside?" she ventured, her nerves twitching, but she knew she had to ask.

He nodded easily. "Blue sky just as far as the eye can see." His phone pinged, and he glanced to the screen. "Dalia."

"Something up?" Hailey asked, expecting it would be about the deal with Riley. This would be a perfect opportunity for Parker to tell her he'd bought into Rapid Release.

"Lucky Breach, I expect. She wants me to call her."

"Oh." Hailey nodded, picking up her coffee cup to take a sip.

Parker didn't move to make the call.

"Are you going to call her?"

"Not right away. You hungry? We can toast some bagels."

"No thanks." The last thing she wanted to do right now was eat.

"Okay." He rose and carried his cup to the coffee maker. "Ready for a warm-up?"

"Not yet."

He filled his own cup and returned.

"I don't want to stop you," she said.

He raised his brow in a question.

"From calling Dalia. I mean, if you have work to do."

"There's no rush."

"It might be important."

He took her hand again, lifting it to his lips to kiss her fingers. "Nothing's more important than you."

Her discomfort increasing, she used a sip of her coffee as an excuse to retrieve her hand. She pushed a little harder. "Anything else going on? New deals?"

His brow furrowed for a moment, but then he shook his head. "Nothing noteworthy. Pretty much business as usual."

She tried to come at it another way. "You'd mentioned wilderness tourism."

He frowned.

She backpedaled to keep from giving herself away. "At Wildflower Lake Lodge."

"It's true. I did think about investing in Wildflower Lake Lodge." His gaze went warmer still. "I have very fond memories. But I decided against it. Tourism's a bit of a stretch for me right now."

"And Rapid Release?" She went for broke.

Again, Parker shook his head. "Riley's got his financials under control."

"So, you didn't invest."

"I didn't invest."

As he lied to Hailey's face, Parker's phone rang.

Dalia's name came up on the screen.

"I guess it was more important than you thought," Hailey said as her heart sank fast and deep.

Parker had just sat there without flinching and lied to her face.

"I better take this," he said, and rose from the table, heading outside for privacy.

Hailey's brain began processing fast. She dumped the rest of her coffee in the sink, rinsed her cup and pocketed her phone before heading out the door behind Parker.

She didn't know what all was going on here, but none of it could be good. He'd bulldozed Raven into prioritizing his needs at Galina, pushed Hugh into paying for a crappy airstrip, and now he was lying about his business with Riley.

She'd hoped to sneak past him, head for Willow's cabin and catch a ride home. But he spotted her.

He said something into the phone, then held it against his chest, quickly approaching her. "I have to say goodbye for a while." He pulled her into a hug.

She didn't resist, although his hug didn't feel secure anymore. It wasn't comforting. It wasn't safe.

"Just a couple days in Anchorage," he told her, giving her a kiss.

"Okay," she managed.

"I'll be back soon."

"Sure." She broke away, nodding to his phone. "Willow will take me into town."

He frowned, looking pained. "You're sure? Because I can—"

"I'm sure. Go. Do what you need to do."

"Okay." He nodded. "Bye." He gave her another quick kiss.

Afraid to try to speak, she took a step back and gave him a wave as she turned to walk away.

She swore silently inside her head, feeling him watching her and berating herself for being so gullible. Her emotions had clouded out her business sense. Worse, she'd let her heart get involved as well.

There was nothing she could do about her heart, but she

might still be able to warn her friends. Burned once by her own bad judgment, she knew she needed help, expert help.

Good thing she knew the experts.

"Hailey?" Her sister picked up on the first ring, sounding both rushed and concerned. "What's wrong?"

"I'm not . . . sure," Hailey answered, still sorting through the confusing series of events as she walked.

Background chatter came up behind Amber.

"Is this a bad time?" Hailey hesitated, feeling guilty now for calling her sister out of the blue. Then she heard a door shut and the background noise disappeared.

"No. Never." Amber sounded adamant. "I was looking for an excuse to ditch the meeting anyway. How can I help?"

Hailey stopped walking and blew out a breath. "I'm really not sure where to start."

"Try the beginning." The calm in Amber's voice was exactly what Hailey needed.

"Okay. Remember I mentioned a guy?"

The interest level in Amber's voice went up another notch. "That one you kissed?"

Hailey realized she'd started in the wrong place. "Yes. That's the guy. But that's not the thing."

"Okay. What's the thing?"

Hailey took a few more paces, sitting down on the steps of a silent cabin. "Remember I asked you about warehouses, and you said you'd build your own and undermine the competition?"

"I did?" Her sister sounded confused now.

"In real life, it's not warehouses. It's an expediting business. The guy is buying into an expediting business and trying to undermine the existing owners."

"Okay, got it." Amber paused. "Hang on. Whose side are we on in this?"

"The existing owners. A friend is the operations manager."

"I'm going to need a lot more detail."

"There are a bunch of threads," Hailey said, thinking through the complex web.

"There always are."

Hailey knew she'd made a mistake in calling Amber so impulsively. She should have waited, pulled her thoughts together, set up a video chat later. "You know what? Let's postpone this."

"What? No. You don't sound so good."

"I'm fine." Hailey attempted a laugh but knew she'd failed. "We can talk later on."

"Why not now?"

"Can you video chat tonight or maybe tomorrow?"

"I have a better idea."

Hailey pressed her palm against her head, her voice going strained. "Amber."

"You sit tight." Amber sounded suddenly energized. "Because I'm coming to you."

Hailey froze. "What?"

"I've been looking for an excuse to visit Paradise for a long time now."

Hailey's heart leapt in reflexive panic. "Wait. No, you can't—"

"I know you need your space and you don't want us interfering in your life. But this is different."

"Different how?"

"You *need* me." Amber's voice went singsong with joy. "My baby sister needs me."

Hailey's brain scrambled for a solution. She'd purposely kept her two lives separate. And now her sister was trying to pierce the wall. "We can video chat. I'll—"

"I'm already setting up a flight."

"Amber, seriously—"

"It's done! I'll text you my ETA along the way."

Chapter Fifteen

HAILEY BROKE INTO A TROT AS AMBER TRUDGED DOWN the airstrip access road. Struggling to keep her disappointment in Parker at bay, she was unexpectedly happy to see her sister. The first officer from the private jet walked along beside Amber, carrying a suitcase while the pilot waited with the airplane up on the strip.

Hailey could only imagine the pilot's reaction to the prospect of taxiing down to the hangar. In fact, she was surprised he hadn't done a flyover of the Paradise strip and diverted to Fairbanks instead of landing on it.

She made it to Amber and threw herself into a hug, while Amber staggered a little on the high-heeled ankle boots she'd worn over her designer jeans. Her dangling silver purse brushed Hailey's waist.

The first officer frowned reproachfully at Hailey.

"I warned your dispatcher it was a rural strip," she told him over Amber's shoulder.

"She said it was maintained," he answered.

"It is maintained."

The man looked pointedly at the aging heavy equipment in the parking lot, obviously also critical of their maintenance fleet.

"We all run on bush wheels," Hailey added, giving her sister a final squeeze.

"It's so great to see you," Amber said, breaking away to study Hailey. Then she switched her attention to the mountains and forest around them. "Wow. Just wow."

"It's the wilderness," Hailey said on a laugh, taking in her sister for the first time in well over a year.

"I can't believe I'm really here."

"Your bag?" the first officer questioned.

"I'll take it." Hailey held out her hand.

"No need," the man said. "Where would you like me to put it?"

"Don't be ridiculous." Hailey stepped forward and whisked it from his hands. "I do this all day long."

"This is Kevin." Amber waved away a mosquito as she introduced him. "Kevin, my sister, Hailey."

"Nice to meet you, Kevin." Hailey settled the bag in her hand. It was heavier than she'd expected. Amber was likely to be disappointed by the slim opportunities to wear whatever nice clothes she'd brought along.

Another mosquito buzzed around Amber, and Hailey guessed she was wearing perfume.

"Tell your pilot the west end of the strip is rough in the midsection," Hailey told Kevin. "If he needs the length, he should skew north of center."

Kevin shook his head in apparent exasperation, but he looked like he was fighting a smile. He took in the assortment of bush planes in the parking lot. "I can only imagine this is an adventure."

"There's no life like it," Hailey agreed.

He glanced at the bag in her hand. "You're sure?"

"Not a problem. Are you holding in Fairbanks?"

Kevin looked to Amber. "Ma'am?"

"They're going back to Atlanta," Amber said breezily, her hands in almost perpetual motion against the bugs now.

"You won't want to stay that long," Hailey warned her.

"I haven't decided how long to stay."

"Fairbanks," Hailey told Kevin in all seriousness, since Amber was already frustrated by the insects and was sure to hate her room in WSA housing. "See if you can get rooms at the Maple Grove. It's nice."

"Don't be silly," Amber said, linking an arm with Hailey. "Somebody might need the jet."

"Give her a day," Hailey told the pilot. "She'll be begging you to come get her."

Kevin's grin was full-on this time. "I'll confer with the captain."

Amber urged Hailey into a walk, waving her hand once more in front of her face. "This is going to be fun."

Fun wasn't the word Hailey would have used.

"I mean, the visit," Amber quickly clarified. "Not your business problem."

Hailey had brought Raven up to speed on the Rapid Release deal and her new worries about Parker, and now she was waiting for them in the parking lot.

Hailey dropped Amber's suitcase into the pickup box, then slid across to the middle of the bench seat, leaving room for Amber.

Amber gamely hopped in and shut the door, only to have it bounce open again.

"The door handle sticks," Raven warned her as she coaxed the engine to start. "Hold on to it then press it in."

"Okay." Amber tucked her purse between her thighs and reached out to give it another try. She fumbled, but got it closed.

Hailey reached across her to test it to be sure.

With so few roads, and so little traffic, nobody bothered with seat belts. Raven's hadn't worked in years.

"Raven, this is my sister, Amber."

"Great to meet you, Amber." Raven reached over to shake her hand. "Welcome to Paradise." She pressed on the gas pedal, churning up dust and gravel as they passed the open overhead door of the hangar, heading for the road.

"Is that meant to sound ironic?" Amber asked in a light-hearted tone as she took in the rather industrial feel.

"We love it here," Hailey said, struggling to keep a hitch from her voice. She hoped the wound from Parker's deception didn't linger.

"Sorry." Amber looked contrite.

"It's okay to joke," Raven said. "We don't take ourselves too seriously."

"Great. Good." Amber rubbed her hands together. "Now tell me more about your Galina Expediting conundrum."

As they bounced along the gravel road from the airstrip to town, Hailey, then Raven, then Hailey again, outlined the situation with Hugh's financial problems and Parker's investment into Galina.

By the time they pulled up in front of WSA housing, Amber was agreeing with their assessment.

"You need a competing offer," she said as they climbed out of the vehicle.

"Thirsty?" Raven asked, pointing to the Bear and Bar sundeck.

Amber glanced into the truck box. "What about my suitcase?"

"It's fine to leave it out here," Hailey said.

Amber looked at her like she'd lost her mind.

"Really," Hailey repeated. "I know it's hard to believe. But it's fine."

"Sun's over the yardarm somewhere in the south," Raven said, heading for the short staircase from the wooden sidewalk to the sundeck.

Amber gazed at the utilitarian WSA housing building and took a long look at the cafeteria at the far end.

"That's where I live," Hailey told her.

"Ha-ha," Amber said with a smirk.

"Seriously."

"Right." Amber chuckled with obvious disbelief as she followed Raven to the sundeck.

Hailey shook her head as she fell in behind, sincerely hoping Kevin and the pilot were bound for Fairbanks right now.

"This good?" Raven called out, choosing a corner table.

Only two of the dozen sundeck tables were occupied, so they'd be able to converse in privacy.

Hailey gave her a thumbs-up and they all settled down at the round slatted-wood table.

"Has Hugh looked into getting interest from other investors?" Amber asked Raven.

Raven shook her head. "It wasn't until Parker came to him that Hugh really started thinking about an investor as an option."

Amber gave Hailey a meaningful look.

"What?" Raven asked, looking back and forth between them.

"He's smart," Amber said. "He identified Galina as a prospect before you even understood the magnitude of your own problem, putting him in the driver's seat."

"I should have pushed harder to figure him out," Hailey said, regretting getting sidetracked by her attraction.

"You killed the deal," Raven said. "How much harder could you push?"

"Then I resuscitated it," Hailey said with a frown.

"There's no point in looking backward," Amber said briskly.

Raven came to her feet. "I'll take a trip to the bar. What are we drinking?"

"What's good here?" Amber glanced over the bare table like she expected a drink menu to appear.

"They have Amber Ice on tap," Raven answered. "It's local."

"Great name. But not beer, thanks. How about . . ." Amber screwed up her face as she pondered. "A golden margarita."

"I doubt Badger gets that request very often," Raven said, amused.

"Works for me," Hailey said. Tequila was a solid choice for a difficult day.

"Coming up." Raven headed inside.

"So," Amber gazed around at the gravel street, WSA housing and the vacant field that opened up to the schoolyard in the distance. "This is home."

"I don't expect any of you to understand."

Amber reached for her hand and gave it a squeeze. "We don't have to understand. I am realizing we have to accept your choice."

Hailey felt a rush of warmth at the concession. "Thanks."

"I should have said so a long time ago." Amber sat back then and considered Hailey. "So, you kissed the guy who's messing with your friend's business."

"Worse," Hailey said, seeing no point in holding back. If she wanted Amber's help, she needed to be honest. "I slept with the guy who's messing with my friend's business."

Amber's gaze narrowed. "You mean the guy slept with you."

"Isn't that the same thing?"

"No. It's not the same thing. He knew what he was doing. He *knew* all along he was—" Amber stopped abruptly, and her blue eyes went hard and cold. "That's it. I'm takin' him out."

"Taking him *out*? What are we, the mob?" Hailey assumed it was a joke. Her family might be ruthless, but she was confident they drew the line at killing the competition.

"He won't be dead when I'm finished with him." Amber tapped her manicured fingernails on the tabletop. "But he'll wish he was."

"I'm not looking for revenge. The sex part is on me. I

mean, I should have known better, but he's a really hot guy, and he comes across as a nice guy, a smart, funny guy. Still—" Hailey was embarrassed by her behavior. "I really should have known better."

"Hey," Amber said, looking concerned. "It's okay that you fell for him."

Hailey shook her head to stop the conversation. She was focused on helping Raven here. The last thing she wanted was to think about her own feelings.

"You liked him," Amber said softly.

Hailey swallowed a lump in her throat. "I wouldn't have slept with him if I didn't like him."

"Oh, honey. You really liked him."

Emotion pressing hard against her chest, Hailey didn't trust herself to speak. She nodded instead.

"That son of a bitch," Amber said.

"He was so good," Hailey said, half to herself as she remembered how natural their attraction had felt to her. "I called him on his motives at first, but then—"

"He backed off, regrouped and came at you from another angle."

"It's like I learned nothing growing up."

Amber's eyes were filled with sympathy. "It's like you're a decent person who knows how to trust."

"And look where it got me." There were moments when Hailey's heart actually hurt from his betrayal.

The door to the lounge opened and Raven appeared with three golden margaritas clustered between her hands.

"Whoa." Amber was on her feet in a second to take one of the tall, icy drinks.

"Thanks," Raven said. "They were getting slippery."

She set one down for Hailey and shook off her damp hands while taking her seat.

"What did I miss?" she asked eagerly.

"How would Hugh like a new offer?" Amber asked matter-of-factly, dabbing her straw into the slushy drink.

Hailey stilled, shocked by the thought of where Amber might be heading.

"Hang on," Raven said, obviously feeling as stunned as Hailey. She took a swallow of her drink. Then she took another and a third before looking up. "Okay, say that again?"

"I'll match Parker's offer," Amber said. "You know, without those pesky little clauses that give him far too much wiggle room and control in the deal."

Raven looked to Hailey, clearly perplexed. "Did you expect—"

"*No.*" Hailey hadn't expected anything remotely like this. She turned to her sister. "Amber, seriously, you can't—"

"I do have some conditions of my own," Amber said.

"Fire away," Raven said.

Hailey braced herself.

"You," Amber said with a waggle of her finger in Hailey's direction. "Take care of Magnolia Twenty's interests here in Paradise."

"Hailey can do that," Raven was quick to offer.

Hailey was less sure. "What would that mean?" Her first thought was that Amber was using this as an opportunity to get her back into the corporate fold.

"You know what it means," Amber said with a sly smile. "I'm not going to lie. It brings you back into our orbit."

Hailey opened her mouth to protest.

"You can deal directly with me," Amber continued. "It won't mean you have anything to do with the Atlanta-based companies. I promise."

Hailey was wary, but she knew she could live with that condition. It wasn't too high a price to pay to save Raven and Hugh.

"Okay," Hailey said. Then she took a deep drink of her own tequila-laced beverage.

"And two," Amber said more softly. "You come down

and visit, now and at least once a year for the shareholders' meeting."

Hailey's whole body deflated. *Every* year? It took her months to recover from her family's emotional machinations and get back on an even keel. If she went back on a regular basis, she'd keep re-upping the problem.

"Could you?" Raven asked Hailey, a hopeful note to her voice.

"You're as bad as him," Hailey said to Amber, knowing her sister had seen an opportunity to push her own agenda and had taken full advantage of it.

"Oh, I'm much worse than him," Amber responded with a satisfied smile. "But I'm on your side. I promise, I'm on your side."

Hailey did trust her sister. When the chips were down, she realized she could trust Amber.

FINALLY BACK IN PARADISE AND DRIVING FROM THE airstrip with Dalia, Parker couldn't wait to see Hailey again. Her answers to his texts had been sporadic and brief for the past few days, and he guessed she'd been busy flying. That was a good sign. It meant the Paradise economy was already picking up.

The Halstead International deal was tricky, but they'd managed to finalize it, and his lawyer, Simon, was now back working on Galina. They'd also had some preliminary discussions with the owners of the Broken Branch airstrip, and Dalia was elbow deep in the rollout of the field laboratory.

The elements of his world were coming together. Adding to its successes were the two matched gold nuggets Colin had found at the Lucky Breach mine, which Parker was having made into earrings for Hailey.

As they turned onto Riley's property, Dalia's phone rang.

"Simon," she told Parker as she answered the call.

"Hope it's more good news."

"Hi, Simon," Dalia said into the phone.

Parker headed for the parking lot thinking he'd drop a few things off at the trailer, then check with someone at WSA to see when Hailey would be back in town. He'd tried her when they landed but the call had gone straight to her voice mail.

Dalia's tone turned worried. "That doesn't make any sense." She glanced Parker's way, her brow furrowing.

Parker pulled into the space between their two trailers and stopped the truck.

"He's right here, but—"

She stilled, listening closely. "Did you talk directly to Hugh?"

Parker shut off the engine. "What's up?"

"I will. Right now." She tucked the phone below her chin. "Hugh's backing out of the deal."

Parker couldn't believe he'd heard right.

Dalia nodded to confirm. "He took another offer. His lawyer sent a notification to Simon this morning."

"Why?" Parker asked, hearing the shock in his own voice.

Dalia shook her head, incomprehension in her expression. "But did you *try* calling Hugh directly?"

Parker pulled out his phone to call Hugh himself.

"Parker's trying now," Dalia said to Simon.

Hugh's number rang in Parker's ear.

"We'll call you back if we find out," Dalia said.

Then Hugh's voice mail picked up.

"What the hell?" Parker stared at his phone in frustration. He didn't bother leaving a message.

"What do you want to do?" Dalia asked him.

"How did they have another offer? Where did that come from?" He smacked his hand down on the steering wheel.

"They should have countered to us," Dalia said, her tone hard.

Parker restarted the truck and pulled the shifter into reverse, peeling backward to turn around. Raven would be at Galina, and she'd know what was going on.

They powered down the main road and swung into the Galina parking lot.

Dalia had to scramble to keep up as Parker strode through the door and down the walkway to Raven's office. But halfway there he spotted her. She was out on the floor talking to AJ.

He grabbed himself a hard hat and headed for her.

Dalia hung back—probably a good idea.

"Raven," Parker called out.

When she turned his way, her face told the whole story. They'd betrayed him, and she was bracing herself for his anger.

He stopped a few feet away and forcibly modulated his voice. "*What* happened?"

"Parker," she said.

AJ glanced surreptitiously between them, obviously feeling the tension and wondering what to do.

"It's okay, AJ," she said.

"You sure, boss?" he asked.

She nodded, her expression tight, and AJ slowly drew away.

"You should talk to your lawyer," she said to Parker.

"I *did*."

"Then you know."

"I know *what*. I don't know *why*."

"It was just business," she said evenly. "A better offer came along."

"We had a deal."

"You should talk to Hugh."

"I wouldn't be here if I had gotten in touch with him."

"There's nothing more I can tell you, Parker."

She'd called it just business, but it felt personal to Parker.

He was obviously missing something here. "Where's Hailey?"

"Gone."

"Where? Viking Mine? Wildflower Lake? When will she be back?"

"She's in Atlanta."

Parker was stunned to silence by that.

"What?" he finally rasped, his anger replaced by confusion and a growing sense of dread.

"She's with her sister."

"Parker," Dalia called from the side of the warehouse.

He waved her off. Now was not the time for an interruption. Something had happened with Hailey, and he was determined to find out what it was.

"Parker!" Dalia's tone was adamant.

"Why did Hailey leave town?"

"Because she's got you pegged," Raven said with condemnation.

"Pegged for *what*?"

"Parker." Dalia appeared beside him, touching his arm. "We need to talk."

"For what?" he repeated to Raven.

"Now," Dalia insisted.

He glared at her, and she looked back with a hard expression, canting her head to the side in a way that said they needed to leave.

His jaw clenched and fists balled at his side, Parker marched away with her.

"What?" he demanded as they headed for the exit.

"The other offer," Dalia said. "It was from Magnolia Twenty."

"Who?" He pushed the spring-loaded door open and exited to the parking lot.

"Magnolia Twenty. It's mostly a food-services conglomerate out of Atlanta."

Parker stopped, turning to stare at Dalia. *Atlanta?* Hailey was in Atlanta.

Dalia faced her phone screen his way. "Magnolia Twenty is owned by the Barrosse family."

Everything inside Parker turned to ice. His voice went hoarse. "This was Hailey? *Hailey?*"

Dalia nodded. "This was Hailey."

Parker's brain recalibrated at about a hundred miles an hour. "She scooped me on a mediocre business deal?"

Sure, *he* wanted to be involved in Galina, but he had mining interests that would benefit from the partnership. Unless they'd settled on a far lower price, there was no benefit he could see to Magnolia Twenty partnering up with Galina, no benefit at all.

"Was it revenge?" Dalia asked.

"For *what*? I did everything her way. I gave her everything she wanted."

"Do we pack it in?"

Parker started for the pickup again, laughing coldly at himself when he thought about the SUV he'd just bought down in Anchorage. It was already on its way here.

"I don't know what else to do," he said. "Hugh's in Anchorage. Hailey's in Atlanta. There's absolutely nothing for us here."

"YOU'RE *HOME*." HAILEY'S MOTHER PULLED HER INTO A tight, rocking hug in the great room of the family mansion. "Finally, finally. My baby is home."

"It's just a visit," Hailey warned.

"I know that." Her mom stood back to survey her, cradling her face. "But you're here now. Oh, honey, we need to get you cleaned up."

"I am clean." Hailey's skinny jeans and tank top might be casual, but they were perfectly acceptable.

Her mom felt the texture of her ponytail. "When's the last time you had a trim? A deep oil treatment? Amber, make us all appointments at the Sunrise Spa." She squeezed Hailey's arms. "Oh, you're going to love being pampered again, my girl."

Hailey didn't argue. She'd agreed to come home with Amber for a few days. It didn't much matter what she did to pass the time while she was here. A facial and a haircut wouldn't hurt her any.

Her mother looked great, perfectly groomed as always, made up nicely, and without a single gray root showing in her blond hair. She was dressed in a pair of blue linen slacks and a gauzy pastel blouse, as if she was about to do lunch with the girls down at Aldo's on the River.

Footsteps sounded on the polished wood floor of the foyer. The door snapped shut behind whoever had walked inside. Her father's low voice rumbled as he spoke to the staff member who would have rushed to greet him when his car pulled up.

"Amber?" his voice boomed down the grand hallway past the twin staircases that led to the second floor.

"Yes, Dad." Amber fixed her expression and squared her shoulders, clearly ready for his onslaught.

"*This* is what you do?" he asked as he marched toward them.

He spotted Hailey and drew back in surprise. "Hello, Hailey."

"Hi, Dad."

He snapped his fingers in Amber's direction. "Just like that?"

"I have full authority," she countered.

"Hailey's come home," her mother said to her father.

"The ink's barely dry on the new agreement," her father said.

"It's dry enough," Amber said.

Hailey couldn't help but be impressed with her sister's poise in standing up to their father's annoyance.

"Alaska?" he challenged.

"Hailey found us an opportunity up there."

Her father looked sharply Hailey's way, his bushy brows knitting together beneath his frosty head of hair. He was fit for his age, careful about his diet and sure to get exactly the right amount of daily exercise.

"Is that true?" He sounded skeptical.

"Only inadver—"

"Of *course* it's true," Amber interjected. "What do I know about business in Alaska?" She sent an arch look Hailey's way. "And Hailey's going to spend a bit more time at home."

"Oh!" her mother all but squealed.

"Just once a year," Hailey cautioned.

"For the shareholders' meeting," Amber added.

Their father harrumphed. "It's about time." But then he turned on Amber again. "That doesn't excuse such a rash decision. I'm rethinking the new agreement."

"You can't rethink the new agreement," Amber said.

It seemed to take their father a moment to compose his next words. "Well, the autonomy is once a year, and you've had your once for this year."

Hailey looked to her sister. "Is that true?"

Amber had explained that under the new corporate organization both she and their brother, Kent, could make unilateral deals under a certain value. She hadn't said anything about it being limited to once a year. Amber had been even more generous to Hailey than she'd realized.

"*Hailey's* going to look after our interests in Paradise," Amber said to their father.

Hailey's mother gave her a one-armed squeeze. "I knew you'd come around."

"I'm not around," Hailey quickly said, then caught Amber's

warning expression. "I mean, I'm a little bit around. Amber and I have it worked out, and I will come home for the shareholders' meetings."

"We'll plan a dinner to celebrate," her mother pronounced. "Tomorrow, after our spa appointments."

"The company is in *Paradise*?" their father asked with a frown.

"The mining region is up-and-coming," Amber said. "There have been some impressive gold discoveries in the past couple of years. Rare earth exploration too. And Galina is poised at the center of it all. They have a long-standing business relationship with West Slope Aviation, and Hailey knows that business, plus the whole area inside out."

Hailey supposed that wasn't a lie. She did know a lot about WSA's operations, and she certainly knew central Alaska as well as any pilot.

And it was true about the mining opportunities. After all, those opportunities were what had lured Parker there. As soon as the thought formed, she steeled herself against it.

She was determined to ignore him, not miss him. The man didn't deserve to be missed. She knew now he was a fraud. She'd fallen for a sham and a ruse, and he'd only manipulated her feelings to get what he wanted.

Even when he'd walked away from the Galina deal. She'd bet now that it was calculated. Maybe he'd taken a risk, but he knew Hugh's financial straits and he knew Hailey would be forced to come running back, making her think it was her idea and leaving her grateful to him.

She'd been grateful all right, letting it cloud her emotions and fuel her desire. And her emotions still felt cloudy. She might not want to miss him, but she couldn't seem to stop herself.

PARKER WAS STILL KICKING HIMSELF FOR THE CATAS-trophe that had been his venture into Paradise. He was doing a final walk-through of the trailer to make sure he hadn't forgotten anything important when a knock on the door interrupted him.

"Yeah?" he called out from the kitchen, wondering why Dalia would bother to knock.

The door yawned open, and Riley stuck his head inside.

He looked both hesitant and uncomfortable, so Parker could tell he'd already heard the news.

"Come on in," Parker said fatalistically. He had no quarrel with Riley.

Riley stepped up and closed the door, standing with his back to it. "I hear the Galina deal is off."

"Was I the last person in town to know?" Parker's tone was bitter.

Riley shook his head. "I don't think many people know yet. Willow said something to me."

Sure. Of course. Because when she wasn't being a stunt-woman, Willow was best friends with Hailey.

Parker paused, seeing an opportunity.

Maybe Willow knew why Hailey had done it. Maybe he could get some answers through her. Because while business was business, he couldn't accept that Hailey had walked away from their relationship without a reason.

He kept imagining her in his arms, remembering the scent of her skin and the taste of her lips. It was impossible to accept that he'd never hold her again.

"I'll refund your deposit," Riley offered. "It might take me a few days—"

Parker tuned in to Riley's words. "What?"

"I'd give it to you all right away, but my cashflow is—"

"No, no." Parker hadn't even thought about the real estate deal with Riley. He sure didn't want to screw up Riley's world.

Riley seemed alarmed, and Parker realized he'd misunderstood.

"I mean I don't need my deposit back. It's still a good

piece of land." Parker could probably sit on it for a few years and make a profit if nothing else. Whether or not he invested in Galina, Paradise was still poised for a boom.

Riley seemed shocked. "You don't want to back out?"

Parker shook his head. "Enough has gone wrong here already. You don't need to be dragged down as well."

"But—" Riley looked guilty. He also looked like he had something more to say, so Parker waited.

Riley cleared his throat. "You should know I was partly the cause."

A tingle ran up Parker's spine. His first instinct was to demand an explanation. He'd been looking for a place to vent for hours now. But Riley didn't deserve the brunt.

"I didn't think much of it at the time," Riley continued, taking a step into the trailer. "But Hailey mentioned our contract to Willow."

"Hailey knew about the land?"

"I thought you'd told her. But the way she said it." Riley moved to prop himself against the end of the counter. "Looking back, I think she thought you'd bought into Rapid Release."

"I considered offering at one point, but—" Parker's memory flashed back to Hailey's questions the morning before he'd left. "She overheard us talking."

"About the contract."

"And misunderstood." Parker reached behind and gripped the lip of the counter. "She could have asked me. Why didn't she just *ask* me?"

He snapped his jaw shut, remembering. She had asked him. But she'd done it so obliquely, he hadn't gotten the chance to explain.

"She didn't trust you," Riley said.

"No shit." Parker glared at the man for that one, even though he was just the messenger.

"You really liked her."

Parker saw no reason to lie about that. "I really liked her."

Riley looked like he was making up his mind about saying something.

"Spit it out," Parker said with a sigh.

"She was also upset about the airstrip."

"The airstrip?" What had Parker done at the airstrip?

"Broken Branch. You were somehow forcing Galina to blow money on it?"

Dalia opened the door then. "Parker, are you ready?"

"No!" Parker barked. "Sorry." He moderated his voice. "They weren't blowing money on Broken Branch."

Dalia looked back and forth between the two men while Parker continued. "Broken Branch is going to make a fortune."

Riley paused. "That's not what they thought. Plus, with you cutting Raven out of the picture."

"Where are they *getting* this stuff?"

"Parker?" Dalia ventured into the silence.

"She really thought I'd screw her," Parker spat out bitterly. "The second something looked hinky, that suspicious mind of hers started churning and she dumped everything she ever learned about me, everything I ever proved to her." Disappointment ate at his gut. "It's just as well, I suppose. Better to learn that now."

"Listen, Parker—" Riley began.

"Nothing to do with you." Parker held up his palms. "Our deal stands."

Riley gave a nod. "Okay." He stayed put, looking like he wanted to say more.

Parker lifted his brow in an invitation.

"Just . . . it made some sense the way they put it all together."

"It would have made perfect sense if I was corrupt and underhanded. But I'm neither. She should have trusted that

I was neither." It galled him that Hailey had thrown away whatever it was that had been growing between them—if she ever really wanted it in the first place.

At this point, he'd completely lost track of what was real and what was a ruse.

"You want me to—"

Parker waited for Riley to finish.

He didn't. So Parker took a guess. "Tell Hailey she was wrong?"

"I'd like to help."

"It's not your fault. She'll figure it out soon enough. Or she won't. Whatever."

He'd still buy and improve the Broken Branch strip. He'd set up the field lab and expand his exploration around Lucky Breach. He might even use Galina for his expediting needs. He'd probably get richer. But no matter how it went, he wasn't coming back in person. His misadventure here in Paradise was well and truly over.

Chapter Sixteen

THE DINNER AT THE BARROSSE MANSION HAD EX-
panded in size. By the time Hailey got home from the day
spa and changed her clothes, conversation was rising up the
staircase and along the hall to her bedroom. She'd borrowed a blue scoop-neck A-line dress from her sister. The
lace bodice and cap sleeves made her look completely un-
like her usual self, like she had on the date with Parker.

Parker.

She shook away the memories, forcing herself to think
about the party downstairs.

Her hair was freshly trimmed and blow-dried, feeling
light and bouncy around her face. Her mani-pedi was a
subtle glittering blush. Her mother had insisted they have
their makeup done after their facials.

It might have taken skilled professionals the better part
of the day to get her looking this way, but at least she'd
blend with the rest of the guests.

"Hailey?" Amber called through the door, rapping
sharply before turning the handle. "Are you ready?"

The conversation grew even louder as Amber opened the bedroom door.

"How many people are down there?" Hailey asked cheerfully, forcing herself into a good mood. She crossed to a small armchair to slip into a pair of silver and blue open-toed heels. She was lucky her feet were the same size as Amber's, adding to the things she could borrow from her sister.

"I haven't looked." Amber closed the door behind her. "The Bennetts for sure. And the Carmichael clan. And if Roger Carmichael is invited, then Seth Winters has to be included. The neighbors, because they'll see something's going on and get their noses out of joint if they're not here. And Dad will definitely have the crew from the head office. He wants to show you off."

"Why would he want to show me off?" Her dad had never been proud of her.

"Because with Kent and Sophie here, he's got the whole family in one room at the same time for once."

"It'll be nice to see Sophie," Hailey said. Her brother, Kent, might be a stuffy, serious, mini version of her father, but his wife was bright and lively. Hailey wouldn't have put the two of them together in a million years, but they seemed happy.

She rose to her feet.

"You look fabulous!" Amber enthused. "But I knew you would. You've got the foundation. You just need a little help bringing it all out."

"I feel like I'm in costume."

Amber linked her arm with Hailey's. "You *are* in costume. You never did get that, did you?"

"Get what?"

"It's all an act."

"You're not acting. You're genuinely gracious and glamorous."

"Only because I learned how to do it. Now, let's go wow them downstairs."

"Don't walk too fast," Hailey warned as they headed for the door. "I'm not used to heels."

"It's some kind of life you're leading up there." Amber had balked, then laughed at her tiny room in WSA housing. And she'd stared in slack-jawed amazement when Hailey tucked into a burger and fries at the Bear and Bar.

"I told you, I like my life up there."

"It strikes me as . . ." Amber wrinkled her nose. "Dusty."

"But delicious."

"Wait until you try Chef Roland's crab puffs. I know he'll make them for a night like this."

Hailey steadied herself on the wooden handrail as they started down the stairs, drawing the attention of some in the glittering crowd in the grand hall.

"Seriously," Hailey whispered. "*How* many people did Mom invite?"

"Not bad for twenty-four hours' notice, is it? The Barrosse name still works its magic."

"There's more people here than in my entire Alaskan town."

Amber laughed.

Hailey recognized many of the people attending—her parents' old friends and business associates and members of their families. Some looked older. Others looked like they hadn't aged a day. Then her gaze caught on one particular man.

"Walton Henke?" she asked Amber with a groan.

"Our mother lives in hope."

Hailey's mother had tried valiantly to match her up with Walton ever since she turned sixteen. He was four years older, a college student at the time, taking economics, being groomed to take over his family's aerospace corporation. She supposed in a different lifetime the two of them might have a few things in common—aircraft, anyway.

He saw her looking, said something to his conversation companion and started their way.

"He spotted you," Amber said on a laugh.

"This is embarrassing."

"You didn't do anything to be embarrassed about." Amber paused and took in Hailey's expression. "Did you?"

"No. He tried to kiss me once, out on the patio. I ducked."

"Hello, Hailey," Walton said as they made it to the bottom of the stairs. "It's been years."

"Quite a few years." Hailey couldn't help but notice the friendly glint in his hazel eyes.

He was a handsome man, always had been, with thick blond hair and a compelling smile that made mothers dote on him and fathers trust him.

Hailey had nothing against him, except for the fact that her mother had constantly thrown the two of them together. She realized now that she'd never stopped to wonder if Walton liked or hated being paired with her at every possible moment.

"Catch you later," Amber said, and headed into the crowd.

"This feels familiar," Hailey said to Walton.

He took the comment with good humor. "Are you asking if your mother sent me over to talk to you?"

"Please tell me she didn't." That would be the height of mortification.

He chuckled. "She didn't. Can I get you a drink?" He nodded to a makeshift bar beneath one of the staircases.

"Sure." Drinking seemed like a good idea.

They made their way to the bartender.

"Sir, ma'am," the man greeted them. "What can I offer you?"

Walton looked to her.

"Something white," Hailey said. "A Chablis?"

"Coming right up." The bartender turned over a wineglass and selected a chilled bottle. "And you, sir?"

"Bourbon," Walton answered. "On the rocks, please."

The man efficiently poured the drinks.

"So, Alaska?" Walton opened the conversation as they moved along the grand hallway toward the great room. The doors were open to the patio, letting in the sultry night air. White lights decorated the palm trees around the pool, the flowering shrubs and the expanse of lawn beyond.

"Paradise, Alaska. It's a small town. I'm a bush pilot."

He nodded. "I know. We all know."

"And you?" Hailey took a sip of her wine, slightly embarrassed she hadn't kept up on the lives of people in Atlanta.

"Production Director for North America. As you can imagine, I'm on the executive management track."

"I can imagine," she agreed.

"I don't suppose you fly any of the Henke aircraft."

"Mid-size passenger jets?"

"The new Arbor is a light passenger."

"You should see the strips I land on."

"I'd like to." The friendly glint came back to his eyes.

"Walton," she warned.

"Too much, too soon?" he asked, swirling the ice cubes in his glass.

"You don't even know me anymore."

"I never really knew you." He lifted his brow. "Not that I didn't try."

Hailey had to stop herself from stepping backward. Walton suddenly seemed too close and too friendly. His banter was harmless, but she didn't want to flirt with him. She wanted to flirt with Parker.

This time when Parker entered her mind, he stuck there—his soft gray eyes, his slow smile, the sound of his voice and the touch of his fingertips. A ripple of emotion went through her.

"—I really wouldn't," Walton was saying just as she caught sight of her mother headed their way.

She blinked, scrambling to catch up in the conversation.

"It's not like I don't have easy access to a jet," he said.

Hailey had missed the first part of what he'd said, but she feared he was offering to fly to Paradise. Her mother was only steps away, and she was sure to encourage him in whatever nutty idea he'd come up with.

Hailey desperately scanned the room for a familiar face, spotting Holt Maxwell, the son of another of her parents' friends and another would-be boyfriend in her mother's eyes. Not the perfect escape route, but Hailey didn't have time to be choosy.

"Look," she said to Walton with a bright smile. "There's Holt Maxwell. I promised Mom I'd say hi to him. I better go do that. Thank you so much for the drink." She backed away as she talked, flashed a final smile at his startled expression and turned away.

Holt was talking with two women, and Hailey wouldn't normally have interrupted him, but she could feel both Walton and her mother watching her from behind her.

"Hello, Holt," she opened.

His eyes widened in surprise, and then his smile curved up. "Hailey Barrosse. I can't believe it's you."

Before she could react, he'd leaned in to kiss her cheek.

"Nice to see you, Holt." She forced a bright smile.

"Holt, Hailey." Her mother slid smoothly in front of the other two women, cutting them off from the conversation.

"Hi, Mom." Hailey should have known she wouldn't outmaneuver her mother.

Her mom smoothed her hair and beamed. "Doesn't our Hailey look wonderful?"

"She looks spectacular," Holt agreed. Though Hailey couldn't imagine what else a man could say in response to a prompt like that. "It must be the healthy air up there in Alaska."

"How are things at Beaumont Financial?" her mother asked him.

"Very well, thank you, Mrs. Barrosse. We weathered the downturn, and I was able to take advantage of some bargains in the commodities markets. I recently bought a piece of land up at Tim Nester, looking to break ground in the fall."

"A new house?" her mother asked, looking impressed, then glancing to see Hailey's reaction.

"I'm thinking colonial with some nice stonework."

"Doesn't that sound wonderful?" her mother asked her.

"It sounds large," Hailey answered.

Holt laughed. "The property is over three acres."

"Room for a growing family," her mother felt the need to point out.

"That's the intention," Holt said. "I'm coming up on thirty. I can't waste too much more time."

Her mother rubbed Hailey's arm. "Thirty is the *perfect* time to start a family."

Hailey began to seriously regret ditching Walton.

PARKER CONSIDERED TOSSING THE GOLD NUGGET earrings in the trash. But he knew that would be ridiculously wasteful. He knew he could sell them or give them away. But then they'd be out there, always out there, Hailey's earrings on someone else's ears.

Or he could melt them down. He wondered if that would be satisfying or just damn depressing—seeing them melted into a pool of nothing, like his relationship with Hailey.

Dalia strode through his office door, halting when she took in his expression. "Something wrong?" Her gaze went to the purple velvet box and the earrings sitting against the puff of dark satin. "Oh."

He snapped the lid shut.

"Hailey's earrings," she said.

"Don't say her name."

"Parker."

He glared at Dalia, knowing the steel in his eyes would shut down the conversation.

"Seriously," she said, taking one of the guest chairs in front of his desk. "Quit with the self-pity."

"*Excuse* me?"

"You act like it's all her fault." Dalia reached for the small case, opening it to look at the earrings. "These turned out nice."

"It *is* all her fault—jumping to conclusions, convicting me without a shred of evidence."

"I'd take them," Dalia said, fingering the earrings.

"No," he snapped.

She shut the box with a pitying smile, setting it back on his desk. "I've tried to keep my mouth shut."

"Keep trying."

"Because you're a grown man."

He gave a curt nod to that.

"But look at it from her perspective." Dalia sat back, crossing her legs as if she was settling in for the long haul.

"Did you review the profit and loss statement for the Fairbanks machine shop?"

"You bribed her to date you." The way Dalia said it made it sound sinister.

"That was all in fun," Parker defended himself.

Hailey had known he wasn't serious about that. Well, he was a little bit serious. He was serious in wanting to date her, but he wouldn't have pushed if she'd been unwilling.

"Uh-huh." Dalia's tone was beyond skeptical.

"*She* came back to *me* on Galina." And he'd walked away from the lucrative deal just to earn her trust.

"She was afraid you were trying to control the business. You know that."

"She has a suspicious mind." That couldn't be put on Parker.

"And you can be—"

"*What*? I can be what?" He was getting tired of the constant character assassination.

"At the risk of getting fired—"

"You might not want to risk that," he warned. Although the idea that Dalia could say something to get herself fired was preposterous.

She didn't take his warning. "You can be . . . persistent."

"So what?" How was that a negative?

"Okay." She arched forward. "How about insistent, unrelenting, overbearing."

"What are you even talking about? Do I not give you flexibility, responsibility, autonomy?" He couldn't believe she was accusing him of being a bad boss.

"I'm not talking about me."

"It was *a joke*," he defended himself all over again. "Hailey knew she didn't have to date me if she didn't want to."

Dalia was silent for a moment, looking reflective.

Parker braced himself for whatever Dalia would say next.

"You're the kind of man who knows when he's right," she said.

"Sure." He could agree to that.

"And you know how to get things done."

"Okay."

"And sometimes, just sometimes, Parker, you leave other people behind you in the dust."

"They catch up."

"Not until you let them. Broken Branch airstrip," she said meaningfully.

He wasn't getting her point. "Having Galina buy it was to their benefit."

"Did you explain that?"

"You know why I couldn't explain everything up front."

He knew word would get around if he started sharing. The bonds ran deep in that small town.

"So, all Raven knew was that you'd used the fine print to force her hand and push your way to the front of the line."

"What line?"

"You essentially told Raven to drop everything and cater to your needs."

"I didn't tell her to drop everything." Parker struggled to come up with the right words to defend himself. "You're taking bits and pieces of information and putting them together in a pattern that doesn't exist."

She nodded, as if to say he was finally getting it.

He wasn't getting anything.

"The pattern obviously existed for Hailey," Dalia clarified. "You said she suspected your motives from the start."

"I proved she was wrong."

"And then you turned around and proved she was right."

Parker smacked his hand down on the desktop. "You are twisting what happened."

"I'm trying to show you what happened inside Hailey's mind." She tapped her forehead. "You scared her half to death. She saw you moving in and taking over Galina, moving in and taking over Paradise, doing exactly what she feared you'd do, the thing she'd seen her family do dozens of times in Atlanta. She was defending Raven and all of her other friends."

Parker rocked back in his chair under the onslaught. Could it have looked that damning?

"Do you miss her?" Dalia asked.

Hell, yes, he missed her. He missed her every damn minute of every damn day.

Dalia reopened the earring box. "These really are beautiful."

Looking at the earrings, Parker felt a knife twist in his

heart. He desperately wanted Dalia to be wrong, but he knew she was right.

He'd loved the design of the earrings, each a loop of gold with the polished nugget nestled inside. He'd pictured Hailey's smile when she opened the box. He'd offer to make her Lucky Breach nugget into a matching necklace. He loved the thought of her wearing it next to her heart.

Thinking back, it had been the light in her eyes when that nugget appeared. That was the exact moment when he'd—

He stopped himself short.

"Are you in love with her?" Dalia asked.

"No." He'd fallen for Hailey. He'd admit that. But he hadn't fallen in love with her. There hadn't been time for that . . . had there? "She's not who she pretended to be." But as he said the words, he was less convinced than ever.

"Maybe," Dalia allowed. "But don't you want to find out for sure?"

He did. More than anything, he wanted another chance with Hailey. "It's too late."

"You don't know that."

"I do know that." He reached out to shut the earring box, finding it physically painful to look at them now.

Dalia shook her head pityingly. "Coward."

His spine stiffened. "Excuse me?"

"You're a coward. You'll take any chance in the world in business, but you won't take the slightest risk with your heart."

"I told you, I'm not—"

"Not in love with her." Dalia waved a dismissive hand. "Yeah, yeah. How could it possibly be that simple?"

There was nothing remotely simple about his problem.

"Talk to her," Dalia said. "Find out what you did wrong."

"I didn't—"

"Yes, you did. Because by all accounts Hailey is a wonderful person, and I'm pretty sure she's in love with you.

So, if she walked away, you screwed up big-time. Admit it and apologize."

"Apologize?" He was supposed to apologize for trying to help Galina? For leaving a business deal for Hailey, then walking back to it again for *her*?

"Or don't," Dalia said, snatching up the earring box. "Want me to get rid of these for you?"

Parker reflexively lunged forward, suddenly feeling like the earrings were his last link to Hailey.

Dalia smiled broadly and took a step back, waggling the box in the air. "You want to fight me for them?"

He clenched his jaw. He *did* want to fight her for them. And he wanted to fight for Hailey. But he had no idea how to even start.

"Tell her the truth," Dalia said, seeming to read his mind.

"What if she won't believe me?" He tried to imagine how a conversation like that would go. Given how suspicious she'd been of him all along, he couldn't see it going well.

"Convince her," Dalia said.

His chuckle was cold. "*That's* your advice?"

"Go talk to her."

"She's in Atlanta."

"Then wait."

He didn't want to wait. He rose and walked around the desk to pluck the earrings from Dalia's hand.

The amusement in her eyes told him she had his number. "Do you want to fly private or commercial? There's a four-hour layover in Seattle for commercial."

"I don't want to wait four hours." The statement popped out of him before he could censor it. He was as much as admitting she'd had it right all along.

Dalia's grin widened. "Good thing I called Ice Executive for a jet."

"You didn't." He was hoping she had.

She looked at her watch. "You might want to head for the airport."

"How did you know—"

"That you'd cave and go after her?" She blew out a breath and shook her head. "I expected it to happen long before this."

Chapter Seventeen

HAILEY EXECUTED A DIVE INTO THE BACKYARD POOL, the water refreshing in the ninety-degree heat.

"You still got it," Amber called from the edge of the deep end.

"You sure can't do this in Paradise," Hailey called back, paddling her way to her sister. She was wearing a years-old mint-green bathing suit from her dresser drawer. It was skimpier than the clothes she was used to wearing, but she and Amber had the whole backyard to themselves.

"Why not?" Amber asked.

"No pools. There's a lake, but the water never warms up much past freezing."

Amber gave a shudder. "So, you don't swim at all?"

"I dip in the hot springs every once in a while."

"Do you miss it? You must miss it."

Growing up, Hailey and Amber had spent hours and days in the family pool. A lot of their friends had pools too, and pool parties were declared most weekend nights when they were teenagers. Swimming was one of the most popular recreational activities in a city with long hot summers.

"I don't think about it much," Hailey answered. "We don't have scorching days like this in Paradise."

"I guess not." Amber stretched her arms across the edge of the pool, gently bicycling her legs to keep herself stable.

Hailey propped one elbow on the painted concrete. "Snowmobiling is fun," she offered. "There are lots of hills to climb and trails to follow."

"And plenty of snow, I'm sure."

"Plenty of that," Hailey said on a laugh.

"You don't mind being so cold?"

"You have to dress for it."

"I'd much rather dress like this."

Hailey didn't have a good argument against wearing a whisper-soft bikini, bobbing around in a pool in the sunny warm weather. "You got me there. But, you know, there's the rest."

Amber gave a sly grin. "I saw Mom pushing you together with Walton and Holt at the party."

"Don't forget Samson." Hailey grimaced. "Could she *be* any more embarrassing?"

"She thinks a man will lure you back home for good."

Hailey's thoughts turned reflexively to Parker. "A man won't lure me anywhere."

Even at the height of their fling, Hailey hadn't imagined moving to Anchorage. Not that their relationship had gotten that serious, nowhere near that serious. But it had been heady and consuming while it lasted, and she had easily pictured herself spending weeks, months, even years dating Parker.

She hated that she still missed him, that he invaded her dreams, that she wondered where he was and what he was doing and exactly how angry he'd been when he found out Magnolia Twenty now owned 45 percent of Galina instead of him.

Then she wondered if he'd ever come back to Paradise, and how she'd react if she saw him there.

"What are you thinking?" Amber asked, peering closely at Hailey's expression.

Hailey gave her head a little shake to erase the image of Parker. Then she grabbed a random thought from last night's party. "That Cassie Whittington has gone way too blond."

Amber splashed some water at Hailey's face. "You were not."

"You don't think she should have gone more honey than platinum?"

"Who cares? What were you really thinking about?"

Hailey paused, not wanting to lie to Amber and feeling the urge to talk.

"Parker," she admitted.

"Ahh." Amber gave a sage nod. "So it was more than just a fling."

"It was," Hailey admitted, gazing at the azalea bushes in a distant garden until the crimson blooms went blurry in her vision.

"How much more?"

Hailey's memories bloomed and she couldn't seem to stop them. "So much . . ."

"And you can't dial it back," Amber guessed softly.

"Trouble is . . ." Hailey took a stab at being honest. "I don't seem to *want* to dial it back."

"But you had doubts from the start."

"I knew he couldn't be as perfect as he seemed."

"Nobody is."

"I know."

"You like hardworking, you end up with driven," Amber said philosophically. "You like smart, you end up with scheming. You like handsome, you end up with vain."

"Parker's not vain." Hailey thought about his perfect suits and shoes and ties, not to mention his haircut. "I mean, he's cultivated an image thanks to Dalia, but that was a business thing. He'd dress down when it made sense. He'd even dig into work at the mine in his good clothes. I saw him do that. We found a nugget. Well, I found a nugget. It was his claim, his nugget, but he let me keep it."

"He was probably co-opting you to his cause."

"I know." Hailey knew that now. At the time, he just seemed like a fun guy who'd finally let his guard down. "I feel like a fool for falling for it."

Amber reached out to touch her arm. "You're not a fool. You're maybe a bit too trusting."

"I am not."

"You've been away from my influence for too long."

"Now you sound like Mom. Is she paying you?"

The distinctive lilt of their mother's laugh wafted over from the patio, which was screened from the pool by a deep green barberry hedge.

Hailey moved closer to her sister. "Seriously, are you trying to help them lure me home?"

"I'd never do that. Or at least I'd tell you if I was."

Another voice sounded from the patio, deep but indistinct, sending a shiver up Hailey's spine.

"What?" Amber asked, looking worried.

"I think I might be losing my mind."

Amber looked around them. "Are you hallucinating?" She put her hand on top of Hailey's head. "Should we get you out of the sun?"

"I'm hearing voices."

"That's Mom."

"And . . ." Hailey paused to listen, and the man's voice rumbled again. "I swear—"

"Who *is* that?"

A wave of emotion sank from Hailey's chest to her toes. "I think it's him."

"Walton? I don't think so. Not Holt for sure."

"Parker," Hailey said.

Amber's eyes went wide. *"Here?"*

"I don't know." Hailey scrambled for the ladder. "Exactly how angry would he have to be to fly all the way to Atlanta."

"Let me talk to him," Amber said, climbing quickly up behind her. "It doesn't need to be you. I'm the one who undermined him."

"It was my idea."

"It was *my* idea." Amber ran a towel over her wet body.

Hailey did the same. "I'm the one who called you in."

"It's not like he can *do* anything. Let him rip me a new one. He won't be the first guy who tried."

Their mother laughed again in the distance.

"She obviously doesn't know who he is," Amber said, pulling a blue cover-up over her head.

Hailey shrugged into a silky white tank that clung to her green bathing suit from the water. She raked her fingers through her hair. "That's him being charming. He's damn good at it."

"Mom's pretty easy to charm."

"She's probably charming him right back—doesn't mean she trusts him."

"True," Amber agreed.

Their mother was a master of being charming to anyone and everyone who came into her orbit. She said you never knew what you'd need from someone in the future.

"You ready?" Amber asked.

"Do I look ready?"

Amber smoothed a whisp of hair from Hailey's cheek. "You look fabulous."

"I want to look tough."

Amber looked her up and down, from her bare feet to her wet hair and the flimsy little cover-up in between. "You look tough enough."

Parker looked up as soon as they walked onto the patio.

His gazed zeroed in on Hailey, making goose bumps rise on her skin.

He rose quickly, looking both out of place and perfect at the same time. He wore lightweight gray slacks and a pin-striped dress shirt, open at the collar. There was no getting away from his good looks and his athletic physique. His dark hair was neat as ever, his face clean-shaven, his gray eyes lighter in the bright sunshine.

Beside Hailey, Amber looked him up and down. She was probably surprised at how easily he fit in here. Hailey wasn't surprised at all. She'd always known he'd slide right into her family's world.

Hailey braced herself. But he didn't look angry. If any-thing, he looked . . . satisfied. Which made no sense.

"Hailey," he greeted her, his deep voice sending an extra buzz along her heightened nerve endings.

"Hailey, honey," her mother said in a cheerful voice. "Parker here was just telling me he knows you from Alaska."

Hailey raised a brow at that description.

"Parker, I'd like you to meet my other daughter, Amber."

"Hello, Parker." Amber's tone was flat. "Mom, did Parker tell you he was also in the running for Galina Expe-diting?"

Parker flinched, and Hailey knew he hadn't shared that little fact with her mother.

"Can we talk?" he asked Hailey.

"That company in Alaska?" Her mother looked at Parker in puzzlement.

"I had a deal in the works," he admitted. "Amber obvi-ously offered them something they liked better."

"Obviously," Amber said.

"And now you're here." Their mother's voice was searching.

"I'm hoping to talk to Hailey."

"You can talk to me," Amber said, taking a step forward. "I'm the one who made the deal on Galina."

"I'm not here to talk about Galina." His gaze stayed locked over Amber's shoulder, squarely on Hailey.

"Then why are you here?" Amber pressed, taking another step.

He spared her a glance. "I'll explain that to Hailey."

"You can explain to me." Amber jabbed her thumb against her chest.

"Amber," their mother admonished.

"It's okay," Hailey said, accepting the inevitable and stepping past her sister. "We can talk."

ONCE PARKER HAD HAILEY ALONE, HE STRUGGLED FOR a place to start. He wasn't used to admitting he'd been flat dead wrong. How did a guy go about saying that?

They'd left the patio to walk the smooth carpet of a lawn, coming to a shaded gazebo beneath a pair of oak trees.

"I really don't understand why you're here," she said, pausing at the gazebo entrance and looking up at him.

She was more beautiful than he remembered, with the little sheath of a cover-up clinging to her shoulders, her breasts and her waist. He could see the ghost outline of a bikini through the sheer fabric. Her face was flushed, sunkissed, her freckles more pronounced, her hair slightly damp, framing her face.

"To apologize," he said, thinking this was going to be easier than he'd thought.

Her blue-green eyes darkened a shade. "For conning everyone?" She made to toss her hair, but it was damp, so it only stuck to her cheek.

He had to resist an urge to brush it away.

"No need," she added. "You already paid a price."

"I did," he agreed, but it wasn't the price she was thinking.

"So, why come here?"

"To explain."

"I already understand."

"You don't."

She blew out a deep sigh. "Here we go again."

"What does that mean?"

"You don't see it?" she asked. "Back and forth. Up and down. You parry, I return, and we never really get anywhere."

He couldn't help but smile.

"Stop," she ordered.

But he couldn't. She was right. But this wasn't going to be that kind of an argument. She'd already won.

"It's been brought to my attention," he said, "that I can sometimes be overbearing."

"That had to be brought to your attention?"

"Are you going to let me talk?"

She tilted her head. "That depends."

"On what?"

"On what you have to say."

"I don't care about losing Galina."

The statement seemed to give her pause. "Then why are you here?"

"I care about losing you."

She shook her head, not believing for a second he was being straight with her. "I was a means to an end."

"I walked away from the deal for you."

"You knew you'd get it back."

"I didn't. Not then. I left it for you, Hailey. I came back to it for you. Remember my condition? *You* were my condition."

She opened her mouth again, but she didn't say anything.

It gave him hope that she might be thinking it through.

He pushed forward. "I had reasons for everything I did. I bought the Broken Branch airstrip because I'd just bought

the Halstead International property and registered a crap-
ton of new claims."

"You didn't buy it. We stopped you."

"No. You stopped Galina from buying it. I still bought it."

Her expression turned puzzled.

"I pushed Raven on those deliveries because we needed
to set up a lab to keep the water licenses to bring the whole
deal together."

"But—"

"And I bought Riley's property so I could build a house.
So I'd have somewhere to live in Paradise. So I could be
closer to you."

She gazed at him in silence for a minute, a gust of wind
lifting her damp hair. "His *property*?" she finally asked in
a small voice.

"Yes."

"Not his business."

"No."

"Not Rapid Release."

"No. I didn't lie about that. I didn't tell you about the
land only because, well, I didn't want to jinx anything or
come on too strong when we were just starting out. Plus,
the thing is, I stop thinking about much of anything when
I'm around you."

He watched closely, desperately hoping he wasn't imagining the softening of her expression.

He dared to take a step closer. "You can trust me, Hailey. If only because you've got Galina, and there's nothing
more I want."

"But . . . you . . ." She seemed to be searching for his
motives, for his hidden agenda.

"Let me rephrase that. There is one thing I want." He
gave in to temptation and cradled her face with his palm.
"You, Hailey. I love you, and I want you in my life."

He forced himself to stop talking, to wait, to give her a
chance for the declaration to sink in and to decide what she

wanted to do with it. It was the hardest few seconds of his life.

"Are you serious?" she asked.

"Yes, I'm completely serious." He tried his hardest to wait longer for her response, but he couldn't do it. "Dalia thinks you love me back."

Hailey rested her head against his palm. Her gaze warmed and a small smile curved her lips. "She does, does she."

He moved closer still, encouraged by her expression. "And Dalia's a very smart woman. She graduated sixth in her class at Harvard."

"Only sixth?"

"Tell me you love me, Hailey."

"Oh, Parker. I do love you." Her arms looped around his neck. "I love you so much."

He bent down to kiss her lips.

Elation washed through him. Desire washed through him. Love and hope and pleasure invaded every fiber of his being as he kissed her deeply.

When they finally parted, he held her tight, unwilling to let her go.

She finally drew back. "I don't know what happens now."

He knew one thing that happened now, something he'd looked forward to the whole trip here. "I brought you something." He drew the jeweler's box from his pocket.

Her eyes widened in shock. "It's not—"

"No, no," he quickly assured her. "It's not that. Wow, that would be overbearing, wouldn't it?" He grinned and flipped open the box for her to see. "Colin sent them down." He paused a moment. "I thought we could make a matching necklace with your nugget."

"They're beautiful," she said, touching the smooth, shiny gold with her fingertip. "They're an almost perfect match."

"Like us?" he said with a smirk.

"Nothing like us. We're . . . I don't know . . ."

"Opposites that attracted?"

"Let's go with that. I like that." She sighed and snuggled into his embrace. "My family is going to love you."

HAILEY RINSED AND BLOW-DRIED HER HAIR, CHANGing from her bathing suit into a simple aqua and lilac halter dress from her closet and a pair of wedge sandals. Her heart was light as she put on the gold nugget earrings and relived those moments with Parker.

She was in love. They were in love. He loved her, and he'd come all the way to Atlanta to explain. Everything made sense now. Her suspicions that had seemed so rational at the time were just plain wrong. Parker hadn't been operating against her or anyone else in Paradise.

She tucked her hair behind her ears and looked in the mirror, first one way, then the other. The gold sparkled against her lobes. She touched her bare chest, anxious to get the necklace made to match.

Then she all but floated down the stairs, hearing her brother Kent's voice in the great room as she came to the bottom.

"That much in one year?" he was asking.

"And that's with a short northern season," Parker answered.

"Without access roads?" This time it was her father Griffin's voice as she cut through the grand hallway.

"We put in roads on the mine site. We can barge heavy equipment in when the river is high. Then we service it there on site to keep everything running."

"But the ongoing supply route is by plane?" Griffin asked.

Parker looked up and saw Hailey appear. He smiled, a glow coming into his eyes as he reached his hand out to her.

"That's where your daughter comes in," Parker said. "She's an amazing pilot."

Her father looked her way and took in her appearance.

She knew he'd be glad to see her in a dress. He'd have liked it even better if she'd done up her hair and layered on some makeup.

"Isn't that expensive?" he asked Parker.

"Gold is valuable enough to support the business case," Parker said.

Hailey went to his side.

He took her hand. "You look beautiful."

Her father seemed to take that as a prompt. "You look very nice, Hailey."

"Thank you," she said to them both.

"So, the airstrip?" Kent asked, clearly fascinated by what Parker had to say.

"Paradise will be the goods transportation hub," Parker said, drawing Hailey against him. "With Galina at its center. But the Broken Branch airstrip will service Lucky Breach, the old Halstead International property, and all the new claims in between, which my geologists assure me are prime gold ground, given the discoveries we've made in the past few months."

"You don't let any grass grow under your feet," Griffin observed.

"No, sir," Parker said.

"And now we have an interest in Galina." Kent looked at Hailey with new admiration.

"*I* have an interest in Galina," Amber announced as she breezed in from the hallway.

"Same thing," Kent said.

"Not quite," Amber told him. "Hailey and I are going to take care of that investment. You two can keep your hands off."

"You should get Parker to help you," their father said.

"They don't need my help," Parker said with a wry grin.
He lifted his chin to Amber. "You've met Raven Westberg."

"Raven's a force of nature," Amber said. To their father
she said, "She's been running the place for years."

"You plan to keep her?" he asked.

"Raven stays," Hailey stated with conviction, daring
anyone to disagree with her.

Her father smiled at her with obvious pride. "That's my
girl."

Parker gave her hand a squeeze, and Hailey realized
what she'd just done. She was firmly back in the family
fold. At least her father thought she was firmly back in the
fold.

Parker leaned down to surreptitiously whisper, "It won't
be so bad."

Hailey heaved a sigh. For better or worse, she'd agreed
to help with Galina. She couldn't go back on it now.

Oddly, the walls didn't feel like they were closing in.
Maybe because Parker was with her now. She had a partner
who'd support her flying career along with anything she did
for the family.

She squeezed his hand back.

"This calls for a celebration," her father said.

"A celebration?" Her mother chose that moment to enter
the room, sounding delighted by the prospect. "The rooftop
room at the White Bay Grille, I hope."

"Wherever you want to go, darling." Her father's voice
was affectionate when he spoke to her mother.

"Definitely the rooftop room," her mother called out as
she headed for the kitchen. "Roland? Can you call Pierre at
the White Bay?"

"I can't believe we've never thought about Alaska before," Kent said to their father.

"It's Alaska," Griffin replied. "Who thinks about it from
here?"

"But Hailey was there," Amber put in.

"Looks like we're celebrating," Parker whispered to Hailey as the conversation flowed around them.

"I feel like celebrating," she answered, feeling the urge to kiss him, then wondering when they'd get a chance to be truly alone. Her family might be celebrating business tonight, but she and Parker would be thinking about their love for each other.

"So, champagne?" he asked as he drew back to look at the earrings. He reached out to circle one with the tip of his finger.

"We have so much to celebrate," she said with a smile.

"I need to get you alone."

She nodded to that, while thinking it might be tough to orchestrate tonight. "I was planning to fly back tomorrow."

He seemed satisfied with the plan. "Good. Dalia will rent us another jet."

"My family has a jet." Hailey was sure they'd insist she use it—if only to reinforce the perks of being actively involved in the Barrosse family business. They wouldn't understand the trappings still meant nothing to her.

"How discreet is your family's pilot?" Parker asked in a tone laced with sensuality.

"Rental jet it is," she said, agreeing they might want some anonymity on the trip home.

IN PARADISE, PARKER WORRIED HIS RV TRAILER WAS too small to house both of them, but Hailey laughed off his concern since it was approximately four times the size of her WSA room. Plus, it had a kitchen. She hadn't done any real cooking in years, but she was looking forward to making meals for the two of them, especially a good breakfast before leaving their warm home on cold fall mornings.

Parker was anxious to get started on construction, and

Cobra suggested they tour his and Marnie's new house for ideas. Mia had jumped in, insisting their house was superior and offering a comprehensive tour.

Hailey planned to use the best ideas from both—plus build around the stellar hillside view. Parker was planning three floors with plenty of glass to take in the views of the river valley.

"This is the part I liked best," Marnie was saying as she led them through a sitting area in the roomy master bedroom and onto a glassed-in balcony.

The screened windows were open on the warm afternoon, letting the fresh air flow through.

"You cannot beat that for a view," Parker said, moving to stand in front of the glass wall.

"Yours will be even better. Take a look." Cobra pointed out the south side to where they could just make out the bluff where Parker and Hailey planned to build.

"And this is really fun," Marnie said to Hailey, putting her hand on the telescope set up in one corner and pointing across the river. "We can usually see mountain sheep in the morning."

Hailey bent forward, focusing her eye through the glass.

"Can you make out the waterfall?" Marnie asked.

"I can." The cascading falls dropped into a wide pool that drained into a creek down the mountainside.

"Bears come there, so do moose and wolves."

"Can we get one of these?" Hailey asked Parker. She saw animals from the air quite often, but the idea of being able to sit back and watch them close-up like this appealed to her.

"We sure can." He came up behind her and she moved to step aside.

"No rush," he quickly told her, putting a hand on her arm to stop her.

"Check this out," Cobra said. He lifted and moved the

telescope to the north end of the porch, steadying it, then focusing in.

After a moment, he stood back and gestured to Hailey.

Marnie grinned in anticipation.

Hailey wondered what the surprise might be. She approached and looked through the lens.

"Is this legal?" she asked on a laugh, seeing Mia and Silas's yard with the film crew in full detail.

"They know we can see them."

"It's not like we spy every day," Marnie was quick to put in.

"It's been interesting for the film shoot," Cobra said.

"There's Willow," Hailey noted. "She's halfway in the river."

"It must be another stunt shoot," Marnie said. "I watched a romantic moment with Aurora and Dax the other day."

Hailey looked up. "There's a romance with the villain?"

"Unrequited. But Dax is semi-redeemed in the end, I'm told."

"Wait, no sequel?" Hailey had been hopeful they'd plan for one.

"They're talking about having a common enemy for Dax and Aurora in the next script, upping the romantic ante."

"I like it," Hailey said with a smile.

She saw Parker and Cobra exchange a look.

"Don't pretend you're not a romantic," she said to Parker, sidling up to him and linking her arm with his.

He wrapped an arm around her waist and kissed her hairline, then whispered, "I'm a hopeless romantic."

Cobra clearly overheard and chuckled.

Marnie moved his way. "Got something to say there, Snake-Man?"

Cobra held up his palms in surrender. "Nothing to say."

"So, what do you think of the glass porch?" Marnie asked as she settled into Cobra's arms.

"I'm sold," Hailey answered.

"So, we're changing the plans again?" Parker asked with mock exasperation.

Cobra laughed and gave Marnie a hug.

"We can always make the kitchen smaller," Hailey offered, plucking playfully at the buttons of Parker's shirt.

"We don't have to make the kitchen smaller." He covered her hand with his and lowered his voice. "You want another porch? We'll build another porch."

"You *are* a hopeless romantic," she said, coming up on her toes to give him a quick kiss.

"I'll be any kind of romantic you want," Parker whispered.

"I'll take you just the way you are," Hailey said, meaning it with all her heart.

ACKNOWLEDGMENTS

A huge thank-you to my editor, Angela Kim, and my agent, Laura Bradford, who helped immensely through the first book of the series and the others that followed.

To my husband, Gordon Dunlop, and his fellow northern bush pilots, thanks for the inspiration and especially for all you do to help remote miners, tourists, researchers, and artists. You are heroes to all.

As always, a special thank-you to the entire Berkley team from editing and cover design to marketing and distribution for turning my stories into such wonderful packages.

Finally, thanks to all the Paradise, Alaska, readers. So many have reached out with words of encouragement. I appreciate that more than you know!

Ready to find
your next great read?

Let us help.

Visit prh.com/nextread

Penguin
Random
House